WHEN THE LIGHTS GO OUT

MICHAEL FARRELL

NFB
Buffalo, New York

NFB
<<<>>>
No Frills Buffalo/Amelia Press
119 Dorchester Road
Buffalo, New York 14213

For more information visit
nofrillsbuffalo.com

And if the whole world's singing your songs
And all of your paintings have been hung, just remember
What was yours is everyone's from now on

-Jeff Tweedy, "What Light"

WHEN THE LIGHTS GO OUT

1

Once upon a time
I had a life in mind
But then one day along the way
That dream was left behind
-"What I Lost" by J. Nolan

Four years ago, I was someone else.

I was Johnny Nolan, an acoustic guitarist who performed at the Nighthawk, a glorious and dingy downtown rock hole in Buffalo, New York. Every Friday night it used to be just me, isolated on stage, straddling a creaky stool in front of a white backdrop. The heat from overhead yellow, blue and red bulbs burned my eyelids. My left fingers aligned between frets on Deirdre, my Martin D-15 guitar. My right index finger and thumb clasped a small orange pick. The microphone waited, alive and hot. When I would glance out over the bar, I'd see strangers clutching beer bottles and pint glasses, taking sips of semi-cold Old Vienna and waiting for action. They'd shout together, join in a rhythmic arena-like chant of "Johnny Nolan" then clap five times (like *John-nee No-lan, clap, clap, clap-clap-clap*).

After the chant circulated five or six times, I'd bring the guitar to my knee and begin to strum, slowly but fluidly. The first line of lyrics, then the second. During the breaks in vocals, I'd shake my head around, like I was winding up for the next lyrical delivery. Every line would pour out, would wail through the crowded barroom, wrap around neon Budweiser signs and seep through the hairline cracks of windows weathered from harsh winters. The guitar chords bounced off steel coolers littered with Avail and Trashcan Sinatra stickers, walls that donned mounted Fender guitars and a framed Elvis concert poster from 1957. One cover song, then another. Once in a while, I'd throw in a Johnny Nolan original, just to make things interesting. Pretty girls in the front gazed and smiled. Tough guys in back nodded approval while ordering another round of beers. To others, those nights may have seemed insignificant or amateur. To me, those Fridays meant everything.

On one of those nights, I attracted a fan, a wiry blonde named Sara.

"With no 'h'," she insisted.

She had a sweet, bright smile when she laughed and cornflower blue eyes that opened wide when she emphasized the last word of every sentence. She also spoke about old punk music at such a frenetic and jittery pace I feared she'd collapse mid-sentence. Still, two hours after I stepped off stage that Friday, I sat in front of her on a leather-seated barstool, listening. She just rolled along, standing up straight for delivery.

"I love, love, love, love the Ramones and I hate people that say all their songs sound the same because, yeah, I know they sound the same because they're all, like, totally fucking awesome and I'm not sure they've ever made a bad song, except maybe 'Pet Cemetery,' but I still like that song, but I don't love it, and I want to love it, but I used to have this dog named Charlie who was hit by a school bus and every time I hear that song it reminds me of poor little Charlie getting run over, and I cry and cry and I don't want to cry because I love the Ramones and all their songs and how fucking awesome they are, you know?"

I listened to her talk and nodded along between sips of beer. She was definitely a shade off, maybe on something. On Friday nights, I'd met girls way crazier, even ones who straddled the line between odd and socially problematic. There was the angry girl who gave a detailed explanation of the motivation behind her demonic wrist tattoo; the Jack Daniel's drinker who moaned about my lack of inspired Bon Jovi numbers; the overtly flirtatious college student who'd send provocative pictures of herself to my cell phone every Wednesday. When my guitar was near me, I was approached by all types. Sara was one of them, and those hypnotic eyes were one reason I didn't grab my guitar and split for the door.

That night, after the Nighthawk closed, we sat on the bar's curb, sharing a cigarette just down the street from Lafayette Square. We exchanged drags, exhaled before we kissed, then repeated through a warm lakefront breeze. During breaks in the action, she rambled on about an old band called Brent's TV who played California laundromats. I nodded politely while intermittently kissing her neck and cheeks between sentences. Eventually, she jumped up from the curb.

"Do you want to do something crazy, like, right now?"

"Sure," I said. "What and where?"

"We have to go to my car. It's across from the square."

She walked quickly ahead of me as I plodded behind her, carrying my guitar case and wondering what she had hiding in her car. Would we up the ante on the curb fondling, or did she plan on taking this night in a whole new direction? Heavy drugs? Petty vandalism? She seemed crazy enough that nothing aside from homicide was off limits. When I got to her white Grand Am, though, she was already in the back seat, taking off her pants. When I saw this, I lightly rapped on the window.

"Um, should I come in?"

"No," she answered. "Just wait out there, please. I don't want to ruin the surprise."

I turned my back to the car and let Sara finish whatever it was she was doing. I could hear her shifting and struggling, her bare skin squeaking against the leather upholstery while she prepared for whatever crazy thing we were about to do.

"Tell you what," she said. "Why don't you wait for me in the square? I'll be over in a minute."

Under a bright, full moon that shined on the windows of shuttered storefronts and closed convenience shops, I headed over to the small park, complete with empty benches and strewn debris from recent outdoor concerts. The sun would soon sneak up to find me standing in the middle of a vacant park, waiting for this Sara. As I leaned against a tree, hands in my jean pockets, I lit another cigarette before she began her approach from across the street. In each of her hands, she held a short rope with dripping, softball-sized spheres attached to the ends. In place of the tight black pants and simple white T-shirt she wore in the bar were a long-sleeved fitted orange tee and free-flowing, bell-bottomed nylon windpants, navy blue with orange flames stitched on the outer seams. Her earlobe-length blonde hair was now pulled back tightly into a ponytail to reveal dark roots. When she reached me, she grinned mischievously.

"Can I use your lighter?"

"Can I ask for what?"

"Just give me the lighter and back up," she said, like she was warning me to look both ways before crossing the street.

I handed over my green Bic and took a few steps back. With the lighter, Sara lit the end of the first rope, saturated in kerosene. With one rope ablaze, she ignited the other. When flames engulfed both rope ends, she began a maniacal dance, flinging the ropes over her shoulders and around her legs. She tossed one up in the air, then the other as I covered my face. Twirling the flames, she whirled around like some fanatical dervish. With her blue eyes now wide to emphasize nothing but fevered insanity, she was celebrating for whatever occasion the ropes and kerosene and firepants were trotted out. Finally, as she spun both ropes around, a portion of one of the fireballs detached and landed on a tree branch above my head, sending down a rush of sparks. After I ducked, I darted to the right, away from the tree. Sara was unfazed and continued to flip the ropes, despite the detachment. For her finale, she rapidly and simultaneously twirled both ropes at her sides, then dropped them to the ground. She leapt into the air, touching her toes in a full split. When her feet came down, she landed on the ropes' lit ends and extinguished each with a single plant of her fireproof shoes. Standing atop each, she posed, arms raised to the night sky, under the stars and moonlight of downtown Buffalo. I clapped wildly while walking toward her as she smiled and laughed.

"Very impressive," I said. "Definitely don't think I'll ever experience a show like that again."

"Well," she said, grasping my hips before pulling me close to her, "if you think that show was impressive, prepare to be dazzled twice in one night."

She grabbed me by my shirt and pulled me down to the shadowed grass. After mounting herself on top of me, her thighs straddling my hips, she ripped off my T-shirt and flung it toward a nearby bench. She ran her hands over my chest before she took off her top and tossed it toward mine. As her soft hands ran over the inked outlines on my arms, her mouth found my chest to kiss and gently nibble every inch of it she could find. I lay on my back and grasped her hips, staring into the sky and loving every second before a thick aroma overtook the moment.

"Do you smell something burning?" I asked.

"I was just tossing some burning ropes around. You think that might be it?" she deadpanned, then brought her lips back to my chest before her fingers left to fiddle with my belt.

"No, no," I said. "I think it's something else."

After I said this, I looked to my right. In the leaves of a large nearby oak tree, smoke wafted out as small flames emerged within. It had taken a few minutes, but that detached fireball from Sara's dance routine had ignited the fresh leaves and branches above.

"Um, Sara?" I said. "What do you say we go back to my place?"

"What? Why? This is so—," she said, then turned to see the nearby smoke and flames. "Oh shit! Yeah, we should go."

She hopped off me, tossed me my shirt and feverishly pulled her own back on. I jumped to my feet, buckled my pants and grabbed my guitar. I took hold of Sara's hand before she ran me to her car across the street. At the doors of her Grand Am, we heard a police siren wailing, approaching in the distance. We slammed both doors behind us, Sara hit the gas, and we fled a scene of accidental arson while laughing hysterically. The next morning, Sara the Fire Dancer was gone. I never saw her again, and our fling existed as a one-night affair. Unfortunately, that downtown tree was irrevocably affected. Our evening generated a giant bare spot it still has within its branches today.

These days, when I stroll past that Lafayette Square tree, I remember those wild Nighthawk nights, when everything was still carefree and unhinged. But those Fridays have been gone for four years now. They were the nights before I was married, before I prepared to become a father; before I left the stage and found a desk. It was a time before everything changed and transitioned as quickly as power chords, sliding from fret to fret. It was before the diagnosis, the hospital bed, the endless tears from the eyes of my father, my uncle Finn, my sister Meghan. It was before breast cancer snatched my mother, before a clutching hand on the chest of a navy ski vest became the last living image I'd have of my father. It was before everything in my life was transformed in a matter of weeks. It was before things that once seemed so important were dwarfed by the enormity of death and loss.

My mother went first, lying emaciated and still in a Mercy Hospital bed on a cold December day. As I peered down at the once beautiful Colleen Nolan, her pale, freckled skin yellowed and thin, the memories flowed forth. The nights she served up cold Dr. Peppers and Neil Young records on our front porch as Lake Erie breezes whisked up our street and kissed our faces; the frosty winter mornings she stirred up bowls of apple cinnamon oatmeal and mugs of hot chocolate. The sight of my mother as she took her last breaths curdled my stomach. The harsh realization that the aforementioned maternal moments would never be replicated stabbed it, ignited a sharp pain in my right side. Instead of succumbing to the sting, I clutched my mother's limp hand, moved my fingers around in her palm and hoped her eyes would flutter open one last time. When I watched Finn walk into her room dressed in his blacks and Catholic collar, I knew it was too late.

"I know this is hard on everyone," said Finn, standing at bedside with the three of us. "But we have to trust there's a reason for this, a reason only God understands. Please, somewhere in your broken hearts, try to believe. Let us pray."

Tears streamed down Meg's face as she reached for my hand. My father clenched his teeth, held back his tears. Looking out a window and into the falling South Buffalo snow, he grabbed for Meg's hand before he clutched onto Finn's. I still held my mother's hand, staring into her closed eyelids as I panned across her freckled forehead, her hanging auburn locks that dusted each mark. I reluctantly closed my eyelids and bowed my head under Finn's prayers. For one moment, I stopped my mind from spiraling wildly into darkness, into pain and hopelessness. For one moment, I reached out to God and asked him to take my mother into his welcoming embrace. And just like that, she was his. Not mine. Not ours.

A month later, it was my father, struck with a heart attack as he shoveled the heavy lake-effect snow at the end of our driveway. As I cleared our sidewalk, I saw him drop the metal shovel before he tumbled helplessly into a snow pile. I ran to him and found him struggling to breathe, his hand scratching at his chest as his body lay twitching, encased in white. When I leaned over him to help, he grabbed my navy pea coat collar and pulled me down to his face as I struggled to break free and get to a phone. With his teeth clenched tight and his dark Irish eyes frightened, he stared right through me, but wouldn't let go. He let the pain in his eyes act as the saddened and desperate voice he didn't have.

"Pops," I yelled. "Pops, you gotta let me go. Pops!"

With his grip still tight, his dying sight emitted one more glare, one more emotive stare that said goodbye. Those browns rolled to the side under weakened lids and I stared at him, petrified. His clutch on my coat loosened and I broke free. I tore up the driveway and into the kitchen, grabbed a phone and called for an ambulance. I screamed into the receiver with frightening urgency, stammering details. Then, I ran back outside to find Tom Nolan unconscious, his eyelids closed as his face rested in the snow, with more falling from the sky to sprinkle across his navy vest and brown wool cap.

Frozen in shock, I could only stare at his body and mumble inaudible hopes. I could only hope for some spiritual intervention to right this cruel injustice. I could only linger until God realized his mistake. There was no way he was taking them both. No fucking way. As minutes disappeared with my father motionless, my mind raced with evaporating moments. Paul Simon's voice soothing from the old man's stereo and out a screen window, over his canned beer and into our backyard; the sight of him at the Nighthawk, leaning against the bar with a bottle of Genesee, nodding approval as I sat on the stage. As those times were fading, my father slipped away, unable to be awoken by my screaming pleas or the blaring sirens that arrived too late.

And this was when the lights went out, when the darkness of loss dimmed the Nighthawk bulbs and transitioned me toward another life, another existence. It pushed me away from the stage and into the arms of family, into an embrace that soothed the trauma of absence. That absence irrevocably loomed over the isolated stool and microphone that projected my voice over the Nighthawk's revelers. I could no longer appreciate the adulation of the beer sluggers and booze sippers who huddled in the bar's dark corners and yelled for Springsteen covers. From my spot on that stage, I stopped enjoying the cheers of those present and became hollowed by the evidence of those missing, the empty spaces once filled by my mother and father. In this state, I walked away from the Nighthawk. I packed up Deirdre and let my moments of Friday mayhem fade into memory. As painful as it was to exit, it had to happen. The act of performing had merged with a pain too significant to play through.

There was a time when I could play through any problem, when one strum of my guitar cured all. When I clutched that Martin's mahogany, all worries dissipated with a simple touch of its rosewood fingerboard. I didn't care about anything except the strings, the chords, or the sounds; every issue I had disappeared. These days, I bring that guitar into my kitchen, set it on my lap and tune the strings. I caress the brown finish, run my fingers over the Nolan family crest sticker still clinging to the back. I run my left hand down the seductive neck, feel the nicks and splintered spots on the wood. I line up a chord and flick my fingernails against the strings. I slide from one chord to another and ignite a sound that doesn't bring about sadness, but recollection.

Each note ushers in a moment from those Friday nights at the Nighthawk, the nights sweat glazed my Celtic arm tattoos, rolled down my long brown hair and collected on the stubble of my unshaven face. I think of the bottle of Budweiser that rested next to my stool's leg. I'd pick it up, take a swig under the burning bulbs. If I took a long drink, hoots came from the back to encourage a finish. Someone else would yell out and jokingly ask me to play "Freebird." After I put down the beer, I'd run my hand through my hair, flip the long strands away from my eyes. I'd start to strum, concentrate on the chord changes before I glared out to the crowd and exhaled one of their favorites. As I sang, people stood clapping, stomping and singing. Couples would swing around as my strings jangled and twanged. When I finished, drinkers applauded my homage to another great, to a group of geniuses so brilliant that their song was replicated on a dusty, sweat-soaked Buffalo stage. This was my release, my drug that made cheap Canadian beer taste like honey. Made the stale, sweat-tinged barroom breeze smell like cinnamon. Made dilapidated Rust Belt streets into parade routes. This was my life, and I loved every minute of it.

But that was four years ago. I was someone else then, an unscathed idealist addicted to the euphoria a crowd's roar could instill in a man. I had to move on from nights infused with intoxicating rhythm, the mornings filled with sporadic reverberations. I don't play at the Nighthawk anymore. Those nights are gone.

2

When my world went goodbye
I took a look inside
To find what kind of truths
I'd face or try to hide
-"My New Dawn" by J. Nolan

After my parents died, my family joined every October for their memorial Mass inside Uncle Finn's South Buffalo parish, St. Stephen's. He'd conduct the annual service, donning his green Celtic vestment as he commemorated Colleen and Thomas Nolan, the faithfully departed. He'd echo their names over his congregation, who'd bow their heads and pray for God's blessings upon those Colleen and Tom left behind. We accepted these sentiments every year.

It was the fourth Nolan memorial Mass. I stood at the end of a pew next to my sister Meg and her two boys, six-year-old Mickey and newly ten-year-old Brendan, just a few hours into his birthday. After the service, we'd head downtown to balance the morning's somber beginning with an afternoon celebration of Brendan's birthday. Until then, we had to endure the Mass and prayers, as well as the memories the mention of my parents' names would elicit.

"And *this* is the Gospel of the Lord," said Finn.

"Praise to you, Lord Jesus Christ."

After I took my seat, I dangled my right Doc Marten

boot into the center aisle and slouched into the corner of the pew as surrounding parishioners nestled into their seats, awaiting the always-intriguing homily of Father Finn.

No matter how many Sundays I saw him in that flowing vestment, his life's designation always seemed odd to me. My mother had told us of the heartthrob Finn was in his youth, how he spent very few Friday nights throughout high school or college without a date. When Meg and I were younger, we witnessed his popularity in person, before he became a priest. In his early and mid-twenties, he occasionally brought women—ones he said he'd met through volunteering at St. Stephen's or working as coordinator downtown at St. Jude's Community Center—to dinner. Devising activities and community outreach efforts appeared to have scored him an attractive date or three. When he reached his late twenties and announced his decision to enroll in the seminary, these memories of his popularity with the ladies made his vocational direction that much more confusing. Yet soon enough, there he was, patrolling the altar of our neighborhood parish as the noteworthy Father Finn.

Only in his early forties, he appeared and acted more like a gregarious corner tavern bartender than a respected priest. He stood tall and burly, with wavy salt-and-pepper hair tickling the eartops that flanked his round Irish head. As St. Stephen's young and exuberant pastor, he made the most of his hours on the altar. In that time, he'd stress selflessness, love and community. He'd speak of how we all must honor God by reaching our potential not only spiritually, but also socially and professionally. He stressed compassion at every turn, especially when considering all sides of controversial wedge issues like abortion, gay marriage or divorce. Even in the face of intense dissention and diocesan backlash, he'd openly discuss difficult topics to elicit sincere and rational thought within his parishioners. In front of a weekly standing-room-only crowd, Father Finn used means neither conventional nor boring to regularly dismiss attendees inspired and contemplative. And if the number of these attendees weren't as great as they were, if they didn't ante up and stuff those collection boxes every week, the diocese would have removed him years ago.

"Okay," he began, strolling off the altar with a gold Celtic cross stitched at the center of his vestment to represent St. Stephen's surrounding Irish-American neighborhood. "Who here listens to the great Neil Young? C'mon, let's see some hands, people. Don't be shy, get 'em in the air."

After a simmer of commotion around us, I raised my hand, as did Meg and Brendan. Before Mickey followed, he looked at me to make sure he'd listened to Neil Young before. I nodded, so his hand went up. With arms rising around us, the church was buzzing. Unpredictable sermons were one reason Finn was so wildly popular with St. Stephen's parishioners. He often referenced topical examples from music, literature, film, and sports to relay the day's message. On some Sundays, he would even play pop songs on his acoustic guitar or the choir piano and sing whatever lyrics helped facilitate his message.

"Now, you're all probably wondering why I'm asking you about Neil, a guy born just a smooth drive up the Q.E.W. in Toronto," he said. "Because as we sit here today and remember the lives of my sister Colleen and her husband, Tom, I remember my own things about them. Personal things, like how much the two of them—particularly Colleen—loved to listen to Neil Young. I'll never forget the stack of his albums she had. If he recorded something, anything, she had it."

After The Goldrush. Everybody Knows This Is Nowhere.

On The Beach. Zuma. Tonight's The Night. I glanced down the pew to Meg and smiled. We remembered all the albums and their jacket covers. We remembered how many times my mother spun each on the rickety turntable in our living room.

"Yesterday, I'm over in the rectory, thinking of Colleen and Tom and what I'm going to say today. This is the fourth year we've done this, so you'd think this whole exercise would get easier with time, right? It doesn't," said Finn. "Whether you're a priest or a plumber, losing a loved one is never easy to handle. As the years pass, the severity of the pain associated with their absence varies from tough to tougher. And some days, man, the pain is downright excruciating."

About midway down the center aisle, he stopped walking and talking to scan the crowd, to look over the pews of men dressed in blue oxfords and Notre Dame sweatshirts, women clad in barn coats and khaki pants.

"Unfortunately, there is no universal answer to alleviate this pain. There's no prayer to say, no spell to cast and no drug to take it all away. As long as you remember the loved ones you lost, remember how much they meant to you, how much you miss them, there's going to be a sting right here," he said, pointing to his heart, "and right here," he said, clutching his stomach.

At the end of that sentence, I peered down the pew at Meg again. Looking forward to Finn, she was biting the inside of her mouth, holding in her emotions as best she could. Despite her efforts, a single tear slid down her right cheek, causing me to look away before I duplicated her reaction.

"Over these past four years, I can assure each of you that I've felt that sting many times, too many times to count. But the only way I've ever been able to alleviate that sting, that pain, is to do something that made those lost loved ones happy; something that made them sing or dance or laugh. Though I may be hurting, they're the ones who are gone, the ones not around to bask in the things we can enjoy every day," he said. "So yesterday, I played a little Neil Young in the rectory, for Colleen and Tom. I turned it up nice and loud, even opened a window or two to get the music out to Okell Street. One of the songs I played was a little number called 'Long May You Run.' Has anyone heard it?"

A few nods and smiles greeted his question. Most faces seemed frozen, anticipatory of where Finn was going with all of this. Waiting, they watched as he walked back up to the altar and over to its podium.

"If you haven't heard it, you're about to hear it from me and my old Fender here," he said, reaching under the podium to pull out his chipped and scuffed acoustic guitar. "When I think of my sister and her husband, I think of music like this and the happy times they spent listening to it, together. I also think of Colleen playing this song over and over again when we were younger and—"

He stopped to let a laugh slip, then paused to scratch the back of his head and gather himself. Before he could let his own tears slip down his face, he inhaled and looked up through St. Stephen's ceiling, then back to his waiting parishioners.

"Now, if I can just get through this song in one piece, maybe I can give the two of them something to smile about as they look down on us all, okay?" he said before another deep, composing breath. "All right then."

He tossed his guitar's leather strap over his shoulder, and applause erupted throughout the congregation, a Catholic oddity that was a mere regularity at St. Stephen's. After he tossed a harmonica harness around his neck to perform some of the song's most memorable instrumentation, he got another rousing ovation before he strummed and sang about things to do in stormy weather, about changes that have come. I didn't look to Meg throughout his performance. I didn't need to. As I absorbed every sound that soothed from Finn's Fender, I knew we were channeling the same memories of our smiling parents. The same nights when they danced around our kitchen together to this same Neil Young song. Instead of turning to my left, I bit the inside of my mouth and enjoyed those chords as they bounced down side aisles and off stained-glass windows.

After Finn clipped his last note, he talked about how some of the song's lyrics connected to his points about the pain of loss, about honoring our lost. This elicited more nods of recognition and understanding, then a shower of applause at the sermon's end. In the entire diocese, St. Stephen's was the only Catholic church where cheers after the homily were expected and accepted. But in the entire Diocese of Buffalo, there was only one Father Finn Leary. With him, you always expected the unexpected.

After Mass, I headed downtown to the corner of Allen Street and Elmwood Avenue with Meg and the boys to find the sunlit interiors of Jim's Steakout, a downtown Mecca for loyal bleu cheese and hot sauce-soaked chicken finger sub disciples like Brendan. After local taverns' nightly last call at four a.m., Steakout routinely became packed with intoxicated loyalists, hungry for greasy wings and subs. Thankful that no one from that crowd was still hanging around, we huddled into a wooden booth for Brendan's birthday celebration. Every Nolan was present—except one.

"It's a real shame she couldn't be here," said Meg of my

expectant wife, Dana. "What happened again?"

"She got called into work," I said, frustrated as I straightened myself up in the bench and took a sip of my Dr. Pepper.
"Guess the staff's post-work drinking got out of hand last night
and left a few waitresses violently ill this morning. Her boss
called frantic at around ten, so she has to serve through lunch and
dinner. She sends her birthday wishes, though. She really wanted
to be here, and felt worse about having to miss the Mass."

"Should we go over there and say hello?" she asked
before sipping her Diet Coke.

"If you were three months pregnant and exhausted,
would you want people to come visit you at work?" I asked.
"Trust me, we're better off here. She was pretty pissed this morning, so we should definitely give her the day to cool off."

Meg smiled while extending a sympathetic hand to my
shoulder. After I took a deep, composing breath, I looked out
one of the restaurant's windows to see a young couple walking
up Elmwood together. Both in black T-shirts and exposing their
tattooed arms, they wrapped those limbs around each other's
waist as the strolled through the crosswalk at Allen and kissed on
the opposite corner. Together on a Sunday; together to laugh and
touch and feel in front of strangers, in front of passing motorists
and mountain bikes. For a brief moment, I imagined myself on
that Allen corner, clutching Dana absent of inconvenient obstruc-
tions that intruded on our lives. There'd be no Sunday shifts,
no tables to wait on. There'd be no other place to be than that
street corner, holding and touching and kissing within our own
black-and-white photograph. Absent this desire, I let the couple
walk from my view and continue up the avenue. I instead turned
to focus on my reality, one that sat my nephews across the table
from me.

"Okay, boys," I said, extending my knuckles to both their fists for a bump. "Are we ready for a birthday lunch or what?"

"Yeah," they said, then reached around their Cokes and connected with my fists.

"So, what are we ordering? Brendan, since you're the man of the hour, I think you can do the honors and start us off."

"How about a large pizza with extra pepperoni, waffle fries with gravy, and a chicken finger sub for me?"

Quieter than Mickey, Brendan had sandy blond hair and freckles across his face, marks poached from his mother. Thin but growing, he was already the star forward for his youth hockey team, the Hawks. Though emotionally reserved, the slick lefty was all heart on the ice, shining with grit and hustle when he'd fly after a loose puck and ignite a breakaway. After he'd flip a wrist shot over the shoulder of an opposing goaltender, he'd skate along the boards and flash a wide grin underneath his wire facemask. Once the season ended, he'd spend proceeding months repetitiously shooting an orange street hockey ball at a tape square on his battered garage door. Meg grew tired of making him come into the house at nightfall, so she had a garage spotlight installed to shine on Brendan and his target. She said it helped him see the square better, but I think she wanted a brighter view of the kid, a way to keep him closer as she watched from the kitchen window. Growing older and ordering saucy, scalding chicken finger subs, he was growing up fast. Meg knew it.

"And who do you think is going to eat all this food, mister?" she asked.

"Yeah," I added. "You think the Mick's gonna eat half a pizza himself?"

"I could do it," said Mickey, sitting up straight and

putting his small hands on the table. "I went to my friend's house last week and had three pieces of pizza all by myself."

"It was a sheet pizza, Mickey," Brendan said before leaning forward to dismiss his baby brother's significant achievement. "Those pieces are smaller, so they don't count as whole slices."

"Yes they do," screamed Mickey. "Mommy, tell Brendan they count. They count!"

With floppy brown hair tickling his eyebrows and covering forehead freckles, Mickey was feisty, tough and shorter than his brother. The kid looked like he'd be a fighter one day, the type whose forearms would breathe out of black rolled-up sleeves in the doorway of a downtown tavern. Though only in the first grade, he didn't let Brendan push him around. Dealing with his mother was a different story.

"Michael Patrick Nolan, you will lower your voice right now," Meg calmly scolded, with dark eyes opened wide and use of the boy's full, baptismal name. "Do you want me to take you out of here before we order even a slice of pizza?"

"No, Mommy."

What made Meg such a good single mother was the line she drew between playmate and policeman, a distinction that earned her the simultaneous adoration and respect of her boys. In her early thirties, she looked younger. Her brown hair dropped to her shoulders and complemented scattered freckles over smooth, soft skin. She should have appeared more worn, working long hours as a court stenographer downtown. As a woman who'd been left alone to raise two boys, she should have stood angrier, full of a jaded distrust. It would have been understandable. The boys' father, a loathsome fucker named Billy Doyle, fled Buffalo's city limits in an F-150 pick-up before Mickey was born and hadn't been heard from since. Billy and Meg didn't marry before or after Brendan was born, so Meg attached our surname to her newborn boy. Maybe she did this because, somewhere deep down, she knew Billy would eventually split—and fulfill the underwhelming promise of every guy she drew close.

Meg knew how to be a mother; she was good at it. She was terrible at picking men, and had a tremendous knack for scooping the wrong ones. Before Billy Doyle, there was Joey Braun, a long-haired Lynyrd Skynyrd guy who drank frightening amounts of Southern Comfort—even for a Buffalonian. After Joe came Bobby Collins, a huge fan of Rush, jean jackets and cocaine. He stuffed about a thousand dollars of Meg's money into one of his denim pockets before eventually landing in rehab. Finally, the quick-fisted Kevin Quinn stormed into Meg's life to the thirsty licks of Van Halen's "Panama." A month into their relationship, Quinn earned a week's stay at the Erie County Holding Center for instigating a massive drunken brawl inside Ralph Wilson Stadium. Shortly after, he earned the boot from Meg. His incarceration sucked all the promise out of their relationship.

Next to that calamitous trio, Billy seemed God-sent. Unfortunately, while she was pregnant with Mickey, Meg endured while Billy fulfilled his predictable destiny. He left her, split town without warning, and without leaving a forwarding address. If there were any positives to be taken from the situation, it was Meg's tremendous foresight in legally making Brendan a Nolan, not a Doyle. When Mickey was born, he too became a Nolan, one more to add to Brendan, Meg and me.

When our parents died, we became the final four, the only Nolans left. Meg and I got over the loss partly by putting everything we had into her boys, who needed the love and guidance our parents gave to us. Every day, Meg and I thought about that guidance, thought about the things we'd have to do to honor our parents' memory. There were the children's books they read us, the open-air folk concerts they walked us to. There was the night our mother blindfolded us, put us in the car and drove us out to a surprise double-feature at the Buffalo Drive-In. There was our trip to old War Memorial Stadium to see The Beach Boys play, that humid summer night our father danced with us in the aisle. These were the memories we laughed and cried inside of before taking a deep breath and wishing they were each still alive, still around to be grandparents to Brendan and Mickey. With my fatherhood approaching, I wondered how I'd ever approach my parents' dedication, their selflessness. With two boys already under her tutelage, Meg's actions were her answers. She handled her boys masterfully, just like our parents would have.

"And Brendan," she continued, "I don't care if it is your birthday. You don't embarrass your brother in front of Uncle John. Three pieces of sheet pizza is plenty in my book."

"Mine too," I said to Mickey.

I offered my fist across the table again to meet his kid-sized version before he flashed his tough, first-grade smile. After civility was restored, I went to the counter, put our order in and returned to the booth to settle in.

"So," I said, tapping my fingertips on the table, "are we doing presents now or are we waiting until after we eat?"

"What do you want to do, Brendan?" said Meg. "It's your day, so it's your choice."

Her sentence was barely finished before Brendan decided.

"Can we do the presents now, please?"

Such polite kids. If I thought Meg would let me, I'd have bought them presents every week. As the dominant male presence in their lives, I wanted to make up for the guy who wasn't there, the coward who hit the road when reality became inconvenient. She wouldn't have any of that. No charity for her or the boys. Just familial love, doled out in reasonable portions on weekdays, birthdays and holidays.

"Here's mine, pal." I pushed a two-tiered package across the table. First was the small square on top, which he tore open. Holding the gift, he seemed grateful, yet unfamiliar with the disc case in his hands.

"Who is the Sam Roberts Band?"

"Group I've been listening to, from Canada," I said. "Rock and roll, lots of guitar. You'll love it, I promise you. If it's nice out this weekend, we'll take a ride to the skate park and listen to it in the car together, okay?"

"Sure, Uncle John, sure," he said, politely smiling like he did at some of the other albums I'd given him over the previous nine years of his life. "Thank you."

"Uncle John, can I listen too?" asked Mickey. "I like rock and roll."

"Sure thing, Mick."

Meg and I grew up with the music of our parents, addicted to their Beatles and Bob Dylan records, their piles of Paul Simon cassette tapes. Music was a Nolan tradition, so for every one of the boys' birthdays, I bought them each a CD or two to go with whatever toys or clothes or sports equipment they actually wanted. What I didn't give them, Meg played for them, spinning the Grateful Dead's hazy jams or Neil Young's acoustical yearn on vinyl in place of bedtime stories. Unfortunately, both were too young to have seen me play the Nighthawk, but they'd heard the stories from their mother. Meg also had a bootleg recording of one of my shows, one she had the bar's sound guys rip from the soundboard years back. When she played it for Brendan and Mickey, they loved it, so I broke out Deirdre from time to time and played a few of the tunes I used to cover on those Friday nights. On these occasions, I was their rocker uncle. On their birthdays, I was their music teacher.

When Brendan opened the second box, he was as excited as ever. Folded under tissue paper, he found a throwback royal blue and gold Sabres hockey jersey adorned with the name and number of his favorite Sabre, forward Derek Roy. With eyes wide and mouth agape, pure jubilation radiated as he pulled the jersey over his head and slid his arms into the sleeves. A perfect fit.

"So that's why you wanted to open the presents, huh?" hushed Meg. "You show-off. How am I supposed to compete with that?"

"Sorry," I said, even though I wasn't. I basked in Brendan's satisfaction and youthful awe. "I saw it and had to grab it. What do you think, Brendan?"

"Thank you so much," he said before sliding over to give me another knuckle pound. "Thank you, thank you, thank you."

With wrapping paper, tissue and box strewn across the table, Brendan ran his fingers over the stitched logo on the front of the jersey, the raging white buffalo and the crossed swords. When he found the gold stripes on the sleeves, he went over those as well, entranced. He didn't even look up to see our bounty of food arrive.

"Brendan, you should take that jersey off and put it back in the box before you start eating," said Meg. "You don't want to get bleu cheese or pizza sauce on it, do you?"

"I don't care," Brendan said, smiling while he puffed out his chest and ran his hands over the front of the jersey again.

"I'm never taking this off, Ma. Never."

Meg sighed, then relented.

"Fine, but tuck that napkin into the neck and put another on your lap. Right now."

We dug into the pizza and let the birthday boy pound down his bleu cheese-soaked chicken finger sub. Delicious grease coated each pizza slice's layer of cheese and pepperoni, and dripped from our chins to the tabletop when we took bites. Mickey tried to eat his first slice fast, storing each large bite in the sides of his mouth like a greedy chipmunk. When one side of his mouth was packed, he jammed bites of mozzarella and tomato sauce in the other. He lowered his eyebrows to glare at Brendan through every bite.

"Mickey, don't be a little pig," said Meg. "Chew every bite and swallow before adding another. This isn't some sort of race. Chew. Chew. Swallow."

While scolding Mickey, she missed Brendan devouring his sandwich, pushing Frank's hot sauce, bits of creamy bleu cheese and shards of lettuce out the back of his sub roll with every bite. After we finished, our table lay in ruins, with soda and hot sauce and bits of chicken strewn about the tabletop. On the tin pizza tray laid a single pepperoni. Mickey snatched it up, tossed it into his mouth and smiled wide: all teeth. Just as I was about to get up to clear this damage, a large hand from behind me touched my shoulder before a voice joined it.

"You can't have a birthday without a cake, right?" said Finn in his deep baritone as he held a white and green frosted cake with 10 unlit candles above my head.

"Uncle Finn," the boys yelled and jumped from their seats to hand out low-fives.

"What do you say, men?" he asked. He always called

the boys *men*. After he handed me the cake, he mussed Mickey's floppy hair and gave Brendan a pat on the back. Finn was our mother's only brother, the last close relative we had to share birthdays and holidays with. That morning, he was a popular clergyman. In Jim's Steakout, wearing blue jeans, a red flannel shirt and his brown secondhand overcoat, he was Uncle Finn. That was enough for us.

"So what is a great uncle to give his great nephew on such a great birthday?"

Brendan shrugged, waiting. Finn reached behind our wooden booth's wall and revealed a hockey stick with a red bow attached to the top. When Brendan gripped the handle, his eyes lit up wide. Again.

"A buddy of mine at the arena owed me a favor," said Finn, a smile curling the corner of his mouth. "On that stick are the autographs of every Sabre on last year's team, even that defenseman who was traded to San Jose."

"Brian Campbell?"

"You got it."

"Wow," said Brendan, his mouth open as he read every name scribbled on the stick. "Thanks, Uncle Finn. Thanks a lot."

After I pushed the cake to the center of the table, I folded my arms across my chest and turned to shake my head.

"Nice try," I whispered, "but he can't wear that stick. I bought him the Roy sweater, so I win this year."

"Sure, John. Sure." He put both hands on my shoulders and leaned toward my ear. "But what if I told you my arena buddy got that stick from Roy's locker? What would the score be then?"

"Um, call it even?"

"Deal," he laughed, then turned his attention back to the

boys. "I see I missed the feeding frenzy, but do you think there's room for cake?"

Finn headed to the front counter to grab five forks and a plastic knife, then returned to light the cake's candles with the royal blue lighter he pulled from his pocket. After we sang the birthday song, Brendan extinguished the candles and Finn served each sliced section on a napkin.

"So, did you hear about the gig we booked?" he said, sliding into the bench across from me.

"What gig?"

"We slid into a spot for Strummerville, the Joe Strummer tribute night in December at your old stomping grounds, the Nighthawk," he said. "We go on around 10-ish, after some old ska band called Mustache Tango. We've been practicing a bunch of Clash covers, so it should be pretty wild."

Many things made Finn popular within the St. Stephen's community, but nothing made him more notable with the parish's youth and music enthusiasts than his wildly entertaining side gig. In local wedding halls, bars and the occasional downtown rock hole, Father Finn Leary was the only Buffalo priest who punched keys for a rollicking, non-denominational, piano-infused punk rock band called the Nickel City Kings.

In the years before he entered the priesthood, Finn was a normal, scruffy guy who played piano for a variety of local bands. After working with the city's youth at St. Jude's during the day, he spent his nights toiling in the smoke-filled bars and clubs that shook with Buffalo's rock and blues acts of the late 1980s. He was just a passionate musician, one tinkling ivory keys behind gravely vocals and spastic guitar work; one trying to emulate the work of his vinyl heroes like Richard Manuel and Roy Bittan.

That was before Finn's moment, before the transformational minutes of an event that led him away from his nights as a side musician and toward his unforeseen spiritual calling. He never told me the specifics of those minutes, the exact details of a scene that transformed his existence. All he ever said was it was as if a light switch was flipped on, as if his situational darkness was lifted and illuminated by an idea that seemed so right, so absolutely necessary. And so began the merger of the piano man with the priest, a union that instilled Finn with a duality that unconventionally augmented his position as the latter. His whole musical presence made him more relatable, more human to his parishioners. But for Buffalo's tattooed barflies, jukebox armies and blues junkies, they could care less about Finn's odd spiritual balancing act. As long as he was around to mash those black and whites, to hit those keys with the same fervor as he had before he donned the blacks and white, he'd have crowds to bask in his rhythmic presence.

"We picked up a new bass player, this big Jamaican named Neko," said Finn. "Guy's got a decent handle and a phenomenal stage presence. He just stalks his stage corner, slaps his strings and swings his dreads. The kids at our last show loved him."

"Nobody threw a shoe at him?"

"No one," he said, laughing. "But honestly, how many bands have lost two bass players to shoe-induced injuries? It has to mean something, right?"

"Punishment from the Almighty?" I suggested. "Maybe he's not a fan of the new material."

"If the good Lord wanted to break up the band, he'd have to break my hands." Finn held up his palms up and wiggled his fingers. "Also, our new songs are brilliant. Imagine Mick

Jones riffs married with Billy Joel keys. You'd pay to hear that, right?"

"Who wouldn't?"

"That's why you have to come out to the Strummerville show," he replied, then slapped the tabletop for emphasis. "We're going to slide in a few new numbers among Clash covers, so it's going to be great. Bring Dana and we'll make a night of it."

"I'll get back to you on that," I said before slouching in my bench. "Dana will be almost five months in by then, so it could be dicey. She's been having a tough go of it, carrying the pregnancy through school and work. I could use a few prayers for the two, er, three or us. Please."

"You got it, kid," he said, then reached across the table and slapped my arm. "I pray for you guys every day, but I'll put in a special call to the boss tonight."

He always referred to God as *the boss*.

"By late December," he said, "you'll be relaxed, the little Nolan won't be stirring, and the wife will be begging you, *pleading* with you for a night of top-rate piano playing at the Nighthawk. Priest and uncle's promise."

"Tell the boss I give my best," I said, smiling. "And say hello to my parents, too, will you?"

"I always do, John," he said. "I always do."

3

I look into your eyes
See you standing by the bar
Wonder if you'll have the time
To dance with this young rock star
-"Nights of You & Me" by J. Nolan

My alarm clock was beeping and squealing as sunlight joined a wailing car alarm outside my window shades. When I glared at the clock, it read 7:23 a.m. Again.

The day was Monday, which was nowhere near Friday. On Fridays, I could slip out after work for an exhale away from the job, away from home. At the end of the week, McGinty's Pub on Swan Street featured five-dollar Miller Lite pitchers to accompany its world-class jukebox, full of rock legends and undiscovered Canadian guitar magicians. But Monday was not Friday. The frustration of this reality brought my palm down hard on the clock, which silenced the cacophony and elicited grumblings from my wife, Dana.

"Why do you have to smack the shit out of that snooze every morning?"

I caught my first glimpse of a tanned twenty-one-year-old named Dana Morelli a little over four years ago, back in the thick of my Nighthawk residency. I remember exactly what she wore that night. I remember the way her raven hair hung past her emerald eyes and over her shoulders, covering the first and last letters of "CBGB" across the chest of her tight black T-shirt. I remember how she moved and swayed a few rows back from the front edge of stage. I even remember her vodka tonic and how she held her straw during every sip. Most of all, I'll never forget her sharp green gaze, a look that didn't burn as much as it warmed. When a look like that connects, it's like a lightning bolt that staggers before it injects a dizzying sense of drug-free alteration. It's hard to shake off, harder to forget. Still, I gathered myself, let that look wash over me. Once stable, I returned a glance of my own, one that connected and locked before I spoke up and took a chance.

"For my last one tonight, I want to take a request," I said into the mic, looking right into her eyes. "How about you, miss? You in the black tee. Do you have a song you want to hear?"

She smiled, embarrassed at the attention.

"How about 'American Woman'," she asked. "Do you know that one?"

"Do I know it?" I asked, adjusting myself on the stool. "Sweetheart, after this rendition, you're going to think I wrote it."

Laughs, claps, hoots from the floor joined her smile as she took another sip from her drink. After my left hand was set on the guitar neck and my boot soles were planted comfortably on the stage, I began finger picking the loose strings, plucking lightly to incite the emanation of a sultry blues walk-down to a G. After I repeated this progression a few times, I replicated the humming and the doo-doos famous in the song's introduction. I soothed out lyrics about an American woman and how she can mess your mind before I spelled out "American" letter-by-letter.

The crowd swayed in anticipation of what was coming— the visceral thrust forward that followed the tame picking and humming and singing. When I hit the last string of the lead-in, I paused, looked at her again. She was waiting. I pulled an orange pick from my pocket and stomped my black Doc Marten boot on the stage four times—THUMP, THUMP, THUMP, THUMP— before thundering down on the heavier acoustic strings to reach the power of the song's electric guitar work. My fingers slid up and down the neck, through the frets, changing chords and manipulating strings to stir patrons into a head-bobbing lather. I continued to stomp the stage planks and replicate a beat in the absence of a bass drum.

I leaned into the mic to wail out the opening lyrics about an American woman, how she should stay away from me and let me be. This song wasn't exactly conducive to what I hoped to achieve with my request solicitation. As the divisive lyrics hit her ears, I hoped she didn't get the wrong idea. Even though I didn't know anything about her, I knew I wanted her to stay. But she requested the song, so I played the shit out of it, regardless of the nasty lyrical connotations. Strumming and singing, I caught sight of her again. She was rocking back and forth, flailing her wiry arms above her head and calling for more, loving every second of it. At the end of the song, I struck a string so hard it snapped and curled up the neck, effectively ending the performance. When I stood to take a bow, sweat dropped from my shoul- der-length black hair and stung my eyes. After I rubbed them dry, I opened them to see Dana, smiling and clapping. She waved me over to the bar, so I stashed my guitar before stepping off the stage. When I reached her, she already had a bottle of Budweiser waiting for me.

"For my request," she said, holding out the beer to me. We did introductions. I was Johnny. She was Dana.

"Interesting take on that song," she said. "I saw Lenny in

concert last year and he doesn't perform it like that at all."

"Lenny?" I asked. "Lenny Kravitz?"

"Of course. Who else would sing his song?"

I turned my head to the side and took a long, deep swig. Annoyance, confusion and irritation were all simmering. I tossed strands of my sweaty hair away from my face.

"Kravitz's version is a cover," I said. "It's originally sung by the Guess Who, from Canada. You've never heard the original version?"

She paused, perplexed.

"I guess not," she said, looking a bit embarrassed. "When I think of that song, I think of the video with Lenny, the American flag, and Heather Graham gyrating on the roof of a school bus. He doesn't do a bad version, though, right?"

It was the worst cover. Ever. Worse than Madonna's cover of Don McLean's "American Pie." Worse than U2's cover of the Beatles' "Helter Skelter." This was fact, not opinion, but I still shrugged with indifference. Damn those eyes of hers. Every time I locked with them, that radiating euphoria returned to my head and chest.

"This is my first time here," she said. "My friend has been begging me to come with her for weeks, and she finally broke me down. She's over there, at the high top with that guy."

I turned to see a mass of snarled dyed blonde hair being cradled and led by a tattooed forearm. The girl's lips were mashed into the face belonging to the inked forearm, and the pace the two moved with was aggressive and impressive. Even prudes throughout the barroom had to be inspired.

"Couple?"

"No," she said. "They just met a little while ago. She's quick like that, I guess."

"Decisive, for damn sure," I said, smirking before I took another swig. "You two don't go out much together?"

"Not really. Like I said, this is my first time here. After seeing you perform, though, maybe I'll be back again. You play every Friday?"

"You got it. I tend to attract the heaviest drinkers on the scene, so that's how I nailed down the Friday slot," I said. "It's not CBGB's, but it'll do."

She looked at me, perplexed again.

"CBGB's? Is that another rock joint around here? I don't hang around this area of downtown too much."

"Are you kidding?" I said, looking down and pinching her shirtsleeve. "You're *wearing* the bar's shirt. You didn't know what this shirt was for when you bought it?"

"Not really, no. I got it at Urban Outfitters for twenty-eight bucks. It fits nice, looks cool. Don't you think it looks good on me?"

And I did. I liked how tightly it fit over her breasts, how cool it looked with her skinny-legged black jeans, her black strap heels. I liked the depth in those emeralds, the style of her raven hair. The way her scent intermixed with the Nighthawk's tobacco and Southern Comfort-tinged interior breeze; the way her delicate hand grazed my arm to send soothing warmth through my chest. I loved all of it.

Later that night, we sat outside the bar and shared a few cigarettes before we made out against a parked Honda. I kissed her left cheek before she pulled back and told me she had a boyfriend. I told her I didn't care. She smiled at my confidence, then leaned toward me so I could move my lips down to her neck. I worked up to her mouth as she slid her fingers across the ink sleeve of Celtic knotting over my entire upper left arm. At four in the morning, we hiked up to my place on Allen Street and made love on the kitchen floor. She broke up with her boyfriend the next weekend.

Over the next year, we had some good times and survived some bad times. I took Dana to rock shows at the Nighthawk, for strolls up Elmwood, down Delaware and around the Erie Basin Marina. We went to Sabres games, grabbed postgame beers at the Swannie House. When my parents died, she was there for the crying, the depression and the hurt. She was there when I needed someone to take away the pain, to coax me toward some path of relevance. About sixteen months after our first night together, we stood in front of Uncle Finn at St. Stephen's and were married. At the reception, we danced to both the Lenny Kravitz and Guess Who version of "American Woman," our first necessary compromise as husband and wife. A little over four years after I played that song for her at the Nighthawk, we slept in the same bed—and dealt with drastically different schedules.

"Do you want me to make you some coffee?" I asked. "I'm gonna go turn the pot on for myself."

"Coffee?" she grumbled. "I'm fucking pregnant. I can't drink caffeine."

"Right, right," I said. Of course she couldn't drink coffee. "Well, you missed out on Brendan's party yesterday. Finn showed up with a cake, we had some laughs. Good times."

"Look, I don't mean to sound like a total rag, but could you please make yourself silent? I worked a double until two last night and my ears are still ringing from all the yelling and screaming during the football game. This talking isn't helping the ringing."

A little over three months into her pregnancy and she was already irritable. I just shook my head, set my feet on the cold hardwood and tucked the comforter tightly under a shivering Dana. She rolled away from me to cradle a body pillow between her arms and legs, cooing and moaning as she adjusted herself back into a sleeping position. I stood there enviously watching her as she jostled about. I leaned over and kissed the back of her head, pulled the window shades down and let her be.

Our schedules weren't always so contrasting. When we started dating, Dana worked as a customer service representative for B&B Collections, located in an office park near downtown's Amtrak station on Exchange Street. Every day, she went to her desk, put on a headset and went down a list of residents who missed payments on phones, cars, credit cards or student loans. She spent her mornings listening to excuses and reluctantly enforcing penalties. Every day, she absorbed the yelling, crying and pleading associated with problems considered bothersome one day, life-threatening the next.

"I'm out of work," they'd say to her. "I'm still looking for work. The wife left me. My husband cheated on me. The kids are in college. The kids are selfish brats. I need my car for work. I need my car for fun. Mother died. Father died. Depression has worn me down. Gonna get paid soon. Have to get paid next week. Give me another week. How about another month? One more chance? Don't you have a soul, you heartless bitch?"

By the time we married, this omnipresent flurry of resident fury buried Dana like a lake-effect snowdrift. Every morning, she walked into work hollowed, numb. The job transformed her, sucked out all that youthful exuberance stowed behind her eyes when we first connected at the Nighthawk. In its place, it instilled an acceptance of life's brutal hand, a jaded attitude to combat a nagging empathy—and such emotions were useless between nine and five. Feeling bad for people didn't relieve debt or remove boots from car tires. Sympathy didn't dismiss the fact that Dana was on the delivering end of a harsh reality. Every evening, she returned to our Allen Street apartment depleted by the job, tortured with the nagging whispers of guilt from the necessary actions of her days.

One day, she decided to revolt.

Dana took her last call at B&B on a Tuesday. After she hung up the phone, she took off her headset, packed up her stuff, and walked right out the door. No goodbyes. No two weeks' notice. No consultation with a boss. She simply left and never went back. She needed a change in her life before it was too late, before the resignation that extinguished the hopes of her methodical coworkers had a chance to douse hers. She wanted satisfaction, fulfillment and all that other shit young idealists want to bask in. She wanted to escape Buffalo, to leave behind the gray skies and long winters that could sap ambition. Dana wanted to work a job she loved under perpetual sunny skies, in a place where overcoats and tanning booths were unnecessary; where flip-flops were the preferable footwear. She wanted to move to Florida, a state her parents had already made home a couple years back, right when we started dating. Every few nights after she left B&B, she'd pitch a move. And every few nights, I talked her down. Eventually, I defeated the relocation idea. I had no interest in leaving my family behind to escape to the south; I didn't intend to leave my birthplace. I wanted to live in Buffalo, raise my kids in Buffalo and be laid to rest in Buffalo. Dana still needed to find a new life path while she was young enough to abruptly change course. So a year into our marriage, she decided to go back to school. She decided to pursue an associate's degree in the Eastern art of massage therapy.

While learning this trade, she needed to work somewhere on the side, somewhere with a flexible schedule and decent pay for someone absorbing the benefits of holism, Oriental anatomy and physiology at the Western New York College of Massage. With these considerations, Dana became a waitress at the White Room, a blues bar down the street from the Nighthawk. The joint was known for its Wednesday karaoke night and killer blues revues on Fridays and Saturdays. Also, according to the *Buffalo Gazette* article framed outside their men's bathroom, the White Room hosted the city's *third* best Sunday Night Football party, making Monday mornings a bleary ordeal for the bar's Sunday evening patrons. Its battered wooden tables played lunch host for area Democrats, salesmen and servicemen, dealing out large portions of crisp, sauce-soaked chicken wings and pulled pork sandwiches, complete with the White Room's own homemade barbeque sauce. These lunch shifts were the safe play for waitresses. With the standard wing and sandwich fare came few drinks and even fewer drunks, a welcome respite from the rowdy biker crowds who frequented the neighboring whiskey dives around Lafayette Square. If a waitress wanted to make some serious money, she'd have to brave the dinner elements, which were fueled by a loud trio of large appetites, leather-clad alcoholics and functional binge drinkers.

When Dana was offered night shifts to balance with her daytime therapy classes, she went for it. Her dark hair wooed older men into generous tips from dinner through the wee morning hours. Her emerald eyes invited even more, ranging from whispered pick-up lines by blue-collared union reps, to phone numbers from white-collared suitors. When she would hustle her delicate frame across the restaurant floor, these men watched and admired. Each kept the wings and pork and beer and liquor coming just to earn a glance in their direction, the same glance that hypnotized me. And Dana knew this. She knew that, every time she grooved her hips from side to side and tapped her heels on the tiles, the tips would pile up. Staged or not, she learned to like it. There were no more repossessions to deal with, no more faceless tears over the telephone. Anything was better than debt collection. Anything. Even working as a waitress through her first trimester.

After I left Dana to sleep that morning, I walked into the bathroom and shut the door behind me. I stepped into the shower and flicked on the waterproof radio, tuned it to 97 Rock and kept the volume low. I turned on the water and made it scalding hot, let it fall down on my dark hair as I listened to three straight wailers from Zeppelin. After ten minutes, I stepped out of the shower, humming the melody of Robert Plant's vocals on "The Ocean." Once toweled off, I returned to the bedroom to quietly grab a pair of navy blue pants from my dresser. Dana was still clutching the elongated pillow and was curled up next to it while rhythmically breathing. She had entered the heightened relaxation of back-to-sleep sleep, a state that elicits the most vivid dreams, the most tempting fantasies. Those were my Saturday mornings, the early hours I'd lie under the sheets and slip into dreams until thoughts of coffee and a newspaper put my feet on the floor. Watching Dana adjust herself under the sheets again, I wanted the rest she was having, the sleep she was lost in. I delicately crawled atop the sheets to sit next to her and watch her serene temperament until she felt my gaze on her lids. Her eyelids fluttered open, wearily.

"What?" she growled, her voice muffled as her face was still plowed into her pillow.

"I'm just watching you sleep," I whispered.

"Great. Have fun with that."

"Oh, I almost forgot," I said. "Finn's band scored a spot on the bill for the annual Joe Strummer tribute night and wants us to go."

"Isn't that show around Christmas?"

"A little after Christmas, at the Nighthawk. Finn would never do a show in the middle of Advent, so I imagine it's a few days after. What do you think?"

"What do I think? I think it's fucking October," she said. "Ask me a little closer to the date, preferably when I'm not freezing and telling you to leave me alone. If I was forced into an answer right now, I'd tell you I have no interest in trudging through the snow to watch Clash covers before another one of your uncle's bass players gets clipped by a shoe."

"No, no. He said this new guy is—"

"I don't care," she interrupted. "Can't you tell me this later? Also, why are you still here? Aren't you going to be late for work?"

"That all depends," I said. "Do you want me to go? I could stay home today, call in sick."

"Are you joking?" she said, then turned over to yank the covers down to her waist. "Why the hell do you want to stay home from work?"

"I haven't seen you in a while. I could stay in bed with you all day, keep you warm. Maybe you can practice your massage techniques on me. What do you think?"

"What do I *think*?" she said. "I think you're talking like an asshole who's thinking with his cock, not his brain. I'm a student and a waitress, pregnant and attached to your health insurance. If you lose your job, we're completely screwed."

"Dana, c'mon. You think I could get fired for calling in sick? Guys in my building have been lighting up their morning coffees with Jack for decades."

"I don't give a shit about the old drunks in your building," she said. "You're the one I'm depending on, so quit acting like a boy and think like a man, dammit. Get your fucking pants on and get out of here!"

"Fine, I get it. You're in a bad mood." I climbed off the bed and slipped into my pants. "You're overworked. You're tired. You're pregnant. Maybe you'll feel better when you give up some shifts at the bar. Did you tell them about the baby yet?"

"During yesterday's Bills game? No. If I had to break the news during that shit show, my manager would have gone berserk. After we went down by three touchdowns, he looked like he was going to stab himself. I'm lucky I'm not showing that much."

"But you're going have to tell him soon, right?"

"This week. I'll tell him this week."

"And then what? How long can you wait tables pregnant?"

"A few more months, I guess." She pulled the blankets up to her chin and over her shoulders. "I could probably do it for a little longer if I could get some proper rest. Uninterrupted."

"Fine, I'm gone," I said, clapping my hands while backing toward the door. "You need anything else before I go?"

"My God, just go," she said, causing me to grab the bedroom door handle and exit. I had one foot into the kitchen before her voice turned me around.

"Wait, John, hold up a second," she said, then sat up and let the comforter fall off her shoulders and down to her lap. After she flipped the matted black strands of hair from her face, she fluttered her eyelashes at me. "I'm sorry I'm being such a bitch, okay? I'm irritable and spent. Plus, after working the last four nights, my back is fucking killing me. I don't mean to take it out on you; you just happen to be here. You're the one in front of me when I feel like this."

"You know you can quit, right?" I said. "I can go knock on some doors, get a job bartending nights somewhere. I know it's not ideal, but say the word and I'll make it happen."

"I'm not letting you do that. Just let me get a little sleep and I'll be fine, okay?"

"You got it," I said. "And with that, I'm out."

I shut the bedroom door behind me and had a sudden urge to say one more thing to her, just three more words before I let her be. After I turned the knob and poked my head back in, though, I couldn't interrupt the silence. Dana lay curled and serene, utterly peaceful amid her rhythmic breathing. There was something about her exhaustion I found oddly endearing. Whether it was how her black strands lay strewn about the pillow or how she spooned with feathered pillows as if they were people, there was something so alluring it sucked the venom from her earlier attitude. Watching her slip into her therapeutic slumber, I could surrender within this truth and note my attraction as an element of love.

4

When we see our lives go by
See the days roar on past
Do we ever stop and think
Of how to make 'em last?
-"Stop, Feel" by J. Nolan

Later that Monday, a city resident stood in front of me at my office's counter. I tried to ignore the scent of stale cigarettes off his black wool overcoat.

"When I ordered the latex suit, the clerk assured me it would be a tight fit," he said, running his long, black-polished fingernails through the dark, greasy locks flowing past his ears. "It was for a party, so I wanted this cat suit to cling to the skin, you know? Really fucking tight."

"I understand," I said. "So you were dissatisfied with the way the suit fit your wife or girlfriend?"

"My wife or girlfriend?" He put his palms on the counter. "No, no. The suit was for me."

"Oh, I'm sorry. Of course it was. My mistake."

I was officially desensitized to such odd revelations. They had merely become the irregular order of my days. I stood in front of this festive visitor as a consumer mediator for the Consumer Aid and Entertainment Licensing division on the fifth floor of downtown Buffalo's architectural jewel, City Hall. After I retired my guitar, an old high school friend hooked me up with the job. I needed a nine-to-five gig, one that would afford me the time and resources to get married and enjoy a family. After two interviews, I officially became an embedded government drone.

Every day since, I've monotonously dealt with incoming consumer complaints and mechanically issued entertainment licenses to bars and restaurants. Consumers have trudged into our downtown government office from the Metrorail station on Main Street. Tavern owners have strolled in from Niagara Square. On many mornings, I've listened to a litany of local consumers and their problems. I've helped these taxpayers garner refunds from businesses that have wronged them. The unkempt and greasy gentleman in front of me had, in his estimation, been wronged—in multiple ways.

"And the costume's fit was my second problem," he said.

"What was the first?"

"It wasn't anatomically correct."

"Excuse me?"

"Cat penis," he said, scratching his facial stubble. "There wasn't a cat penis on the suit."

I took a deep breath and crossed my arms over my blue dress shirt and navy tie.

"Do cats even have penises?"

"Well, they sure as shit better have something to distinguish themselves from the lady cats, right?" he said, very matter of fact-like. "I mean, I don't want to split hairs here, but I was told I was getting a male cat suit. For three fifty, I want what I was promised."

"Three *hundred* and fifty? Dollars?" I said, wide-eyed. "That's what you paid for a Halloween costume?"

"Who said it was for Halloween?"

"Oh, well, I guess I assumed that—"

"Whatever, whatever," he interrupted. "I bought a latex cat suit, but I wouldn't have paid a goddamn dime if I knew I wasn't getting a cock on it."

"Okay," I sighed, aware that maybe I wasn't *completely* desensitized. "So you want a refund for a three hundred and fifty dollar cat suit because it didn't cling to your skin and, most importantly, lacked proper feline genitalia?"

"That's right."

"Sure," I said. "Could you wait here for a second?"

I walked away from the counter and past my shoulder-high cubicle walls, soft and gray and scattered with pictures of places I'd been and people I should be with. Every day, strangers I didn't want to be with demanded refunds for televisions, radios, vacuums and telephones. Their new car broke down; their old car's repairs weren't performed. They wanted refunds for pants that didn't fit, for winter coats they didn't like. Their landlord's a deadbeat, scumbag or general Nazi prick. A veterinarian killed their cat, Bubbles. Their neighbor scared their dog, Ruffles. They want a refund; they want to press charges, and they need to get paid *right fucking now*. Yelling. Crying. Screaming. As I walked back through our office, past more steel desktops and cube walls and pictures from Florida vacations, all these emotions pinballed through my head.

When I arrived at the back office of my old high school pal Pete Konarski, I found him staring at his computer monitor, stroking his neatly trimmed brown goatee. Without acknowledging him, I found the corner of the room and the six-foot high silver file cabinet tucked into the angle. I clutched its metallic sides and began pounding my head against its flimsy exterior. By the third time my forehead found the cabinet's side, Pete looked up from his monitor.

"Hey, hey, hey," he said, sitting up straight in his powder blue dress shirt and maroon necktie. "What the fuck, Nolan? I'm trying to read about last night's Sabres game here."

After I smashed my head two more times, I looked at Pete, dazed and enjoying the dancing specks floating in front of my sight. Thankfully, they adequately dulled my astonishment.

"I guarantee you can't imagine the level of perversion that's waiting at our counter."

"Christ, don't be so dramatic." He took a sip from his coffee, still steaming in a blue ceramic Sabres mug. "Is this consumer so deranged he's worth a lunchtime concussion?"

"How deranged is it to want a latex cat penis swinging between your legs?"

Pete put down his mug.

"Come again?" he said. "You're kidding, right?"

"Afraid not, captain."

Since he'd worked in our office for nearly six years, a consumer complaint had to be extra strange to pique Pete's interest. He'd read or heard them all. He'd also engaged in his share of questionable adventures, so his understanding of what constitutes crazy was not that of the everyman. The stories about his past—some of which I'd witnessed in person—were giddily rehashed with City Hall employees during my first week of work. Did he really run onto the field during the Bills-Cowboys game on "Monday Night Football"? (Yes, and security mauled him before he hit the twenty.) Was it true that he once ran up a five-hundred-dollar bar tab at McGinty's for himself and five co-workers—at lunch? (Actually, no; the bill was well over six hundred.) And on that Single's Night on the Miss Buffalo cruise ship, the night he housed fifteen rum and cokes before singing karaoke to Bush's "Little Things," did he really jump into the

Niagara River to close his performance? (Absolutely. He also swam back to shore and fell asleep in the Colonel Ward Pumping Station parking lot. That's where I found him the next morning.)

When I first took the job, I enjoyed our Happy Hour trips that ended at last call, our table littered with empty Molson bottles. I played it straight while he convinced unsuspecting girls he was an ex-professional hockey player whose career was cut short by a horrific eye injury. Somehow, it always worked, always suckered some impressionable girl into drunken bar-necking. Then, Pete found Tracy, a rabid hockey fan who knew he'd never skated a professional shift. They dated and fell in love. Tracy became pregnant. Pete found marriage, fatherhood, financial commitments, and modest weight gain. In the throes of these changes, he came to work sober, went home before dark and woke up under moonlight to feed his beautiful baby girl, Mia. He stopped jumping off moving cruise boats, too. He became a regular guy in his early thirties, one who dealt with our derelict consumers better than I could.

"So, a cat dick, huh? Yikes," he said, leaning back in his chair to scratch his small gut. "So what are we dealing with here? Standard goofball or dangerous deviant? The kind we might need to worry about, like a John Wayne Gacy type?"

"I don't have a fucking clue. Why don't you have a look at this dude and make your own judgment. See if this guy's presence gets you to send a few BPD cars to check his litter box."

"But what do *you* think, smartass?"

"Honestly? I think he's another Nickel City weirdo who thinks this office is here to do his perverted bidding. Just like last week. You remember the call I got?"

"The Girls Gone Wild guy," he said, grinned, and cracked his knuckles. "The guy who wanted his money back because the DVDs he ordered weren't smutty enough."

"I was under the impression there'd be actual *sex* in these videos," I said in a mocking, hillbilly voice, mimicking the conversation in question. "You know, like a real porn film, couples just going *at it*. All these were just a guy with a camera, filming girlies showing off their goods at Mardi Gras. Hell, my buddy Tony has tapes like this all over his living room. If I wanted to see some titties, I could borrow one of his tailgating videos from last season's Bills games. Titties *everywhere* on those!"

"That accent is dead on," Pete said, laughing before he sipped his coffee. "But what do you want me to tell you, pal? It is what it is. We get a lot of shitheads who come in here because we're all they have. We're their safety net."

"A safety net for dudes buying cockless cat suits? Christ, the city should commit these lunatics, not shuffle them into our office."

"But he's here, so let's just give him a complaint form to fill out, file it and send him on his way. How long you been here for? Two fucking years?" He rose from his desk chair. "C'mon, I'll show you how it's done. We'll get this pervert out of here, then you and I can jump up to the deck for a smoke. Sound good?"

After Pete took the necessary information from our visitor and sent him on his way, we grabbed our coats for a walk up to the 28th floor observation deck. In the fall, painters occupied the art deco-style civic cathedral's upper stairwells with tarps and tin cans as they added a fresh coat of cream-colored latex to hallways and lobbies traveled by local sight-seers and Canadian tourists during the city's pristine summer months. On a clear August day, one could peer through the deck's protective plexiglass and across Lake Erie to see the sun set over green shores.

In October, one could still find these views, but there were ob-
stacles to avoid, like tarps, pans, brushes, scaffolding, and union
laborers named names like Lou or Carl. If we wanted to feel the
thick autumn breeze off the lake, we headed up the stairs, under
the ladders and outside for a 360-degree view of Western New
York and Southern Ontario. When Pete came along, he bummed
a smoke. He never brought his own. Never.

"So how was Brendan's birthday lunch yesterday?" Pete
said, exhaling smoke toward Lake Erie. "Did he like the Sam
Roberts album?"

"I think," I said, then took a drag as I leaned against the
deck's exterior bricks and looked to the distant Canadian shores.
"He always has the same reaction when I give him a new album.
Grateful confusion, I guess. He was much more excited about the
Sabres jersey. You should have seen the look on his face when he
opened that."

"Hey, how old is he now anyway? Eight? Nine?"

"Ten," I said, smiling. "Can you believe it?"

"Number ten's a big one, man. Double digits. And of
course he liked the jersey better. He's a sports-crazed kid. All
kids don't grow up attached to their guitar like you did."

"I was a sports fanatic, too. Punched things when the
Bills and Sabres lost games, that kind of shit. I did get my first
guitar at ten. I remember borrowing one of my dad's Stones
albums so I could try to play along with the songs."

"Really?" he said, impressed. "At ten, I think I was
listening to dubbed Run DMC tapes I got from some dickhead
neighbor of mine."

"But you remember listening to the tapes, right? That's
the beauty of songs, their ability to help stamp moments in your
memory. Each can attach to an event and align itself with those

minutes forever. For instance, what song was playing the first time you got laid?"

"Honestly? I was so shit-faced the first time I got laid, I barely remember the girl's face, let alone the background noise."

"Mine was Van Morrison, 'Sweet Thing.' I set it up like that, but still. Every time I hear that song, I think of that night and laugh."

"And that's why you give these poor kids Canadian rock albums for their birthdays? Albums they could give two shits about?"

"That's why I give the boys records they don't give two shits about *yet*," I said, flicked my smoke to the ground and stepped on it. "Eventually they will, and they can attach their own memories to the songs."

"And what are you going to do with your own kids? You'll have to be Dad, not the cool rocker uncle. I mean, I love Van Halen, but I don't think Tracy would be cool with me giving Mia her own copy of *1984*. We try to stick to Dora the Explorer. Is Dana going to be cool with you playing Springsteen while Elmo sits on the shelf?"

I turned to my left and took a few seconds to think about the question. Looking down Route Five, toward the Buffalo River and the billowing smoke from the General Mills factory, I thought about my first born flipping through my piles of records, exploring. My little boy or girl will find albums, spin them and ask questions. I'll pull out Deirdre and play along with the songs, maybe even sing a verse or two. I couldn't wait.

"Pete," I said, then walked over and placed my hand on his shoulder, "if I can learn how to appease the wackos who roll into this building, I'm sure I can win over my wife when it comes to our children's upbringing."

"Don't worry, Nolan," said Pete, laughing. "I'll be around to help you with both."

5

The snow will fall down
Start a winter parade
Here in Buffalo
This is how we were made
-"Kings of the Queen" by J. Nolan

When a winter storm blows through Buffalo and the surrounding streets off Lake Erie, it's a harsh, windswept blitzkrieg of snowflakes. It's not a scene out of a Frank Capra film, where gentle white specks drop slowly over lampposts and passing cars. It's frustrating accumulations on roads, yards and rooftops. Snow blows thick, sticks to car windshields so firmly wipers snap off, losers of a fight with an inch-thick layer of ice. When a strong storm relentlessly blows with a foot or more of overnight snow, it's never something so delicate that you're eager to stand outside with your girlfriend, embracing as soft flakes dust your eartops. You look for cover until the winds stop rattling your windows and heavy flakes cease burying your front porch.

The day after the storm? That's the calendar portrait, with white fluff coating everything that sits idle. Men shovel out narrow driveways, with cigars dangling from their mouths as aromatic smoke drifts above their winter caps; children tap plastic orange balls with hockey sticks down plowed side streets. This is the calm after the rage in a region known more for its blizzards than its beauty. And on days like these, it's good to be a Buffalonian.

"You think the Ridge is gonna be packed today, Uncle Finn?" said Brendan, bundled in his red Hawks hockey coat and a winter cap in the backseat of my Subaru Outback. With Finn next to me in shotgun and Mickey in back with his brother, we rolled over layers of Southtowns snow toward Chestnut Ridge Park for a day of sledding, tobogganing and football tosses.

"It's definitely going to be packed," said Finn, who pulled his wool Irish cap down his forehead before he turned to the backseat. "But that's the fun of it, men. It's the whole region together, enjoying conditions the rest of the country cries about. Are you ready, or are you ready?"

"Ready," the boys yelled before each clapped their gloved hands together.

In the summer months, Chestnut Ridge accommodated daily picnics, scenic biking, jogging routes and hiding places for teenagers to polish off a few cases of beer. Winter ushered in a snow-coated wonderland, busy with giggling children gliding down adventurous hills on blue and red plastic sleds, their parents watching while snapping pictures and sipping Tim Horton's coffee. The more adventurous guardians would haul out wooden toboggans, a longer sleigh-like transport to seat two or three at a time, and ride down the park's rickety chutes with their children, hooting the whole way down until the ground became level. In the back of my Outback, we had two sleds and a football, as well as an archaic toboggan strapped atop the car.

When we pulled up the drive and into the Ridge's main parking lot, it was mobbed, with families dragging sleds across icy pavement and toward the top of the park's main run. There, parents and children stood with cocoa and coffee in gloved hands, staying warm inside ski coats and gazing at the panorama of downtown Buffalo in the cloudy distance. After we parked, we grabbed our gear and joined them.

"Should we take the toboggan down?" said Mickey, a royal blue and red Bills ski hat pulled down just above his eyebrows to complement a bulky bright red winter coat.

"Not yet, Mick," I said. "Why don't you grab your sled and go to the hill with Brendan. Finn and I are gonna stay up here and toss the football around."

"Can I play too? I'll sled around later."

"No, Mick. Go with your brother. I'll toss you a few passes later, okay? Nolan promise."

He slumped away with his brother and found a place with the boys and girls playing in the snow. I waited until they were a good distance away to reach underneath my black wool pea coat to pull out a cigarette.

"You're still smoking?" said Finn, zipping up his green ski jacket. "What's wrong with you, kid? I can't imagine you're stressed out about work on a day off, right?"

I lit my cigarette and enjoyed a drag.

"No, no," I said. "I think it's the baby only five months away, that sort of thing."

Finn held the football in his right hand, his fingers lined on the laces.

"What are you worried about? Being a father? You've been in training with Meg's two for years. You'll be fine."

I stepped back, let the cigarette burn between my fingers.

"Look, I know we never talk about this, but can I ask you something?"

"Shoot."

I took another long drag to let a few more seconds pass.

"Do you know why Billy left Meg?"

He glared at me. We never talked about Billy Doyle. Ever.

"Where is this coming from?"

"Meg never wanted to talk about it right after he split," I said. "Hell, she never talks about it now, either, so I've been content assuming he was just another guy who fell in line with the rest of the shitbags she dated over the years."

"There were plenty, sure."

"But he wasn't always a bad guy. You remember how in love he seemed with Meg during their first years dating? The matching Sabres jerseys he bought for the two of them?"

"The Pat LaFontaine ones," he said. "I remember."

"So while this was going on, did you ever sense that Billy was the same as the rest? That he'd eventually split?"

"Not until after Brendan was born, but yeah, I did. I've never told Meg this, but I stopped trusting Billy after he didn't push for marriage after Brendan. I remember talking to him after church one day when Meg was pregnant with Mickey. He was so distant, so off. I could see this glazed fear in his eyes, this intention to bolt out the first open door. I can't explain how I knew; I just did. He was gone soon after that."

"So what do you think happened with the guy? What do you think made him bail on so much?"

"God only knows," he said. "I've seen it happen with so many couples over the years, both young and old. On their wedding day, they're on the altar together, wide-eyed and smiling as they promise to live for each other, through good times and bad. Then one day, one of them decides the deal isn't convenient. One of them decides to reset their life and leave everything else behind. I imagine that's what Billy did. And if you don't mind me saying, good riddance to the bastard."

"No, I don't mind."

I took another drag through a grin.

"So," he said, "are you going to tell me or not? Why are you asking me about a shit like Billy Doyle? Why now?"

He leaned back and threw the ball to me. I caught the pass, looked at the ball and flipped it in the air to myself.

"You remember when we used to come here when I was a kid? My dad brought you and me, we found a picnic site and we'd play one-on-one football in the snow, with Dad as the all-time quarterback."

"He used to always lead you a little bit, so you had to dive into the snow for it," he said and smiled. "Then he'd yell, 'If you can touch it, you can catch it.' What about it?"

"When we were here, tossing that football around, I never wanted to be anywhere else. Never even had a thought about it," I said, then watched Finn catch my toss. "My father didn't, either. He was as enthusiastic as I was, as interested in throwing a pass as I was in catching it."

"Of course he was. Guy was a spark plug. But is that it? Are you afraid you're not going to perform like your father and, instead, wake up as a gutless Billy Doyle? Abandon your wife and kids?"

"I don't know why, but yeah. Ever since my father and mother passed, I've been waiting for this day, waiting for a chance to become the parent they each were for me. Now that it's approaching, I'm scared. Scared that whatever seeps in and infects guys like Billy Doyle will get to me, too. You see where I'm coming from?"

He stood there for a moment of silence, cradling the ball while staring stone-faced at me.

"Not really, no," he said. "I'm a priest, thus preventing

me from starting a family I'd even think about abandoning. The only guardian role I've experienced is being your uncle. When you were younger, I took you to Bills games, even took you down to Home of the Hits to buy you your first cassette tape, remember?"

"It was a double tape. *The River*."

"Good memory," he said, smiling. "I think I was a damn good uncle, right?"

"You bought me my first guitar, too. That old, beat-up Yamaha we picked up at Allentown Music. Of course you were a good uncle. Still are."

"I know," he said. "And do you know why I'm stating these feats?"

"No."

"Because despite all of these things I did for you as a kid, despite all I do for you now, you're ten times the uncle and father figure to the boys that scumbag Doyle left behind than I've ever been to you. You care for them more than you care about yourself, and that's what parental love is. If you can already do that, you're golden, kid. Stop worrying."

"What if I wake up one day, changed?"

"Well, a few things," he said, then put the ball on the ground so he could count on his hands. "One, you look into the eyes of your wife and the faces of your children and know what they mean to you, and what you mean to them. Two, you turn to God and ask for the strength every man can summon. And three, stare into your own reflection and know who you are. You're not a coward, and you're not weak. You're a Leary and a Nolan. Our families have always believed that depth of character defines the virtue of a man. Understand?"

He picked up the ball off the ground and continued.

"Is it going to be easy? No. Are you going to screw up, go through hard times? Absolutely. But please, know where you come from. Your parents are watching down on you, and your sister and I are here for you. We won't let you walk away, ever. Got it?"

"Sure," I said, then tossed my cigarette to the ground. I watched the ice extinguish it for a moment. "Thanks, Finn."

"This is what I'm here for. I just didn't expect to have such an in-depth Saturday discussion outside of a confessional. I'm supposed to be off today, dammit. Are we done?"

"For today, we're done."

"Good." He lined his fingers up on the football's laces again. "Now, you think your black lungs can still go long, past that tree on the left?"

"Never mind if I can get there. Do you think your rusty arm can throw it there?"

"Kid, there isn't an arm like mine in the entire diocese. Just get near the pine tree and look up."

I pulled my navy fleece cap down tight, rubbed my bare hands together and started kicking through the snow and wind, past coffee sippers and young sledders. Approaching the tree, I turned back and looked to the sky. The football was twisting, descending in a perfect spiral inches ahead of me. Before it reached the ground, I dove, arms outstretched and hands open. When the ball touched my fingertips, it bounced off and fell to the snow before my face mashed into the hard, cold ground. Immobile and atop snow, I heard faint cheers through my covered ears as random onlookers applauded my efforts. After the applause, I rolled over on my back and heard Finn in the distance.

"You see? Despite our best efforts, things don't always fall the way we want them to."

"Right," I said, staring up into the light, falling snow.

"But it doesn't mean we quit."

"Nope," I yelled back. "Just let me gain feeling again in my chest before going out for another, okay?"

I sat up to Finn's laughter as an uprising of excited and angry children's voices rose above it, floating up the main hill to the two of us.

"What's going on down there," I said to Finn, who was standing at a better vantage point than I was.

"Some of the kids have gathered around a little brawl. Looks like it could be a good one."

"Finn," I said, jogging toward him. "You see a red Hawks jacket in that mix?"

"No Hawks jacket," he said, then let out a gasp of a laugh. "I do see a little boy in a floppy Bills ski cap, right in the middle of the scrum."

"Mickey," I said. "Dammit, c'mon. And stop laughing."

"I'm sorry," he said, still laughing as we made our way to the wooden stairway built into the side of the hill. "You'll laugh too once you see the size of the other kid."

I ran down the stairs, skipping every other step while holding the side railing to avoid a spill. When Finn and I hit the bottom, we tore toward the gathered circle and shouldered into the front. In the middle of it all was a yelling Mickey, arms flailing as Brendan pulled him backwards by his coattail. On the ground curled in the fetal position and covering his head was a boy a bit bigger than Brendan. Draped in a coat much like Brendan's—except it was navy and read "Stars" on the back instead of "Hawks"—the poor kid laid sniffling and loudly whimpering. I burst through the front line, grabbed both Brendan and Mickey by their coat collars and dragged them out of the circle and away from the boy, who started to wail even louder once we left him alone.

"What's going on down here?" I said. "Finn and I leave you two for five minutes and you're starting fights?"

"But Uncle John, I—"

"No way, Brendan. You're supposed to be watching after Mickey and instead, you're slugging people? Is that kid on a rival hockey team?"

"He is, but I didn't hit him," said Brendan amid another loud wail from the circle.

"So why is that kid crying?" I said, confused. "What happened?"

"Mickey punched him in the stomach."

"What?" I said, eyes wide open. The kid on the ground was at least twice the size of Mickey. "Mickey punched the kid once and he's wailing like that?"

"No. After he fell down, Mick jumped on top of him and hit him in the face a bunch of times until I pulled him off."

I looked down to Mickey, who stood staring at the tops of his boots.

"Why in the world would you pick a fight with a kid that big?"

"He started it," said Mickey, still looking down. "When we got to the bottom of the hill, he saw Brendan's coat and said the Hawks sucked."

"That's why you hit him?"

"Well," he said, kicking some snow with his boot, "then he made fun of my Bills hat. He said it looked like it's from the eighties."

"Wait a minute," I said. "Brendan, where were you when this was all happening?"

"Over there. I heard him say the Hawks sucked, but I ignored him and kept walking. I scored three goals against the Stars earlier this season," he said. "Then I heard some yelling, turned around and saw that kid bawling like a baby. Mickey took him down pretty fast, and I tried to drag him out as fast as I could."

Mickey looked up and exhaled.

"I'm sorry, Uncle John. Should I go apologize to that kid?"

I looked to the circle. The kid had risen under the taunts and laughter of red-faced tweeners in Columbias and Carhardts. To have Mickey approach him would be embarrassing, even more so than getting hammered by a kid half his size. I kept him away until the blubbering kid fled the scene—then felt an odd pride simmering inside me. Mickey defended his older brother. He beat up a kid twice his size. Still, when I looked down at my nephew, I kept that pride from swelling to my face.

"No, no," I said. "Just grab your sleds and get up the stairs. Now."

When the boys were safely in front of me, I turned back to Finn. He didn't even try to hold back his laughter.

"I say we keep the Buffalo Brawler and his floppy hat off the hill before someone claims to be that kid's parent. Deal?"

"Smart thinking, Johnny," he said. "Smart thinking."

We all sat on a bench to the left of the Ridge's old toboggan chutes, recently repaired after years of neglect. Brendan and Mickey were on the inside; Finn and I took the outsides. The boys' sleds were propped against the ends of the bench, dripping with wet snow. The day's crowd had thinned out, leaving a spattering of children sledding and a few couples drinking hot chocolate outdoors with the sun dipping low on the downtown horizon. The four of us each had a hot cup and watched the steam drift out their sipping holes and up into the cold afternoon air.

"So we're all in agreement," I said. "We will not speak of Mickey's little altercation today around Meg?"

"What's an *al-tar-ca-tion*?" said Mickey.

"It's when you have a disagreement with someone and punch that someone—repeatedly," I said. "You're lucky that kid's parents were nowhere to be found."

"But, Uncle John, I—"

"Enough, Mick. And I don't care what he said. You can't just go around punching people. What's a little kid like you ever going to become if you keep swinging like that?"

"A Gold Gloves boxer," said Finn. He mumbled it low enough for the bundled, snow-drenched boys not to hear, their ears now covered with different, non-descript dry ski hats. I bit the inside of my mouth and tried not to laugh at the thought of "Irish" Mickey Nolan.

Finn sat up to speak louder. "Your uncle's right, Mick. Remember what I said before we got here? This is a day to be with our neighbors. And you don't hit your neighbors. You help them."

"Okay," said Mickey. "I'm real sorry."

"Good," I said, then thought of him mercilessly pummeling that bigger kid. I had to take a deep breath to hold in my inflated pride.

"Uncle John," said Brendan, "you and my mom used to come here all the time when you were kids, right?"

"Absolutely," I said. "Your grandpa used to send us down those old chutes over there on the toboggan, the same one strapped to my car. We'd stay out here for hours, freezing and laughing while your grandma snapped her camera. Your mom probably has a bunch of those pictures around your house."

"I've seen them," said Mickey. "You're wearing a hat like mine."

"Not *like* yours, Mick. It *is* yours," I said of the fluffy royal blue and red ski cap now hidden in the car. "That Bills hat used to be mine."

"So it *is* from the eighties?"

"It is."

"Oh. Do you want it back?"

"No," I said, laughing. "You fought for it, so now it's yours."

I turned away from Mickey and leaned back on the bench to look out at the city skyline. I thought more about those days past.

"After we were nice and frozen, we'd go into that building over there," I said, pointing to the hilltop lodge. "We'd sit by the fireplace. They used to have an old piano in there, remember Finn?"

"How could I forget? You and Meg made me play songs on it. You both would jump up and down, singing at the top of your lungs. You two were a spectacle."

"But it was fun, right?"

"Of course it was. You boys should have seen your mother back then. She was quite a little singer."

"She still sings sometimes," said Brendan. "She's been singing that song Mickey loves, by Neil Young."

"Long May You Run," said Mickey. "That's my new favorite song, Uncle John."

"I think it's your mom's favorite, too. Maybe you should spend a little more time listening to Neil. Might mellow you out a bit."

He smiled.

"Maybe."

We all laughed and went back to sipping our drinks and gazing at the skyline. After a few minutes, it was time to leave.

"You guys want to head out of here?" I said. "I think we should call it a day."

"Can we do one more thing before we leave?" said Brendan.

"Like what?"

"Can we take the toboggan off the car and take it for a run? Please?"

"Oh yeah, I forgot about the toboggan," I said. "Sure, let's go get it."

We drained the last of our hot chocolate, untied the toboggan from the luggage rack and dragged it up the steps to the top of the chute. A few brave souls were still gliding through the snow, leaving a wide vacant expanse to openly navigate. After I set the toboggan down for the boys, I backed off and let them mount it. Once Brendan and Mickey were settled in, they looked back at me as I stood off to the side.

"Are you coming or not?" said Brendan.

"Me?" I wondered. "You want me on that thing, too?"

"Sure," he said. "You can show us how you used to ride. Plus, you can stop Mickey if he tries to start another brawl at the bottom."

"I already said I'm sorry," yelled Mickey.

"Alright, alright. Settle down," I said. "I'm in."

I climbed in last to put the bulk of our weight at the back, with Mickey directly in front of me, then Brendan at the front of the toboggan. He grasped the front ropes while I pushed us to the edge and tipped us down the chute. After gliding down the chute's steel track, we went flying through the snow, kicking up flakes with Mickey and Brendan howling. Faster and faster, wind numbed our faces as we slid past kids with sleds, teenagers with snowboards. Finally, we glided to a stop at the level bottom. When I climbed out, I looked back up the hill at Finn and raised my arms. After we were all off and standing in snow a foot high up our legs, Brendan looked up at me.

"That was awesome. Just like when you were a kid, right?"

Clutching the toboggan rope to drag it back up the hill, I laughed again.

"I think this was better," I said. "Much better."

6

Some see this guitar
And hear a distraction
Others see you, girl
A walking attraction
-"You, Girl" by J. Nolan

I stepped to our office's counter and saw her standing there, waiting and smiling.

"Hey, I'm here to pick up the entertainment license for Cigarettes & Coffee," she said. "Do you have it ready?"

Of course it was ready. Any license for the beautiful and mysterious Samantha was made a priority. The only reason I knew her three-syllable name was because it was printed on a yellow Post-it note, stuck to every manila envelope she picked up. One of the functions of our office was to issue one-time licenses for events at city bars and restaurants not zoned for everyday live entertainment. Sometimes we licensed senior dances or college trivia competitions; other times we dealt with singing contests at a coffee shop named after an Otis Redding song. On the second Friday of every month, Samantha came strolling through our glass door to pick up such a license for Cigarettes & Coffee, a soul-themed coffee shop on Allen Street that, ironically, was a non-smoking establishment. The place was famous for its Second Saturday Serenade, which featured musicians and vocalists of varying styles vying for the event's grand prize: free coffee for the year. For this event, the shop needed a license.

Dark brown shoulder-length hair was always slung tightly behind unpierced ears entertained with white iPod ear buds. Her large blue eyes and mascara-laden eyelashes were hidden behind tortoise shell-rimmed rectangular frames, balancing her hip attractiveness with fashionable intelligence. She'd always tap her slim fingers on our countertop and her canvas sneakers on the linoleum both to grab our attention and, presumably, satisfy the beats galloping into her ears. If any other consumer or bar owner tapped that counter, Pete and I purposely ignored them until we heard their frustrated "hell-o?" ring over our cubicle walls. With Samantha, we welcomed the rhythm.

Every time we reached her, she'd remove her earbuds, smile and try to exchange pleasantries, with comments on the weather or football or hockey or music. We kept our daily responses to a minimum, with a stammering "hello," "sounds good" or "goodbye." Samantha would occasionally make appearances in my nightly dreams, cameos likely ignited by my timidity. Remarkably, these dreams weren't salacious; they merely featured her amid typical nonsensical dream imagery and conversations. That Friday, I tried to have real interaction with Samantha, something actual to balance with the exchanges in my sleep.

"Your license is right here," I said, then handed her an envelope with the document inside.

"You know, I'm so sorry," she said. "I always come in here and I have no clue what your name is."

"It's John,' I said, extending my hand. "John Nolan."

"John Nolan? Um, okay." She briefly paused to absorb the answer. "Oh, and I'm Samantha. Sam, actually. But I guess you already know that since I see it's written right here on this envelope. God, I feel stupid."

"Don't worry about it. So, um do you—"

Before I could continue, the door behind Sam swung open to reveal an angry old man. He barreled past her and slapped his wrinkled, heavy hands on the counter.

"Where is Pete?" he said, seemingly unaware of how loud he was talking. "I need to speak with him right now. Imme-diately."

"Sir, if you'll take a seat, I can find Pete and get him out here for you."

"Look," he said, "I don't know who the hell you are, son, but I suggest you get Mr. Konarski out here before I lose my temper. Northtown Windows and their installation department are putting the goddamn screws to me, and Konarski's work on my behalf has been *egregious*. Do you know what the word egregious means?"

"Sir, if you'll calm down I can get Pete out here and—"

"Egregious," he bellowed. Startled co-workers peered over their cube walls at this disturbance before he took a seat and yelled again. "Egregious!"

I glanced toward Sam, standing frightened, albeit still interested. She put the envelope in her bag and backed out of the office, sure to keep her distance from the old man while opening the door.

"Well, hey, you should check out the Serenade some-time. Every now and then, we actually host real-life, skilled musicians," she said. "It's not always just vegan girls crooning Tori Amos numbers."

"Cool," I said, uneasy with the stewing gentleman in front of me. "Maybe I'll pop in sometime."

"All right. Nice," she said, nodding her head. "Until then, it was nice to finally get your name, and I'll see you around, John."

"Bye, Samantha."

"Please," she said. "It's Sam. Just Sam."

She turned and exited. My smile joined a hint of déjà vu, momentarily freezing me before hearing the voice of the day's visitor.

"Hey, Casanova. My taxes aren't paying you to make nice with the broads," he said. "Now either you get Konarski out here or I'll find the mayor's office and make a goddamn stink like you've never smelt before. You'll have all kinds of time to chase skirts after I get your ass tossed out into Niagara Square."

"One minute, sir," I said, then clenched my teeth and walked back to Pete's office.

"Um, Konarski? You've got a real irritated fellow out here demanding to speak with you. Immediately."

"Fuck, is he an elderly guy? Walt Zimmerman?" said Pete. "I heard his gravelly voice from back here."

"He didn't give his name. Whoever he is, he's pissed."

"I guess he never read the specs on his installation agreement, and Northtown apparently switched the brand of window to a more expensive one on him. But he signed it, and now they're scooping him for an extra eight hundred bucks."

"The store won't fix it?"

"Why should they? They have a signed contract, and that'll hold up over this old codger's he-said argument. What can you do, right?"

"You have to come out and talk to him. I don't know how old he is, but I'd bet he's not too old to cause a scene."

"I got that from our phone conversations. Is he a big guy?"

"Not really, but you should see his hands. Looks like they're made of fucking stone. He slapped those mitts down on the counter and the thing nearly caved."

"Oh, that sounds great. Fucking fantastic."

He walked out from behind his desk to follow me through the office and find Walt, still seated and seething.

"Mr. Zimmerman, sir," said Pete, "So, I've talked with North—"

"Save it, Konarski," said Walt. "I don't want to hear a single word of your bullshit excuses. Am I getting a refund from those grifters or not?"

"Well, I—"

"Jesus, what is it about your generation of college-educated babblers? Can't you go a second without filling the air with excuses?" he said, arms folded across his chest. "I want a simple goddamn answer: yes or no."

"No," said Pete. "They're not going to budge, so you'll have to take them to small claims court."

"Small claims court?" Walt stood from his chair. "So let me get this straight: I now have to go waste my time in a courtroom because your gold-bricking, Polak ass didn't lift a finger to handle my case? These crooks pulled a bait-and-switch on me, dammit!"

"Mr. Zimmerman," said Pete before taking a step behind our front counter, "if you can't calm down, I'm going to have to ask you leave."

"Leave? This is my goddamned building!" He slapped his calcified paws on the counter again. "My taxes paid for that chair, that desk and your salary. And what do I get when I need your help? Not an ounce of effort!"

"John, you want to call security up here to escort Mr.

Zimmerman out the door?"

"Sure," I said, then jumped back to my desk and dialed behind their showdown.

"Security? Yeah, bring 'em up here. Maybe they can escort me up to our mayor and I can ask him why city dollars are paying for slobs like Konarski here to get fat on my dime."

Pete took a deep breath. It failed to calm him.

"You know what, you old prick?" said Pete, wide-eyed. "I've heard enough. If you didn't want to get slipped for eight hundred bucks by Northtown, why didn't you read the goddamn contract? The specs were written right there, in black and white. Didn't have your magnifying glass that day, Magoo?"

"Magoo?" said Zimmerman, then folded his arms again across his chest. "Oh, that's sharp. Like the blind cartoon character, right? Who the hell do you think you're talking to, just some cranky old man? What say the two of us head out to Niagara Square and I kick your fat ass down to the naval yard?"

Pete stood firm for a moment, staring at the gentleman before he let out a laugh, one of those you've-got-to-be-kidding-me laughs that bursts out in one pop. He tried to take a step out from behind the counter, but I grabbed his shirttail and yanked him back. Before either party could shout another word, two security guards pushed through the door to flank both sides of Mr. Zimmerman.

"All right, sir," said one of the guards to Zimmerman, "let's take a nice easy stroll to the elevator, okay?"

"Sounds good to me, fellas. Mr. Konarski and I were just talking about taking a little walk outside, weren't we Pete?"

"Goodbye, Mr. Zimmerman," I said, standing next to Pete as he gnashed his teeth, hands in his pockets and breathing heavily. "Thanks for stopping in."

"That's fine, sure," he said. "But God knows where this country would be if men like me were replaced by cowards like you, Konarski. Coward!"

When the door closed, Pete stormed back to his office and slammed the door shut. At first, I heard silence. At second, I heard a loud scream and the sound of a fist repeatedly smashing the side of a filing cabinet. After another moment of silence, the punching resumed.

Later that afternoon, well after North Buffalo resident Walt Zimmerman was ushered out of our office, the encounter with Sam was still swirling inside my head. Pete, sitting at his desk with a bandage wrapped around his bloodied right hand, was still teetering on the edge of rage after being verbally assaulted by a man nearly three times his age. Holding a fresh Tim Horton's coffee, I leaned into his office to see him staring ahead at nothing in particular. He was still breathing heavily.

"You want to take a stroll out to the monument, have a smoke?" I said. "Might calm you down a bit."

"Who the hell does this happen to? What kind of grown man gets verbally undressed by someone's grandfather, then takes out his embarrassment on a filing cabinet?"

"Not sure. Are we talking drunk or sober?"

"Regrettably sober," he said while massaging his knuckles. "Is it wrong that I was scared of that guy?"

"Absolutely not."

"I really thought he might jab a pen into my jugular. Christ, he had to be involved in Korea or some other conflict, right? I'm scared of him, and I don't give a shit who knows it."

"Let's take a stroll, okay?"

"You don't think he's waiting outside the building, do

you?"

"My God, let's just go."

The elevator stopped on the first floor and we exited past the overhead lobby murals of Indians and buffaloes and steelworkers toiling in front of the American flag. Before striding past the busts of former Buffalo mayors Frank Schwab and Grover Cleveland, we stopped and patted their copper scalps before bursting through the revolving doors and down the steps to Niagara Square. Thankfully, Mr. Zimmerman was nowhere to be found. We reached an empty bench, sat down and lit our cigarettes in the shadow of the square's towering McKinley Monument.

"So," I said, "before your scrape with the war vet, you missed an appearance by our Samantha."

"Aw, are you kidding?" he yelled, then took an exasperated drag. "As if things couldn't get any worse. What did you say to her? Anything?"

"It wasn't what I said to her; it was what she said to me. Kind of freaky."

"Explain."

"You know how I told you that she pops into some of my dreams?"

"Sure."

"Well," I said, "today, she said an exact line from one of the dreams."

"Something dirty?"

"No, you fucking creep. In the dream, we were sitting at a table, and I looked at her and said, 'Samantha, my name is John, John Nolan.' Then, she leaned across the table, looked right at me and said, 'It's Sam. Just Sam.'"

"So what?"

"Before she left today, she said the exact same line."

Pete leaned back in his bench and took another drag.

"John, for a married man, you have pretty boring dreams. Maybe after the baby's born, you'll kick it up a notch. I'd be embarrassed to tell you some of the shit I dream about."

"So you don't find this a tad freaky?"

Pete pondered the details and exhaled smoke toward the square's traffic circle.

"What kind of drink did she order at your dream table? Beer, scotch, gin? What?"

"Seriously? You're hauling out your genius drink selection theory on this? It's a yes or no answer. Was this odd or not?"

"Okay, it was odd. Even a tad spooky," he said. "Now, my turn. What was she drinking?"

Pete had this theory about how a man could tell everything he wanted to know about a woman based on her bar drink. Vodka revealed a volatile problem drinker with a torrid past involving bad break-ups. Rum enabled sloppy drunks to recklessly sing karaoke. Whiskey was simply a deal-breaker. And according to Pete, imported beers apparently indicated a heightened level of European traveling experience he didn't want to hear about. With these aforementioned choices all cautionary tales, Pete exclusively gravitated toward ladies drinking the domestic light beer trio of Miller, Coors and Bud Light. He claimed women sipping these selections appreciate the simplistic taste and social compatibility of watered-down American beer. They're not after an escape via Long Island iced teas, or an image afforded through a dry, two-olive martini. These women just want to be; they present themselves as everything every reasonable male has ever searched for. They love dogs, hate cats. They hold doors for the elderly, say, "God bless you" to the sneezes of strangers. They like the Beatles, but live for the scruffy, leather jacket-wearing 1975 version of Bruce Springsteen. When they cry, something is very wrong. When they laugh, the moment is very right. In Pete's estimation, these were the women a man should spend the night and make a life with. To validate his cherished theory, he found his eventual wife sipping a Coors Light under "Jungleland" when he first spotted her across a lakefront barroom. Still, he wanted me to confirm his theory with the images of my dream.

"She wasn't drinking booze or beer. We were sitting in a coffee shop, with coffee," I said. "What's the point of this question, anyway? Are you planning on asking her out?"

"I'm just curious, that's all."

"She sips coffee. How does your compatibility meter read on coffee drinkers?"

Leaning his head to the left, he scratched the back of his neck while contemplating.

"That tells me nothing. If I had to guess, though, I'd say Samantha's a beer girl. If you told me she was drinking a Miller Lite, this little talk of ours would be a lot more interesting."

"Noted."

"Do you remember that one conversation I had with her?"

"You call the exchange you had a conversation?"

"What? We talked, exchanged musical tastes, blessings."

"First of all," I said, "you asked her what she was listening to on her iPod."

"'Torn and Frayed' by the Stones," he remembered, proudly.

"And then, you sneezed a mouthful of coffee all over the front of her winter coat."

He smiled, reminiscing.

"Which she said 'God bless you' to," he said. "And she was wearing a green raincoat, not a winter coat. She was protected."

"Have you noticed how she now flinches whenever you hand her an envelope? Good for you, but that wasn't a conversation. An incredibly embarrassing moment, yes. Not a conversation."

Still, until my recent encounter, Pete's awkward exchange was more communicative than any moment I'd had with her. I usually smiled, handed her the envelope and watched her alluring exit before I retreated to my desk. But why? If I thought she was that cool, that fond of dogs and Springsteen and light beer, why couldn't I simply be friendly? Why couldn't I just ask a question or two to validate Pete's theory and confirm her legitimacy? Maybe because it would spoil the illusion.

Whenever we heard Sam's low-top Chucks come clicking into our civic confines, we needed to believe in her perfection. She was a "what if" girl for two married men, an entity to look to and wonder how our lives would be different if we were dating her. If we asked her too many questions, her answers might prove our idealistic assumptions wrong. We wouldn't admit it to each other, but Pete and I wanted to know as little as possible. This way, we could fill in the details ourselves and mold Samantha into exactly who we wanted her to be. We developed all kinds of scenarios for where she worked and what she did in her free time. The only thing we knew for sure was that she wasn't a cashier at Cigarettes & Coffee. I'd been there on Saturday mornings to read the paper and listen to whatever saxophone-infused soul the baristas soothed through the shop's overhead speakers. If she worked there, she would've been there those mornings.

In our favorite and most detailed fantasy scenario, she works as a cashier at an indie music shop, like Record Theater over by Canisius College. She spends her mornings stocking shelves with Canadian imports before helping some elitist audiophile complete his massive conversion from CDs back to vinyl. When her day is done, she goes back to her downtown loft to write poetry in spiral Mead notebooks and slowly sip from a tall pilsner glass full of ice cold domestic beer. Van Morrison's "St. Dominic's Preview" serenades her scribbling and, a minute into the song, her sublime voice joins the rising percussion, precise guitar picking and piano tinkering to sing only one line:

"And it's a long way to Buffalo."

After filling a few pages with profound stanzas, she takes her male black lab Duke for a walk through her neighborhood full of rockers and painters and writers. And maybe one of her neighbors is the owner of Cigarettes & Coffee. One of the many neighborly favors she does for him or her is a nice stroll over to City Hall, where she takes an elevator ride to the fifth floor and picks up the Second Saturday Serenade entertainment licenses.

This was the kind of bullshit we invented instead of asking her real questions. Since Pete's infamous sneeze, she never got a full sentence from either of us. There was once a time we weren't hesitant to engage a woman like Samantha, a time when the mere chance to talk to any woman like her lured us into pubs and rock clubs. Those nights reigned in a different life, when each of us held idealistic assumptions for how our futures were going to erect themselves. When those assumptions yielded to a different reality, things changed, just as they do in everyone's life. People act, react and absorb the aftermath. They get married, take civilized jobs and try to mature. That's where Pete and I were standing. We were now embedded in a life of obligations, not impulses; a life of responsibilities, not recklessness. Love and commitment had put us on more solid ground. We were thankful for this. Most of the time.

Was I happy to be away from the Nighthawk, away from Lynyrd Skynyrd covers, Genesee pints and insane (yet alluring) pyromaniac jugglers? Sometimes, sure. Was Pete better off cradling a baby girl in his arms instead of being hog-tied on the 20-yard line of a nationally televised football game? Definitely. But despite the security this responsibility afforded, it could never soothe the glaring reality that those old nights of excitement, those hours spent in the early stages of dizzying attraction, were gone forever.

And maybe that's why Samantha's appearance every month was so thrilling for the two of us, so exciting that her voice and image filled the end of my sleep every once in a while. In her, we could see those old tavern nights and unknown possibilities we used to bask in, still right at her delicate fingertips. We could see her at the bar, adhering to some lucky bastard's expectations before eclipsing every last desire. We imagined the moment she looked up through those tortoise shell frames of hers and injected the guy's chest with that nascent warm surge we yearned for. Through our silence, these assumptions remained intact.

If we had a real conversation with her, she might tell us otherwise. She might tell us that her life sucks, that it's complicated and empty and unfulfilling. She might tell us that, on her Friday nights, she drinks chardonnay while watching reality television with her best friend Bentley, her male housecat. She might reveal her life to be not nearly as romantic and reckless as Pete and I remember our own to be. With this remote possibility, we erred on the side of idealism. We needed to recall that euphoria of romantic possibilities.

Once a month, we were able to do that through the beautiful existence of a mysterious entity named Sam.

7

When a young heart finds love
It radiates the soul
Jealousy will steal love
Leave a soul feeling cold
-"Cold" by J. Nolan

When I escaped through the revolving copper doors and exited to a blustery Friday night in Niagara Square, Christmas was over. January approached, and I had a good downtown night ahead of me. After intense negotiations, I'd convinced Dana to go to Finn's Joe Strummer tribute show at the Nighthawk, and needed to pick her up from her lunch shift. In order to be sensitive to her necessary sobriety, I promised to have no more than three tallboys of Genny Cream Ale all night. I also assured her we'd immediately leave the show if the Kings' crowd became unruly. Along with the occasional shoe tossed at the bassist during performances, there was some occasional pushing that broke out between regular rockers and parishioners who'd pop in to see Finn's frenetic, off-the-altar performances. These casual observers, green to the local music scene, weren't aware of the fervor generated by such songs as "Queen City Chaos." Besides a blistering power chord-driven lead, there was well-known, fist-pumping audience participation on the song's chorus:

Go down to the waterfront, just to take a look at us!
Dancing and a singing to the Queen City chaos! Oh, oh, way oh!

Queen City chaos!

Usually, this was the part in the song when casual observers had their beer unintentionally knocked out of their hand by one of the rowdies. This led to words, an odd exchange of shoves and, eventually, a peaceful exit by the parishioner who didn't want to answer to Father Finn on Sunday morning. He'd been known to quell such skirmishes by merely standing off his stool and looking toward the altercation. Local clubs, VFW halls and the Nighthawk appreciated Finn's prominence in such instances.

I lit a cigarette and walked up Court Street, lined by weathered gray buildings on both sides. When I crossed the Main Street Metrorail tracks, I noticed a bundled woman across Lafayette Square tossing a tennis ball across the area's flattened expanse to an enthusiastic black lab. The dog chased the throws over the frozen turf, retrieved and returned it to his owner. When she spotted me, she paused.

"John? John Nolan?"

Samantha. Sam.

"Hey," I said, then ditched my smoke to the street. "I thought that was you. This your dog?"

"Yep," she said, scratching him behind its ears, rubbing his side with mittened hands. "This is Otis, the main man in my life."

"Nice," I said, then leaned down to pet the friendly, tail-wagging dog. "You bring him down to the square a lot?"

"When I have the time, and I try to get down here before everyone gets out of work. Old Otis here loves making new friends, so he runs to anyone with their hand out. I don't mind chasing him, but it gets a little exhausting around five-ish."

"I'm sure."

"Where you headed?" she said. "Off to bust up some bars without entertainment licenses? Saw you walking in the distance. You looked ready for action."

"No, no. I'm going to meet someone at the White Room on Washington Street."

"A hot date, or are you meeting your coworker, Sneezy?"

"Pete? No," I said, then hesitated. "I'm meeting my wife. She's a waitress over there."

"Your wife," she said before she flashed another glance at Otis. "Oh, that's nice. So how long have you been married?"

"About—"

"Wait, no. I'm sorry for being so nosey. I always ask too many questions. Jesus, I finally got your name this week and now I'm dipping into your marital history."

"Don't worry about it. It's fine, really," I said, relaxed. "Otis might mind, though. All these questions are cutting into his fetch time. He looks pretty antsy for a toss."

She laughed and scratched Otis behind his ears.

"You're probably right," she said, then wound up and tossed the ball across the frozen grass. "Plus, he gets jealous when I talk to guys for too long. Even married ones. I'll let you go."

"Sure, sure. Until the next Serenade. See you around?"

"With my man here," she said, taking the ball from Otis's clenched teeth. "Have fun tonight. And oh, one more question."

"Shoot."

"If you see Luther at the White Room, can you tell him I'm a huge fan?"

"Absolutely."

If you grew up in Buffalo, you'd heard of the great Luther White. Not only was he acting owner of the White Room, he'd been playing as a legendary local blues musician for over thirty years, since he was a teenager. My parents used to go on dates to his blues shows. Before he became a priest, Finn occasionally played piano with him, adding another layer of instrumental ambiance to Luther's already commanding presence. When I was a kid, my father took me to his outdoor concerts in Lafayette Square and LaSalle Park to watch him wail on lead guitar or stomp his giant red wingtips on wobbly stage planks. On an isolated stool, he howled about a broken heart on "East Side Lady," about drunken downtown nights on "Beer for Blues." Before he walked off every local stage, he'd rise from his stool and show the crowd he had the size to play offensive line for the Bills. After the applause, his mammoth right paw would grab the mic. He'd look out and, in a voice raspy from singing, smoking and sipping bourbon, say, "I'm the great Luther White. And to you Buffalo, I wish a good night."

When I was twelve years old, I stayed after one of Luther's shows to get his autograph on my program. He eventually emerged from his trailer with Finn, who led him over to the partition gate where I stood. When he looked down and asked for my name, I said, "It's John, and I play the guitar." He smiled, then nodded under a floppy brown driving cap before he took my black Sharpie into his giant right hand. "You keep practicing and make it happen, baby," he said before he handed me my pen and program back. When I looked down at his signature, it was preceded by, *To John, Make it happen, baby*. That night, I framed the autograph and hung it over my bed. I nestled into my pillows and blankets underneath it and played chords until my fingertips blistered.

But Luther never made it out of Buffalo. It was a great local mystery. He was a star, a sound to behold both live and on record. Every few years, a local band or artist was scooped up by a major label and left Buffalo. They'd cut a record, tour the country and name-drop their hometown in *Alternative Press* and *Spin* features. Not Luther. He never left to search for fame in Manhattan or Los Angeles, never strummed tunes on the San Francisco Bay. He peaked years ago in our local smoke-filled bars, and now stood as an Erie relic, found in the *Gazette's* entertainment pages for his performances and in the gossip pages for his unyielding sexual dalliances. He existed as a local commodity while mediocre, out-of-town musicians invaded Buffalo with derivative garbling, and filled local clubs without the talent Luther had in his wingtips. Still, these bands were singing on the radio or dancing on YouTube. Luther? He was at the White Room, Buffalo's Home of the Blues.

After I walked past a row of parked Harleys on Washington and through the bar's front door, I could see the place was already buzzing. It was an odd mix of suited professionals and leather-clad bikers, and all had drinks in their hands as they stood talking and laughing. Loud voices and profanities joined a soothing Duane Allman guitar solo to fill the barroom. Shadowed by framed photos of Buddy Guy, Muddy Waters and Stevie Ray Vaughn, bartenders slid from customer to customer to line up shots of Jack Daniel's and pour pints of Molson Canadian. Every barstool was occupied, as was most of the bar's standing room and small tables. In the thick crowd, I found Kelly, a young waitress who worked with Dana during most of her shifts. I tapped her arm as she walked past me.

"Kelly, have you seen Dana around?"

"I think she's back in the kitchen finishing up. You can

go on back, but watch the floor. I just spilled a bowl of barbeque sauce near the entrance. You'll slip and break your neck if you're not careful."

When I got to the kitchen door, I could see Dana through its small window, marrying her ketchups on the aluminum counter. She looked tired and worn down. She had a visible bump now, albeit a small one muted by her apron. I was watching her pour each bottle into the other, waiting to bust through the door and kiss the back of her neck. I wanted to tell her how all the serving and the beer and the blues and the ketchup would someday be behind her, behind us.

Before I could open the door, I watched Luther walk into frame behind Dana. He was scheduled to perform later that night, so he was dressed accordingly: black dress shirt and red necktie to match his red pants and famous red wingtips. When he reached her, Luther put his gigantic paws on both her upper arms, massaged them and worked up to her shoulders. He talked, smiled and let out a laugh. With Greg Allman's vocals filling my ears, I couldn't hear Luther's words. Whatever they were, they caused Dana to lean her head back, listen and reply. Luther slid his hands down her sides and planted them on her hips before mouthing something else. Before my heart could thump harder, I pushed through the door. After my first step, my right foot planted in barbeque sauce and sent me flying backwards onto the floor, flat on my back. Dana and Luther scurried to hover over me, concerned but confused.

"You okay, baby?" said Luther, offering his hand. He called every man or woman *baby*.

"I'm fine," I said, pushing myself up.

"John, what are you doing back here?" said Dana.

"Kelly told me you were in the kitchen. Just didn't expect to see you on a massage break."

"What's that now?" said Luther, standing straight up, chest out. "I came out my office and Dana looked tense, so I rubbed her shoulders. No big deal. I do that for all my girls. Shit, I do that for my momma. I didn't mean nothing by it."

He stood about five inches taller than me. I looked up to find his eyes.

"Don't bullshit me, Luther. Don't you dare fucking bull-shit me."

"Oh, Luther don't bullshit, baby," he said, moving closer to me. "You should know that by now."

"Luther, please," said Dana before he held up his hand to stop her.

"Settle down, baby. Let me talk to your man here," he said. "Johnny, let me make something real clear to you, just so we understand each other. I'm Luther White. If I wanted to take your little girl here, I'd take her. You and I don't piss in the same pool, let alone the same pot. Never have and never will, so if I were you, I'd think twice about coming into my place and ac-cusing me of moving on your shit. Ever. Instead, how about you take a walk and cool the fuck out."

I stood still, staring up and into his glare.

"John," said Dana. "Can I please talk to you outside, now? Excuse us, Luther."

She took my hand and walked me out the back service entrance. Standing with her, I reached in my pocket with a shaky hand, pulled out a cigarette and lit it with a green Bic. Dana grabbed my shirt to pull me close and angrily stare at me.

"What the fuck was that about? Have you lost your mind?"

"If you walked into my office and saw a girl rubbing my

leg, what would you think?"

"You're joking, right?" she said, head cocked. "You just started a fight with the owner."

"I know who he is. I used to have his fucking autograph hanging on my wall."

"You could have gotten me fired!"

"Holy shit, are you serious? He had his hands all over you! What else could I do? Besides, what the fuck does it matter? You won't be working here too much longer anyway."

"What the hell is that supposed to mean?"

"When the baby comes. You'll be home or elsewhere, away from chicken hawks like Luther White."

"Elsewhere? Like where? Back at a collections desk harassing the poor and unemployed? This is where I'm gonna be until I finish school. They want me back after the baby's born, and I plan to come back."

"And what about the baby?"

"The baby? I'm sorry, but this child isn't going to turn me into some lifelong stay-at-home mom, some sheltered introvert. This baby isn't going to stop me from living, from breathing. From being myself."

"But it's going to change things. It's going to change things significantly."

She crossed her arms and stared back at me.

"Maybe it will and maybe it won't," she said. "You know what? We're not going to talk about this now. I have to get back in there."

"Fine. I'll wait out here for you to finish up."

Before Dana walked through the door, she stopped and turned to me.

"Um, no," she said. "Since you were busy mixing it up

in there, I didn't get to tell you that I'm not going to the Night-hawk. Luther asked me if I could stay, so I'm working the night shift, too. For his show."

"You're kidding, right?" I threw my cigarette to the ground. "Tell me you're fucking kidding."

"That's what we were talking about when you barged into the kitchen. He was asking me to stay. Look, I'm sorry. Tell Finn I'm sorry, too. I gotta go."

"Dana, please. C'mon, please."

She closed the door and was gone. Back to the blues.

8

When the bright lights go dark
A place finds a sound
Come down to the Nighthawk
Take a look around
-"Nighthawk" by J. Nolan

McGinty's Pub is a good place to have a drink by yourself. The clandestine chicken wing dive for downtown's heavy drinkers stood right down the street from the Nighthawk. It had good corner barstools to straddle and old aerial shots of the city lining the walls. There was hockey on its televisions, classic rock on its juke and baskets of salty popcorn from the self-serve machine. If anyone talked to you, they kept it brief; patrons weren't clingy or intrusive. When I was still playing at the Nighthawk, I bartended at McGinty's four nights per week, slinging pitchers of Molson Canadian to boozers in Harley Davidson T-shirts and Sabres hockey jerseys, cargo shorts and blue jeans. A mere sniff of the bar's Marlboro-soaked curtains brought me back to my days of service. After I left Dana to work her night shift, I found my old environs and claimed an open stool. As a McGinty's veteran, I was entitled to a few free Canadian pints and a shot or two of Jameson. I also knew Butch Strombone, a bouncer from my days at the Nighthawk and now the bar's distinctive Friday night bartender.

Butch's tended mullet, studded dog collar and wide array

of colorfully messaged sleeveless tees made him a must-encounter on any Buffalo bar crawl. Ask the man anything about eighties metal, ultimate fighting or the glorious attributes of the Trans-Am, and he'd have your answer. Add his fantastical stories about drunken weekend adventures that may or may not have happened, and Butch was good company. He's also the only guy who'd ever hired me for guitar lessons. This wasn't because I was real selective; Butch just happened to be the only person who'd ever asked. With this relationship, he was always happy to comp my tab, as well as let me use the bar's code for free songs on the juke.

"I don't give a shit what you play," said Butch, behind the bar in a tight black tee with the words *fucking sweet* in red lettering across the front. "Just play one song for me."

"Name it."

"Bobcaygeon, by the Tragically Hip."

"Really?"

"Yeah *really*. Why do you think I've been trying to play the fucking song during our lessons?"

"I know, I know," I said of my only student's emotional turns during our semi-regular weekly guitar sessions, held in a McGinty's back booth on their least busy night. "I just can't get over it. Always struck me as a bit mellow for you. Back in our Nighthawk days, all you listened to was hell-raising shit by Motorhead or Molly Hatchet."

"And you don't think I still dig fucking Hatchet?" He slapped his hands down on the bar. "Did I ever tell you how my dad was their roadie back in the seventies? They called him T-Bone, Johnny. Fucking T-Bone!"

"You've told me about that a few times." I'd heard this no less than a couple dozen times from Butch, but I wanted to be gentle. I didn't want to upset a guy who regularly referred to himself in the third person as *The Bone.*

"Okay, okay," he said before a step back. "But now it's time to get over to that juke and give me some Hip. Bobcaygeon, motherfucker."

"I know who sings it, Butch."

"Not enough people do. Visited my brother in Denver and his Colorado buddies never heard of 'em. How can you not know the Hip? They're like the fucking U2 of Canada. Shit, they're better than U2, those pussies."

"Some great bands just don't make it big everywhere."

"Right on," he said, then flung his bar towel over his shoulder. "Shit, take Luther White. He never made it to Cleveland, let alone Denver."

"Please," I said. "I don't want to even hear the name Luther White tonight."

"Hey, that's fine with me. The Bone don't give a *fuck.*" He crossed his arms across his chest. "I'm a Hip man, so play my fucking tune."

"You got it. And I'll have another Canadian."

I climbed off the stool and went to the juke, an old-style model with knobs, dials, buttons and heavy plastic pages. After I punched in the code, I started flipping the pages to look for songs. I needed relief, something to soothe the Dana-induced acidity still burning my stomach. I wanted to hear the old numbers that tingled my spine when I strummed them in the dark. I wanted to hear the songs that took me back to my days at McGinty's, back when I didn't care about a career, a child or marital complications. I needed to be whisked away from the present, from work, life and Luther White. I flipped past the intensity of Metallica and the chaos of early Zeppelin; I decided against the introspective work of Neil Young. Instead, I went with "Bell Bottom Blues" by Derek & The Dominoes, just to hear the desperation in Eric Clapton's vocals. I wanted to listen to the song and remember when I enviously listened to the lyrics. I once ached to feel the same way about a woman, pained to play any song with the same mastery. After I punched the numbers in, the song came floating out to wash over McGinty's tables and stools. Leaning against the juke to enjoy the opening guitar work, I felt a hand set down on my right shoulder.

"You know I can't stand Clapton, right?"

I turned around to see Finn, dressed in blue jeans, faded green T-shirt and his secondhand brown overcoat.

"How can you not like this song? It's flawless."

"I don't respect musicians who blow off performances," said Finn. "You know how much your parents paid to see him live that time he stumbled out on stage high as a kite? Son of a bitch was so juiced he had to stop in the middle of the show and leave. Didn't give ticket refunds, either."

"C'mon, that was one performance. One amid thousands of others."

"Even one is too many."

"So for that one night, you're willing to deny the man's greatness? Deny the excellence of this tune?"

"Damn right. I'm a forgiving man, but I have no respect for the disrespectful. Can you imagine Springsteen pulling that garbage? Blowing off even one performance?"

"No."

"And that's why he's the Boss," he said with a smile. "So where's Dana?"

"She's not going to making it out tonight." I looked down to McGinty's grime-ridden floor tiles to avoid eye contact with Finn. "Has to stay on at the bar for the night."

"That's too bad. She's going to miss a good one," he said. "Is everything okay?"

I crossed my arms to feign nonchalance.

"Oh yeah, don't worry about it. Think I'd rather be alone tonight, anyway. You want anything from the bar?"

"No, no. We're loading in at the Nighthawk right now. Why don't we go over so you can say hello to the staff. I know they'll want to see Johnny Nolan, the loner."

After I punched in Butch's Tragically Hip tune, I followed Finn out the door and down to the Nighthawk. I found its flyer-covered front entrance and walked under the barroom's low-hanging interior piping and omnipresent aroma: a sublime mixture of spilled Genny Cream, sweat and toilet water. The bar lights were on; its stools sat empty. The walls were still lined with small, framed pictures of past performers and stickers of bands, ones that shook the windows and rattled empty shot glasses with extended bass riffs. Moving through the narrow barroom adorned with beer brands, I briefly thought about the nights I was embraced by these surroundings before Finn interrupted the reveling by rhythmically slapping his palms on the bartop.

"Hey Sues," he said to the bartender, her back to us. "You remember this guy?"

She turned around and brushed her black hair from her face. Her blue eyes and dark eye shadow widened, her silver lip ring shimmering as she curled a smile.

"Jesus, Finn, is this former Nighthawk legend Johnny Nolan? I knew you were a priest, but I didn't know you could raise the dead."

"You're rough, Sues," I said, then reached over the bar to give her a hug. "And you wonder why I haven't been back."

"What the hell, dude? Where have you been hiding? Ever since you got married, you never come by here anymore. I know you're not playing, but you could at least come by for a beer sometime."

"You're right. I should pop in more."

"Damn straight," she said before she cracked open two bottles of Budweiser for us. "I miss you, and so does everyone else around here. And it's not just because of your crowds."

"Thanks, Sues."

"Finn, did you ever come in here back in the day when this guy performed?"

"A few times, yeah."

"He was sick, right? Johnny could pack 'em in on a Friday. Used to have the bar three deep all night. Fucking slammed."

"That's why I dragged him here tonight," said Finn. "Hope his history will rub off on us."

Sues gave me a wink. I followed Finn to the stage and helped his band with their gear. Drums and guitars and amps were being lugged through the side door, along with Finn's piano, a polished ebony Yamaha upright he bought for fifty bucks off a city parishioner fifteen years ago. It was compact, but still heavy and inconvenient, the way most pianos are. We dragged the black box through the door ourselves, running it up a ramp and onto the stage before rolling it over to the far right. With sweat rolling down my face, I looked to Finn.

"Good spot?"

"Perfect," he said, then placed his stool before looking to the bar from the stage. "This is a great venue, isn't it?"

I turned around to see what he saw, the empty floor space and the unmanned soundboard in front of exposed brick; the dirty, vacant high tops; the green street signs for Broadway and Michigan Avenue. I looked out and saw Sues smiling behind the bar. She flicked the switches on the back stage lights before she hit the brighter, multicolored front bulbs. When their glow hit my sight, I squinted and put my right hand above my eyebrows to shield the glare of the yellows, blues and reds. I adjusted to the heat and shine and lowered my hand to my side. I envisioned my old stool, my bottle of beer. I recalled the stomping crowd, the masses that stumbled in from the harsh cold to hear familiar songs and melodies. These thoughts rushed forth to send an inspiring chill through my chest and legs. It felt real and pure, like when I learned how to play my first song, "Satisfaction" by the Rolling Stones; like when I heard my first round of applause. When I looked to the bar again, I found Sues still gazing at me, almost like she knew my thoughts.

"You still look good up there," she said.

She flashed another smile, then switched off the front stage lights to let Finn and the Nickel City Kings tinker in the shadows.

Over two hours later, right around ten o'clock, Finn found his piano stool in front of the roar of a packed Nighthawk. I leaned at a secluded high top on the raised landing at the darkened corner of the stage, nursing another Bud while looking out at the eclectic crowd below. Grizzled, leather-clad rockers mixed with soft-skinned sippers in woolen sweaters and North Face fleeces, all enthusiastic and excited to pay homage to Joe Strummer of The Clash. When Neko strapped on his glistening black bass, a few guys in the thick of the crowd already knew his name.

"Neeeeeeee-kooooo!!"

He gave them a head nod, swung his thick dreads down

and plugged into his amp. On the drums was George, who adjusted his stool and ran a towel over his bald head before he took a swig of Rolling Rock and waited for the cue from singer and lead guitarist, Patty Vee. When his cream-colored Les Paul swung at the right length in front of him, Patty found the mic.

"People of Buffalo, we're the Nickel City Kings," he said. "And tonight, we are once again kings of the Nickel City."

Screams, hoots, and claps stormed from the floor. George readied his drumsticks and counted it off.

"ONE! TWO! THREE! FOUR!"

Attacking the snare with both sticks, he mixed in the kick drum with every fourth hit. As George worked his kit, Patty jumped in with a G and worked down the two strings to an F before jumping into a B flat. Neko slapped his bass strings with his heavy thumb, thumping each chord while he stared at the crowd through sunglasses. Finn worked the right side of his Yamaha, tinkling the keys in the absence of a rhythm guitar, while also complementing George's percussion work. With Patty's gravelly vocals scratching Joe Strummer lyrics across the faces of drinkers and dancers, the band was tight behind him. Heads were bobbing while Genesee spilled over pint glasses. Fists were pumping while Jack Daniel's slipped down throats.

Watching from my table, I took another swig of beer while tapping my boot with the band's beat. Unfortunately, simmering under the mayhem were the thoughts of the White Room kitchen, the memory of the scene intruding on my attempts to bury it beneath a return to the past. Dana and Luther, standing together in that kitchen. The two of them engaged in what could've been harmless flirtation, your average bar industry interaction. I wondered if that's what I saw, whether I overreacted to something so common. The picture of Luther's hands on

Dana wouldn't disappear; it wouldn't dry up as the Nighthawk heat was rising around me. His were famous hands, ones I saw wield a guitar like a pocket watch and hypnotize local crowds for years. What were those hands to Dana? What did they do for her?

I looked out onto the floor as fans continued to flail about, shaking fists and scuffing floorboards through Clash classics like "Jail Guitar Doors" and "Safe European Home." Dana used to stand on those same boards and watch my left hand slide up and down Deirdre's neck. I'd strum, she'd smile, and I'd toss a wink toward her wide emeralds. I wanted to see that Dana in front of me again, dancing and singing and laughing. I wanted to grab that Dana and replace jealousy with those old innocent feelings. But my hands remained empty, free to tap the tabletop as the Kings ripped through a few more Clash numbers until they reached the end of their set.

"For our last tune, we'd like to hear your voices out there," said Patty. "And Joe Strummer, he'd like to hear you singing, too—up there in heaven."

Screams and hoots followed, as did some boot stomping.

"We know you know this one, you Buffalo bums, so let's hear ya!" he said. "This is one of ours, and it's called Queen City Chaos! ONE! TWO! THREE! FOUR!"

Patty Vee furiously down-picked his Les Paul, flicking his wrist cartoonishly fast as George unleashed his full arsenal, smashing skins and cymbals like he hated them. Finn popped off the stool to his feet, mashing white and black keys wet with the sweat dropping from his bangs. Neko slapped his strings, swung his dreads around and stood straight up to face the crowd. As Patty's vocals worked attendees into a dancing frenzy, they knew their part was coming; they knew it was almost time to sing. But before the chorus, one misguided soul decided to keep with the unfortunate tradition of past Kings shows.

When the lonely brown shoe flew at the stage, it was snatched out of the air by Neko's right paw, right before it hit his face. With the shoe in their bass player's hand, the band played in a loop, waiting to see what he'd do as their fans stood silent, anticipatory. Neko slowly lifted his sunglasses from his face and raised them to his forehead. Staring into the crowd, he focused on the person who threw it. Watching the whole thing go down, I saw this poor kid, paralyzed by what this giant, dreadlocked bass player was going to do to him. He became more frightened when the patrons parted around him, offering him up to the big man. Neko smiled widely, wound up, and plugged the drunken twenty-something in his face with the old, scuffed shoe. When the kid hit the floor, the mob erupted and began dancing around him. Neko pulled his shades back down and resumed slapping his strings. His bandmates stopped circling, and Patty Vee incited crowd participation through his microphone.

"Go down to the waterfront, just to take a look at us! Dancing and a singing to the Queen City chaos! Oh, oh, way oh! Queen City chaos!"

I sang along, pumping my fist while shouting out syllables. I let a laugh slip while remembering the nights I spent on that stage, nights I owned the joint. Picturing myself on that stage, I watched Finn lead his Nickel City Kings and enrapture the crowd with the same brand of unbridled bliss I used to deliver in heaps. As his fingers continued to smash onto his piano keys, he turned his head to find me at my table. I raised my bottle in his direction and nodded approval. After he flashed a grin, he raised his left hand to me and waved goodbye as his right continued to dance across the ivory. He knew I had to slip out and avoid possible attention from a random fan or two from days past, fans who hadn't seen my face at the Nighthawk in years. I left my empty bottle and found the exit while the crowd remained transfixed by the band in front of them.

I stuffed my bare hands into my coat pockets for a walk up to Washington. The sweeping winds outside were so harsh they burned my ears, numbing them in seconds. Hiking toward Lafayette Square, I found the sidewalks empty and desolate under dark skies. I was hoping to see her up the way, outside and waiting. I wanted to see her leaning against a lamppost with co-workers, waiting for me to walk by. When the White Room came into focus, though, Dana wasn't out front. I reached the front door to see the bar lights out, the neon Budweiser and Genesee window signs unplugged. Just to make sure, I gave the door a tug. Locked. I rubbed some of the frost off a front window so I could peer in through cupped hands. The barroom was empty and dark, only barely illuminated by the light dimly emanating from the back office. I exhaled onto the glass, then took a step back. I buried my numb hands back into my pockets and turned to head home through the night's dueling tingles of revival and regret.

9

In the shine of morning light
Things don't feel the same
Thoughts of love have drifted off
To find another name
-"Thoughts of Love" by J. Nolan

Sitting at my kitchen table, I sipped coffee from a cream-colored mug and flipped through the Sunday *Buffalo Gazette*. The sun shining through my apartment's windows confirmed the reports of odd December warmth predicted on the paper's front page. The window behind me faced Elmwood Avenue, and I could hear the sounds of parents and children, laughing and shouting as they kicked around through mild breezes. Their happy voices made me smile; they made me momentarily forget about Dana and our problems.

We hadn't spoken to each other since Friday night's incident in the White Room kitchen. She didn't come home after her shift that night. She didn't walk through our front door to see me passed out on our green corduroy couch while the DVD menu music of Bob Dylan's *No Direction Home* played on a continuous loop. When I awoke on Saturday morning, I walked to our bedroom to find the sheets still tucked. Dana had not come home, but probably went to stay with her co-worker, Kelly. She did that from time to time after a really late shift. I repeatedly called her phone. It was turned off and sent me right to voicemail. After a long walk up Elmwood Avenue to find coffee and clarity, I returned home to evidence that she'd slipped into the apartment to take a shower and change her clothes. When I came back that night, I found her asleep soundly in our bed, curled up with her body pillow as she rhythmically cooed. Instead of waking her to talk, to apologize, I let her be. I watched that Dylan documentary again, switched it off when it was over and slept on the couch again.

That Sunday morning, as I flipped to the sports page to read about Saturday's Sabres game, I sat waiting for our bedroom door to open. Eventually, I heard footsteps on our finished wooden floor and a creak from the doorjamb.

"Good morning," I said. "Do you want some orange juice?"

"Sure," she said, rubbing her eyelids before she mussed her snarled hair and watched me fill her glass. "What time is it?"

"A little after ten. The sun hit me in the face on the couch pretty early, so I decided to get up, grab a paper and make coffee."

"Thanks for the bed last night. You didn't have to do that."

"Yes I did," I said, got up and walked over to her. "After my performance Friday night, figured you deserved some space. I shouldn't have gone off like that with Luther or with you, so I'm sorry. I'm just anxious about the baby, anxious about you working so much. I wish it didn't have to be like this."

She stood silent for a moment, staring past my face and out the window. She crossed her arms under her breasts and looked back to me.

"But it *is* like this. We just have to deal with the situation as best we can, okay? You storming into my job and threatening the owner isn't going to help us out."

"I know, but—" I said, then stopped. I instead swallowed hard, took a deep breath and continued. "You know what? You're right. I just want you to know that I'm sorry and it won't happen again. It's over, so let's move on."

"Fine," she said, then walked down the hallway and into the bathroom. When I heard the shower start flowing, I let my feelings ease; I needed to let whatever anger attached to Friday's scene float away, to melt with resolution. As the shower's steam began to drift into the hallway, the lingering anger attached to the unresolved was rising. I had to speak, had to get one thing out before it exploded inside of me. With this item stewing in my stomach, I walked down the hallway and poked my head into the humidity.

"Dana, I don't want to get into this again, but—"

"But what, John?"

"You know my deal with Luther. You know our past."

"Please," she said. "We're not going to have this conversation again about the pros and cons of Luther White. That crap between the two of you happened years ago. And, might I add, you still have absolutely no proof he had anything to do with it."

I put my coffee down on the toiletry shelf and took another deep breath. I swallowed hard again, trying to think of the big picture. No good. Anger was rising from stomach to shoulders to mouth.

"So you think that beating I took five years back was merely coincidental? You think it was some random occurrence that three White Room regulars jumped me around the same time I stole most of the guy's Friday night music business? The people at the Nighthawk still think he was behind it. That's why it's the only bar in the city that won't pour the guy a free drink."

"Look," Dana said, then pulled the shower curtain back to reveal her shampoo-soaked scalp. "We're not getting into this again. Frankly, I don't give a shit what happened with Luther. It was before you were my boyfriend, before you were my husband, and before he was my fucking *boss*. Now, he signs the checks that pay for my classes, gives me the big money shifts that delivers us some financial breathing room. Do you know anywhere else in Buffalo I can make the kind of waitress cash I make there?"

"No, but—"

"Then we're done with this. We're done with the buts, and we're done discussing Luther," she said. "If you're not going to remember him as your childhood hero, think of him as the guy who helps us pay for a crib, okay?"

I bit my lip and stood silent. Find the high road, I thought. Stay on it and keep moving, dammit.

"Okay?" she yelled again.

"Fine. I'm done," I said. "From this day on, Luther White is our goddamn savior."

Dana retreated back into the shower and I turned toward the door. Before I headed out, I cut one more question through the steam and aroma of lathered eucalyptus oil.

"Dana?"

"If you say either 'Luther' or 'White', I swear to God I will come out there and whip this shampoo bottle at your groin."

"No, no," I said. "I'm just wondering if you'd like to take a walk up Elmwood when you're done, see if we can find a crib. It's a great day for a stroll."

I could only hear water droplets hitting the shower walls and floor amid her pause. I didn't hear her massaging or scrubbing or moving; I only heard falling droplets. I was about to pop my head in to check on her when she finally responded.

"Yes," she said, then poked her rinsed scalp out from behind the curtain. "We can do that."

After she was dried and dressed, Dana joined me outside and we headed to Elmwood. Walking up and away from downtown, we found the street vibrant with walkers, runners and cyclists. A fleeced woman jogged with her energetic yellow Labrador, smiled and nodded hello as she passed us. A young man in a white T-shirt—arms covered in brightly colored tattoos from wrists to tapered short sleeves—pedaled past on a black ten-speed, its thin tires rolling swiftly on ice-free pavement. We passed vintage boutiques and record shops, intimate coffeehouses and subversive taverns. On a Sunday afternoon, all were bustling, filled with friendly conversations that echoed out open doors and windows. Such lively talk bounced around Buffalo sidewalks on unexpectedly temperate winter days, assumed gifts from a sympathetic God. Dana and I walked hand in hand, laughing and talking again as we felt the soft lake breeze blow against our faces.

We passed the darkened windows of Merlin's Tavern and came upon the front window of Evelyn's, an intimate shop specializing in children's furniture and Buffalo-themed household decor. Standing between small oak drawing table and an aluminum rocking horse was a white, spindled crib, fully assembled and reasonably priced. When I saw it, I looked at Dana, who seemed pleased with the appearance and displayed price tag.

"For that price, we could grab the rocking horse, too," she said. "Maybe give it to Mickey for his birthday."

"I think Mickey's too tough to be seen on a rocking horse. And even if he isn't, he'd act like he is."

"Right, right," she said, rubbing her stomach in a circle.

"Well, what do you think? Should we go for it?"

"Absolutely," I said. "Let's get this baby its first bed, Mommy."

Holding the Evelyn's door for her, I heard Dana as she whispered the end of my suggestion to herself.

"Mommy."

For one hundred and fifty dollars, we had our crib, an unassembled version in a large box too heavy to carry back down the street. The cashier agreed to tag it and keep it behind the counter until I came back with my Outback. Before we left, I bought a crib mobile with little hanging blue buffaloes that rotated with a turn of a knob. Outside on Elmwood again, I took hold of Dana's hand for our walk back home. Passing under lines of bare tree limbs, scattered clouds began to float in front of sunlight, blocking the previous array of beams but not eliminating the warmth. Winter would soon return, with its lake-effect snow squalls and icy sidewalks. That day, we were enjoying the meteorological aberration, walking toward Allen Street as she leaned her head on my shoulder. When we reached Allen, we saw tables and chairs being dragged to the sidewalks outside Cigarettes & Coffee. Before anyone else grabbed the few available seats, we snagged two under the fading sunlight. I popped inside the café and grabbed two decaf coffees, then brought them outside to Dana. She cradled her cup in front of her, raised it to her mouth and blew at the rising steam.

"Thank you," she said. "This smells so good. God, I can't wait to have a strong cup of coffee again."

"It'll come soon enough. This time next year, you can strap the baby to your chest, come down here and take a seat inside. Maybe you'll score a corner spot in the Sam Cooke section."

Dana took a deep breath and blankly stared down Allen, sitting silently as she held her cup with two hands.

"What's on your mind?" I said.

"Nothing really. Just thinking about things."

"Baby things?"

"That's part of it, sure," she said, then ran her hand over her stomach again. I leaned across the table to reach out and graze that hand, to bring it off her stomach and into my grasp.

"You know your life isn't just yours anymore, right? When you're in class, at the bar, walking down the street, whatever, your life is now *our* life. Our choices, our responsibilities and our changes, and I'm going to be with you every step of the way on this. If you think there's anything I wouldn't do for you and this child—"

"I don't think that."

"And don't ever," I said, then took a sip of my coffee and gazed down Allen as more children emerged from neighborhood houses to ramble down sidewalks and shout under the sunshine. "On really bad days, those days when I have one idiot after another call my desk about a spoiled carton of milk or faulty brake pads, you know what gets me to five o'clock? What gets me out the door with hair still on my head?"

"What?"

"The thought of this kid," I said. "All that I think about is doing things as a family, doing the same stuff I did as a kid. I think about things like sitting around in our living room and listening to Dylan records until the baby falls asleep."

Dana blew on her coffee again as I continued.

"I think about the three of us walking down to Canalside for music on Thursday nights, going out for Bisons baseball in the summer. I think about our first Bills game."

"You assume I'm carrying a boy. What if it's a girl?"

"What, girls don't like football? When the Bills dropped that first Super Bowl, no one in my family was more upset than Meg. She sat in front of our television and bawled her eyes out."

She flashed me another tiny grin before peering off into the sky as more clouds were gathering off the lake.

"Honestly," I said, "I don't care if you have a boy or girl. Either way, it's going to be a beautiful child, our child. Ever since my dad passed away, I've been waiting for this day, waiting for the hour I could think of him and my mother looking down to see me as a father."

A rush of emotion came up my chest, danced across the back of my scalp and tickled my hairs' roots. I took another deep breath, looked down the street at the children playing and converted my emotion into a grin. My parents liked to see me smile. They enjoyed seeing me show my teeth.

"It still hurts," I said.

"Them being gone?"

"Every once in a while, yeah. It'll come out of nowhere, like when I see a laughing grandmother or a grandfather showing off pictures of their grandchildren in City Hall. The thought of them gone flashes and I'll clutch my stomach. Even after this long, I wonder what it'd be like if they were around, wonder how my life would be different if they hadn't passed away so suddenly."

"They'd be those same type of grandparents," she said. "Probably spoiling Mickey and Brendan worse than you do."

"Right." I let out a quick laugh before glancing up to the sky. "I know they're up there somewhere, sitting amid the clouds or whatever constitutes Heaven. I know it's clichéd, but I really do believe they're around, keeping an eye on us."

"And I bet they're happy with what they see. Happy with their son." She paused to look at the sky, growing darker as the winds down Allen picked up. "These clouds are another story. They're beginning to turn angry, so we should call it a day."

I nodded and took one last sip of coffee before we walked back to our apartment. At the corner of Elmwood and Allen, I stopped Dana, let the Hondas and Fords roll by before I grabbed her hand and led her across the street. It was such a prudish thrill, the touch of another's hand. It was merely heat and oil and sweat and skin mashed up between appendages nowhere near sex organs, but it still meant something; it was a sign of genuine affection between two people who once stood as strangers at opposite ends of a dirty rock bar. Through our fingertips, there was still electricity. I grasped Dana's shoulders and stopped her before we reached our front door. Staring into her eyes, I could feel that vintage charge, that aged, innocent thrill buried behind the green hue.

"So," I said. "I have an idea for tonight."

"And what's that?"

"How about we have a little party? Just you and I."

"Doesn't sound like too much of a party," she said, smiling.

"I'm going to go pick up our crib from Evelyn's, and then I thought I could come back and make us some dinner."

"Oh really? So what are we having? One of your Irish spaghetti specials? I think we're out of Ragu."

"I can come up with something else," I said, laughing. "After dinner, we can put on some music and put that crib together. What do you think?"

"I think that sounds great," she said, then braced for a kiss, my lips already approaching hers. After I walked into our apartment behind her, I heard the muffled ring of Dana's phone, buried deep in her purse. She dug it out, identified the number and slumped.

"Work," she said.

She answered, walked down the hall and into our bedroom, then shut the door behind her. I continued into the living room to put down the buffalo mobile and grab my car keys and navy blue fleece. Before I could slip my hands in the fleece's sleeves, I heard the bedroom door swing open and Dana's footsteps follow down the hall to the living room. She had already changed into a black T-shirt.

"They need me to come in," she said. "One of the girls is sick and they don't want to be understaffed for tonight's game."

I looked at Dana, took a deep breath and exhaled.

"So I guess our party is cancelled."

"I'm sorry, John. Maybe we do this tomorrow night instead."

"Don't worry about it," I said. "I can put the crib together myself, maybe have a few beers. Why don't you grab your stuff and I'll take you down to the bar, okay?"

Standing in the doorway, she glared at me, hands on her hips and head tilted.

"You're mad."

"Mad?" I said, jingling my car keys from my fingertips. "No, I'm not mad. It's just, you know, I wish—"

"You wish it didn't have to be like this."

"Yep."

"Me too."

"Then why don't you call Luther and tell him to fuck off," I said. "Tell him you have plans with your husband tonight."

"Would you stop it? You know I can't do that. If they call, I have to go in. That's the deal. If I don't, some education major from Buff State, an airheaded little pixie with tits falling out of her T-shirt, will take my place in minutes. Maybe even seconds. Are you really going to make a thing out of this?"

I stood silent for a moment, inhaled my anger and tried to bury it.

"I get it, Dana. You need to work. You need money for school, life, whatever you say. Why don't you finish getting dressed and I'll give you a ride down there."

I zipped up my fleece and stayed silent while she stood in the doorway, waiting for me to throw in another comment or final plea. When the silence continued with the passing seconds, she reacted.

"So that's it? You're not going to say another word about this?"

"Like I said earlier, this is our life. This is the way it is, and I just have to deal with it. Biting my tongue and driving you to work is my way of dealing with it, okay?"

Once Dana was dressed, I drove her to the bar, then went to Evelyn's and loaded the crib into my Outback's hatch. Darkness overtook the daylight, and those warm Lake Erie breezes turned cold. I zipped up my fleece collar as a chill went down my chest and legs. I parked along the Allen curb in front of our apartment, grabbed the bulky crib's box from the hatch and hauled it up hallway stairs and through our door. I leaned it against the living room wall and went to the fridge for an ice-cold bottle of Molson. I cracked it open and ripped a quick swig before I grabbed a wrench and screwdriver from my toolbox, then walked back to the living room and the crib's waiting box. I looked across the room to my record shelves, lined with decades of audio poetry. I scanned from section to section until I found John Lennon and pulled out *Double Fantasy*. I took the vinyl from the sleeve and ran it through my hands, searching for scratches. I laid it on the platter, counted the grooved gaps while they eased around. I gently dropped the needle to elicit introductory crackling before Lennon's fingers found piano keys. Andy Newmark's percussion followed and merged with the piano for a sublime instrumental opening. Lennon's lyrics eased out the floor speakers, and I dropped onto the couch to listen.

People say I'm crazy, doing what I'm doing.

"Right on, John," I said. "You and me both."

10

Get ready for change, son
It comes in an instant
But while things are right, kid
Let's try and resist it
-"Stand Strong" by J. Nolan

Meg closed her refrigerator door with a bottle of Molson Canadian in each hand. After she passed one to me, she twisted the cap off hers and clinked her bottle against mine for a toast. Flashing her wide Irish grin in the glare of her kitchen, she gave me a wink before taking a deep, anxiety-relieving swig. Even if I didn't know it, one look at my sister's demeanor made it abundantly clear her date that night would be her first in at least a year. This occasion—combined with my availability to stay with her boys on a Saturday night—demanded a toast.

"So you're sure this is a good idea?" said Meg, standing before me in blue jeans and a long-sleeved brown top.

"Why wouldn't this be a good idea? You think single mothers aren't allowed to go on dates?"

"No, no." She sighed as she leaned against the marble counter and took another drink. "It's just that every time I go out with someone, the boys are with me. Not physically, but they're there, you know? I don't ever have time alone. That's the way it is when you're a parent."

"My God, would you stop being so dramatic? You're

only going out for a few drinks, so enjoy yourself. This is what single adults do, Meg. Speaking of which, who is this guy?"

"Ray Tyler," she said, picking at the label of her beer bottle. "He's a lawyer who works cases in city court from time to time. Real nice guy, and . . ."

I looked to the floor and her words faded from my attention. I stopped listening. I'd heard this "nice guy" tag before. Every guy Meg had gone out with was a nice guy, with a solid past and a promising future. They all turned out to be shits—every last one of them. Thankfully, as Meg grew into her thirties with two Nolan boys at her side, these dates became less frequent. So did the empty preparations.

"So what do you think?" she said.

"About what?"

"Did you even listen to what I just said? About Ray?" she said, hands on her hips.

"Sure, you said he's a lawyer and a nice guy, right? Seems like a good start."

"John, I get it, okay? I don't have the best record in picking men."

"No comment," I said, then took a long pull off my bottle of Canadian.

"None needed. I mean, Christ, I have two examples of my inability to judge character sitting in the living room."

"Meg, I—"

"You don't have to say anything," she said, waving me off. "I know what you think, that this nice guy is just another mistake waiting to happen. And that's fine. You've earned the right to be pessimistic."

"And I shouldn't be with this guy?"

"I'm not," she said. "He seems like a good guy, and he's

a good father. He has two children of his own. Daughters."

"Divorced?"

"Yeah," she said, then took another sip. "He and his wife split about four years back. She left him for another guy, so it was a pretty rough ordeal."

"But he seems to have it together?"

"He has to. Man has children to look after, two little girls to take care of. You can't crawl into a corner and feel sorry for yourself when others are depending on you. That's kind of how we connected, with single parent talk."

"Sounds promising. And hey, if things go well, we can add a lawyer to the family. Wouldn't hurt to have a cheap attorney around for when Mickey gets older."

She slapped me on the arm.

"My God, I'm only having drinks with the guy, right? Slow down. Besides, the boys don't need a new father. They have you, one of the few good men I've ever had in my life."

"You know I'm watching them for free, right? No need to brown-nose," I said. "Besides, with Dana at work for, like, the eighth night in a row, I have nothing to do. You're actually entertaining me with this sitter gig."

"Happy to entertain, little brother," she said, then set her empty bottle on the counter. "And with that, I'm gone. So you're all set for tonight? Food, drinks, money?"

"Good God, just get going." I gave her a friendly push toward the kitchen exit. "We have the Sabres game on in about an hour. We'll order a pizza and all will be fine, just as you left it. Deal?"

"Deal. I'm gone."

We walked out of the kitchen together to find Brendan and Mickey watching television from opposite sides of the brown leather couch. Meg grabbed her car keys and purse off an end table and alternated looks between the two of them.

"So I'm leaving now."

"Uh huh," they each said, staring at the television, not even glancing toward their mother. She walked to stand in front of the television.

"I said I'm leaving. Now."

"Okay," they mumbled, crooking their heads and trying to watch the sports highlights behind her.

"Brendan and Mickey, nothing but your best behavior tonight with Uncle John, you got it? No fighting, no yelling and no wrestling during the game. Understood?"

They nodded again, and Meg kissed them both goodbye before giving me a hug.

"Have a good time tonight, and call me if you need anything," I said. "Also, be careful driving out there. The icy roads aren't suited for your maniac driving style."

She feigned offense at my comment, then pushed out the front door and into the biting South Buffalo cold. When her Ford Escape was safely out of the driveway, I grabbed the television remote and clicked off the tube.

"Hey, c'mon," Mickey yelled, turning with Brendan to face me.

"All right," I said. "I turned the television off because we have to get ourselves situated for the game. The Sabres are playing the Leafs tonight, right?"

They both nodded.

"What are you two going to wear to watch the game? Are you planning to cheer for the home team in those clothes?"

They confusedly looked at each other before looking back at me.

"That's not gonna get it done. You need to show some city pride, boys. Mickey, get upstairs and put on your Sabres sweatshirt. Brendan, go find your Roy sweater and pull it on. Report back to the couch when you're both dressed."

Still confused, they slowly got up from the couch and trudged up the stairs to their bedrooms. Minutes later, both returned ready, dressed in their suggested gear.

"Okay," I said. "That's better. Now, where are we going to sit to watch the game?

They both retreated back to their spots on the couch to claim an armrest at opposite ends. After I saw this, I revealed my secret plan, a play right out of my parents' playbook.

"So you'd rather have those crummy couch spots than seats in the arena?"

Their faces lit up, eyes wide staring at me and waiting for me to confirm the deal.

"Go grab your coats, boys," I said. "We've got a hockey game to get to."

Whooping loudly, they each met my waiting right fist with tough bumps. Once ready, we piled into my Outback to head to the arena for a Sabres showdown with their closest and most hated rival, the Toronto Maple Leafs.

We shuffled through the doors off Perry Street with a mass of Sabres fans, clad in royal blue, navy blue and gold ski caps; oversized jerseys and sweatshirts; team coats and Sabres T-shirts. Before we reached the entry turnstiles, I stood off to the side to search for Pete, who scanned tickets before every home game as a second job. He'd worked at the arena in one position or another since it opened in 1996, so he had the seniority to enjoy a few perks. One of those benefits was the ability to slip three stragglers with no tickets through his turnstile and tell them where to find the night's most vacant sections. When we finally found him, he did that, just as he'd done for us many nights before.

"Brendan, Mickey. What's the word, boys?" he said. "You think we got this one tonight or what?"

"You bet, Mr. Konarski," Brendan said. "Roy's due for a good skate tonight."

"That's what I like to hear," he said. "And Mickey, don't you go quiet tonight, pal. You let those Canadians have it, okay? Tons of Leafs fans in here tonight."

After Mickey nodded and smiled, he pushed through with Brendan, leaving me to talk with Pete as a line of patient ticket holders stood behind me.

"You should be good up in any corner of the 300s," he said. "My guy in the ticket office told me there's a few rows open in each."

"Thanks, pal. You always make me look good in front of those two."

"No problem. Just call me when you find seats so I can come up and see you during the game."

I patted him on the back and took the boys up the escalator to the main concourse, full of Buffalo sports memorabilia lining its walls. They'd seen it all before, and they always wanted to come back. They wanted to study Gilbert Perreault's first Sabres jersey and the picture of Brad May getting mobbed after his famous "May Day" goal against Boston in the 1993 Adams Division semifinals. They needed to see the weathered and chipped sticks of local legends Rick Martin, Alexander Mogilny and Mike Foligno. Brendan always stared at the border of colorful pictures and captions beneath each like he'd never seen them before, like each historic snapshot was a new experience for him to inhale. After he'd seen enough, we made our way up another series of escalators to find three seats high above the ice, against the railing of the first row of Section 323.

"Uncle John," said Mickey. "Do you think anyone is going to come for these seats?"

"Maybe, but it's just like last time we were here. If we're in someone's seat, we'll move somewhere else."

"Kind of like musical chairs, right?"

"I guess, yeah," I laughed. "And hometown rules apply tonight. Brendan, please refresh your brother's memory on this."

"If a Sabres fan says these seats are his, we apologize and move. But if a Maple Leaf fan shows up—"

"I start crying and say these are my favorite seats ever," said Mickey. He sat up straight to smile. "I remember."

"That's good. Let me see your fake crying."

Mickey brought a sour look to his face, like kid actors did on Nickelodeon's after-school lineup. He began rubbing his eyelids with his tiny fists, brought a stuttering wail up from his chest and let it all out.

"Awwwwwwwwwwwwwww," he screamed. "I'll never have seats like this again! Awwwwww-huh-huh-hooo."

Mickey was going for it, and I could see nearby fans look over at us, convinced of how upset he was. Brendan sat still, fighting back laughter by biting his lower lip. I did the same before tapping Mickey on the back so he'd stop the show.

"Okay, enough, you little faker," I said. "Save it for the game. Hopefully we won't need it."

Mickey sat happy with himself while the lights went down for player introductions. Spotlights surveyed the seats as bombastic rock music joined flashing Jumbotron video to electrify a charged home crowd, all on their feet to scream for the Sabres and insult the Leafs. After the introductions, the arena grew silent for the Canadian national anthem, sung sweetly by a high school girl from Hamilton, Ontario. The thousands of Canadians in attendance helped her sing most of the song, loud and proud and standing guard for thee. After their moment closed, they stood silent for the American turn.

"Ladies and gentlemen," boomed the arena's announcer, "to perform tonight's anthem, please welcome a local institution. Singer, songwriter and guitarist, the legendary Luther White."

I clenched my teeth through the roar and tepidly clapped so to join in with the crowd. I watched Luther, who confidently strode across a red carpeted runway laid from the players' entrance to center ice. Clad in a royal blue suit and gold tie to match the Sabres' traditional colors, he clicked his signature red shoes down that carpet as he waved to the crowd, flashing his beaming smile on the overhead Jumbotron. As I crossed my arms, I felt Brendan's hand on my shirttail.

"Wow, Uncle John. The Leafs and Luther White in the same night. Pretty cool, huh?"

"Sure thing, pal." There was no need to let Brendan in on my past with Luther. The benefits of him enjoying such a communal event amid the cheers and chants outweighed my grudges.

After Luther wailed his expected smoky, histrionics-infused anthem under a bright, isolated spotlight, the lights came up with the roar of the crowd. One by one, they joined in on a spontaneous chant of "Loo-ther, Loo-ther, Loo-ther" as he strolled off the ice, pointing and waving to the masses. Thankfully, that chant was quickly overtaken by the customary "Let's go, Buffalo" chant that began every home Sabres game, broken up repetitiously as *let's-go-Buf-fa-lo, clap, clap, clap-clap-clap.* We stayed standing at our seats, clapping and yelling and stomping until the opening puck was dropped at center ice.

I spotted the hot dog vendor once we settled into our seats and signaled him over with three fingers. I ordered three dogs with packets of mustard and ketchup before I waved over the soda vendor and ordered three cokes. We sipped our drinks and dressed our dogs as the Sabres pressed the Leafs defense, pinning them in as they worked the puck around inside the blue line. As I took my first mustard-slathered bite, I felt a hand tap my left shoulder. Dressed in cobalt blue and white, two over-weight Maple Leaf fans stood on the aisle steps, each holding a tall beer in both of their hands.

"Think you're in our seats, guy," said the first one, with dark eyebrows joining his closely cropped goatee.

"No, no, these are definitely our seats," I said. "Section 323, row one, seats one, two and three."

"Well, we got the same tickets as you, there," said the one in back. "Can we see your tickets?"

While I sat searching for ticket stubs I didn't have, I heard the wailing, right on cue.

"Awwwwwwwwwwwwwww!" Mickey cried, letting it go three times as convincingly as he did in the pre-game warm-up. "Awwwwwwwwwwwwww-huh-huh-hooo! Are these men gonna make us leave our seats, daddy? Are they? Awwwwwwwwwwww-www! These are my favorite seats in the whole world! I'll never have seats this nice again! Awwwwww-huh-huh-hooo!"

When the crowd around us heard Mickey, they looked to the two now startled Leaf backers as the ones who made him upset; the sons-of-bitches who made a poor little boy cry at a Sabres game. One by one, surrounding ticket holders rose from their seats to yell at the men, hurling filthy expletives I'd rather

Mickey or Brendan didn't hear. A full beer hit the goateed one in the back and exploded all over his white jersey, splattering on nearby fans. When he turned around to confront his hecklers, a handful of peanuts rained on him and a crumpled beer cup hit his pal in the ear. More expletives joined more shouting, until a majority of our section rose to their feet to point at the two men while rhythmically chanting, "aaaaaaaass-holes, aaaaaaaass-holes." Security guards were scattered in neighboring sections, but nowhere to be found in 323. Finally, the second Leafs fan looked at me to surrender.

"Jeezus, can you get that kid to stop crying before these people kill us?" he quietly pleaded. "The seats are yours, okay? We'll go sit somewhere else. Just settle him down."

With that, I nudged Mickey, who held his face in his hands, his performance totally over the top. Brendan covered his face with his blue jersey, hiding his laughter; he'd never seen Mickey put on a performance like this before. I patted him on the back and leaned down to his ear.

"Alright, let's stop the show before one of these guys gets tossed over the balcony rail."

He looked up at me, nodded and smiled before rubbing his eyelids again for show. The two Leaf fans were exiting up the stairs, off to find some open seats in a worse section as profanity and debris continued to rain down on them. Brendan mussed Mickey's hair as the two sat laughing. Hometown rules were adhered to. I crossed my arms, leaned back in my seat and grinned widely. It wasn't the best example to set, but a necessary lesson in hometown allegiance, best learned at an early age. At six years old, Mickey was already a scholar.

My cell phone still had no reception when the horn sounded at the end of the second period. I couldn't call Pete to find us, but the game's action was more than enough company. Tied at two, each team scored one goal in the period to keep things knotted. I was anxious and nervous, the same as I'd been while watching nearly every Buffalo sports event as a kid. Didn't matter if it was a preseason Bills game or a Sabres playoff; I was always unsettled. Thankfully, the boys appeared unfazed. Mickey flipped popcorn into his mouth as he talked to a younger boy behind us, a friend of his from school. Brendan sat quietly and sipped his Coke, relaxed while looking up at the shot totals on the Jumbotron.

"You think Miller's goaltending is keeping us in this one?"

"Definitely," said Brendan. "They outshot us 17-8 that period, so without some of those saves, we'd be down bad right now. Our offense will pick up in the third, though. They have to start forechecking to open up some space, too. You know Roy can let a few rip with some time to gather and shoot."

"You should get on the phone to the locker room," I said as a highlight reel ran on the scoreboard screen. After another long sip of his Coke, he looked away from the screen to turn back to me again.

"Uncle John, can I ask you a question?"

"Shoot."

"Who's this guy my mom went out with tonight?"

"Just a guy she knows through work. A lawyer named Ray."

"Do you know him?"

"No, but your mother said he's a good guy. She usually makes good decisions about stuff like that."

"Except for my dad."

"Right," I said. As long as he acknowledged the big one, there was no reason to talk about the rest of them—or swap out the word *usually* with *never*. "Everyone makes mistakes."

"So do you think she really likes this guy?"

"It's only a first date, so who knows. You're not worried about this, are you?"

"Well," he said, fidgeting in his seat, "it's just that, with Aunt Dana and you having the baby, maybe Mom thinks she needs to find a husband. A guy to help take care of me and Mickey since you won't be around as much."

"You serious? I mean, have you and Mickey really talked about this?"

"A little bit, yeah," he said, then sipped off his Coke. "Mom doesn't go on that many dates, so we figured this might be the start of things to come, with other guys around who we might have to get used to."

I took a deep breath and looked right to Brendan again.

"After Aunt Dana and I have the baby, it's not going to change things with us. It's just going to expand our family a bit. I'm not going to leave you and Mickey behind. You'll always be my guys, right?"

"I guess. But what if Mom gets along well with this Ray? What are we supposed to do with him?"

"If she says so, we'll let him in, too. In the meantime, relax. It's a first date. Leave those decisions up to your mother. We've got a game going on here."

"Okay," he said, smiling as we exchanged a fist bump before the start of the third period. Just like Brendan urged, the Sabres came out forechecking, laying immense pressure on the Leafs' defensemen to handle the puck in their own zone. All it took for the Sabres to regain the lead was one sloppy clear around the boards. Sabre forward Derek Roy swooped in to handle the loose puck in the Toronto zone, then swept past the Leafs' goalie to stuff a wrist shot home, top shelf over the flailing tender's right shoulder. When the red light flashed, the entire arena went ballistic, screaming and cheering as three horn sounds rattled the farthest reaches of the cavernous upper deck. The boys and I exchanged high fives before turning around to exchange slaps and pounds with the fans around us. Though strangers on the street, we were united in the stands, all Buffalonians wearing the same blue and gold.

After the goal stood to give the Sabres a win, we flowed with the crowd to descend down escalators and exit out onto the now-tolerable chill of Perry Street. While fighting through the lakefront winds whipping around us, I felt my phone vibrating, its reception finally restored. I flipped it open to find twelve new messages waiting, all left during the game. Before I could check even one of them, the phone was ringing again, with Meg calling.

"So I know I have the boys out after their bedtimes," I said after answering, "but did you catch any of that game?"

"Game?" she yelled, her voice shaking. "John, my God, where the hell are you, and why haven't you been answering your phone?"

"Whoa, whoa, settle down," I said, startled. "I took the boys to the Sabres game tonight, and my phone didn't get any reception in our section. Why, what's the problem?"

"I've been calling your cell phone for the past hour. I need you to get down to Mercy Hospital as soon as you can. Please hurry."

"Mercy? Why, what's happened? What's going on?"

"Just get down here as fast as you can," she said. "It's

Dana, John. And the baby."

11

My father always hoped
I'd never see the day
When all the hopes and dreams I had
Would start to fade away
-"Untitled" by J. Nolan

I emerged from the elevator with Brendan and Mickey to see Meg bundled in her winter coat, leaning against a hallway wall and sipping a cup of coffee. She turned to see us as we were approaching her, like she could sense our presence.

"Where is she?" I said. "What room is she in?"

She looked down at the boys and grabbed each of their hands.

"Brendan, take your brother over to those chairs along the wall. I need to talk to your uncle alone, okay?"

Brendan nodded and led Mickey away to the empty chairs and a table full of magazines. After she watched each of them take a seat, Meg grabbed the arm of my coat and led me down the hallway to the spot where she'd been standing. She leaned back against the wall in front of me as I repetitiously rocked on my heels, my arms folded while staring at the paint flecks in the linoleum floor tiles.

"So I've talked with the doctor who worked with Dana, and she said she's going to be fine."

Still staring downward, my sight became blurred, causing the flecks to spin and dance as my mind wandered.

"John? John, look at me. She's going to fine. Dana is going to be okay."

I lifted my head.

"Where is she?"

"She's down the hallway in the recovery unit, sound asleep with strong vitals. The doctor said that if the bar staff hadn't acted so quick in keeping her calm and calling the ambulance, we wouldn't be so lucky."

"Did the doctor tell you who helped?"

She tentatively took a sip from her coffee.

"Two of the younger waitresses," she said. "And Luther."

"Luther?"

"Guess he was over at the arena and walked into the bar as everything was happening. He even rode here in the ambulance with her. Doctor said he kept her calm and helped with information they needed for her until I could get here. She also said that without Luther's help, Dana's eventual recovery wouldn't be so certain. She lost a lot of blood at the bar."

"Meg," I said, scratching the back of my head, "what the hell happened?"

"She had an incomplete miscarriage. Doctor said it's very rare this late in the pregnancy, but it can happen with overexertion or stress."

"From her job?"

"Since this happened at work, yes, it's a possibility. Luther told the medical staff how often Dana had been working lately. It was in the paperwork I went over."

"So what happened tonight? What happened to her at work?"

"The waitresses said Dana had been complaining of back pain at the start of her shift, which can obviously come with being pregnant and on your feet," she said. "About an hour or two later, Dana said her stomach hurt and went into the bathroom. When she didn't come out for twenty minutes or so, a waitress went in to check on her."

"And?"

She looked down at the same tiles I'd been hypnotized by.

"She found her in a stall, bleeding and crying for help," she said. "I guess no one could hear her screaming over the bar's loud music."

"My God, my God, my God," I whispered, lowering my pale face into my hands. "And the baby?"

Meg stood silent, let some of the hospital's surrounding sounds fill the space between us. After a few seconds passed, she looked up and delivered.

"The baby was dead before she entered the emergency room."

I bit the insides of my mouth while clenching my fists, backing away from Meg as she took a deep breath and reached for me. I reluctantly let her snatch my hand, pull me toward her and wrap her arms around me.

"My God, Johnny, I'm so sorry," she whispered as I buried my head into her shoulder. "I love you so much. I'm really hurting for you right now, but I need you to look up at me. Can you please look at me?"

I raised my head, staring through her as my stomach churned and clenched.

"The doctor stressed how many miscarriages happen to young couples who later have multiple children. She also said

Dana suffered no irreparable damage. They're going to keep her here for a few days of recovery. She's going to be fine, and will be more than capable of having another—"

"Can I see her? I know she's asleep, but can I see her now? Please?"

"She's down the way a bit. Room three fifteen." She sympathetically touched my shoulder before I could walk away. "Johnny, stop. Look at me. Look at me, dammit."

"What? What else do I need to hear?"

"You need to know this wasn't your fault. The doctor said that, in cases like this, there are no warning signs for what's about to happen. None. You need to understand this, because I know you. I know what you're thinking right now."

"And what am I thinking?"

"You think there's something you could've done to stop this. I can see that look on your face, the same look you had when dad died," she said. "You told her to slow down on shifts. She went to work anyway. And even if you were in that bar with her, following her around from table to table, you couldn't have stopped her body from miscarrying."

I absorbed these words. They were an attempt to console, but merely joined the surround sound of squeaking wheelchair wheels and tapping fingertips on hospital computer keyboards. My sight fixated on those flecks in the linoleum again, particles of dirt glossed over each tile. I kept staring with unfocused sight, so the spots became blurred and began to move in rhythm with my heartbeat. Teaming with the deafening silence of my guilt, my heartbeat overtook the squeaking, the tapping, the words. It was all I could hear as I stood with Meg.

"You know there's no way I'll ever believe that. You know there's no way I'll ever believe I couldn't have stopped this."

"Try to believe it, because it's true," she said. "Sit with Dana and try, okay?"

Meg grabbed me again and pulled me toward her, holding my lifeless body as I breathed heavily into the shoulder of her wool coat. When we broke apart, I looked into her compassionate eyes, welling up before she took another deep breath to calm herself.

"I'm going to take the boys home," she said "I called Finn, so he should be in here soon to sit with you for as long as you need. I'll call and check on you after I get them to bed."

I nodded and turned to walk down the cold, sallow hallway, staring at the dizzying linoleum as the click of my soles echoed in the empty space. After numerous paces, I scanned the door numbers. Three eleven. Three thirteen. Three fifteen.

When I found the door, I pushed it open slowly, trying not to elicit a creak from the hinges. Thankfully, they were oiled and silent as I found Dana asleep, with sheets and a brown plush blanket pulled up under her chin. Approaching her, I could see her face, her dark hair pulled behind her ears, her eyelids closed. Sunken into the pillows and bed, she looked exhausted. Even with an I.V. tube connected to her exposed left arm, she appeared to be at peace, comfortable. She didn't moan or mumble; she didn't jostle around in the bed. She lay still, breathing rhythmically. I let her be. I pulled up a brown sofa chair to the side of her bed to sit quietly and watch her breathe. I didn't touch her or kiss her or even lean close enough for her to feel the heat of my breath. I sat in the silence, thinking reassuring thoughts.

I tried to embrace the positive as my hands cradled my face. Dana's fine; Dana's alive. We're both alive, and we can do this again. We'll get pregnant again. People have miscarriages all the time. We're going to be fine. God, oh God, tell me I'm going to be fine. Help me believe we're going to be fine.

   I looked over the metallic rail on the side of the bed. Dana was breathing freely through her nose, her soft lips sealed and content. I leaned forward in the chair; one of its legs scratched on the floor to make a sound. Dana gently reacted. Her head rolled away from me, sunk itself into another spot on the pillow. On the wall across from me hung a laminated instructional sheet for new mothers, suggesting that they *welcome baby softly. When the baby is born, hold it against your skin, stroke it softly. Gaze at the child and talk to it softly, lovingly. This time and interaction between child and parent is very important in the bonding process, vital in the first two hours of a baby's life.* Dana didn't even get two seconds, not a mere moment to hold her child, to smell its skin. I watched her nuzzle into her sheets. I arose from the chair, backed out of the room and slowly pulled the door shut behind me.

   I found a hallway window to look out at the traffic intersection at Abbott Road and Cazenovia Street as light snow fell from above. The hospital was cavernous, with silence joining the sterilized scents of clean bed sheets and plastic that floated past rooms filled with patients, asleep or contemplative. Usually, my mind juggled several thoughts while new lyrics or rhythms spontaneously flashed forth. At that moment, my mind didn't race. I didn't think about the miscarriage or what life would deliver next. I could only stare blankly at the traffic or notice a passing black Ford truck and rusted red Honda rumble loudly down Abbott. After I watched those cars pass, I looked past the cars and to the Tosh Collins Community Center across the street. Out of their doors walked fathers and sons, holding ice skates and hockey sticks. When the pairs found their pick-up trucks or

SUVs, the boys threw their skates in the cab or back seat and slid their sticks in after. Fathers and sons, walking and laughing and talking together. When my mind finally absorbed this image, it obliterated my numbness. Realization raced through the engulfing silence as a tear slipped down my face. Fatherhood wasn't approaching. A new Nolan wouldn't appear at Mercy Hospital in a few months. Suddenly, a hand grasped my shoulder.

"I came as soon as I could," said Finn. "Had my damn phone turned off during a Pre-Cana session. Luckily, I was close when I listened to Meg's message. Where is she? She take the boys home?"

"A few minutes ago, yeah."

"So how's Dana doing? How's she taking this?"

"She's sound asleep, so I don't know. I didn't want to wake her. This is probably the earliest she's been to bed in weeks."

I paused to take another deep breath, lean back against the window and stuff my hands into my jean pockets.

"Christ, Finn, what the hell kind of a husband am I to let this happen? At a goddamn hockey game while my pregnant wife's waiting tables."

"Alright, calm down. You didn't let anything happen. This just happened on its own." He put his hand on my shoulder again. "What did the doctor say?"

"Meg talked with her, said she called it an incomplete miscarriage," I said. "Hell of a description to give to something so complete."

"Do they know what caused it?"

"Work, most likely. It's rare, but it does happen, even midway through the second trimester. So that should be of some consolation, right? That I'm not alone? Guess there's plenty of others who've felt as empty as I'm feeling right now."

"John, please—"

After I waved him off, some more silence passed as I faced the window to watch more cars rumble down Abbott. When I turned back to Finn, I crossed my arms and took a deep breath.

"How else should I be feeling?" I bit down on the fleshy inside of my cheek. "You think anything can console me in this Godforsaken place? You think anything can stop me from staring out this window, looking out there onto Abbott and feeling sick? Feeling dead? Why is it that every time I walk into this place something gets taken away from me?"

"John, I know this is—"

"You know *what*, Finn?" I stepped back, keeping my arms crossed. "That this must be tough? Must be a punch in the stomach to find out my wife miscarried our first kid in a bathroom stall while I was watching a fucking hockey game?"

"Just calm down," he said, then stepped forward and extended his hand to my arm. "You can't blame yourself for this. Like the doctor said, this stuff *does* happen."

"But how much more of this can I be expected to take?" I slapped my palm against the bare drywall beside the window. "My mother dies of cancer, my father drops dead in the driveway, right in front of me? Yet here I am again, strolling the halls of Mercy while my wife's in a hospital bed. Really, how much can a man take?"

Standing in front of me, he looked up for a few moments, seemingly collecting his thoughts as they stirred.

"It's not a matter of how much you can take. It's how you handle it. With an unfortunate situation like this, you need to have faith that the pain you feel will serve an eventual purpose."

"A purpose? What the fuck kind of purpose can this have in my life, in Dana's life?"

"I don't have that answer."

"Yeah, well who does? God?"

"I believe he does, yeah."

I took a moment to stare at him, to wonder whether he really believed in such a stock response, in the ridiculously simplistic religious slogan he quickly shoveled at me. With frustration fermenting inside me, I stopped wondering and, instead, exploded.

"Tell you what, Finn. Next time you talk to the boss, you ask him about me. You look up to that gray Buffalo sky and yell, hey God, why do you keep fucking with my nephew? Ask him to give me a break and set fire to someone else's life for a change."

I turned around with my shouting still reverberating through the hallway. I stormed away, down the hallway and toward the stairwell that led out to the street. I put my shoulder into the exit, smashed it open and jumped down the stairs to find the sidewalk at the hospital's main entrance. The snow still fell lightly. I lit a cigarette underneath it, inhaled a deep drag as my hands were shaking. Staring up at the streetlights, I could see the nighttime flakes drift past the bulbs and down Abbott. I soon heard the sound of shoes calmly tapping down that stairwell until the door opened behind me.

"You have an extra smoke, kid?"

I stood silent for a moment, took another long drag and exhaled into the brisk lakefront breeze while Finn waited.

"When was the last time you had a cigarette?"

"When your old man died," he said. "I was standing right here. God, that was a terrible day. I think I must've smoked three butts in ten minutes."

I pulled out a Camel Light and handed it to him with some matches.

"I'm sorry about up there," I said. "It's just that feeling of helplessness. That feeling that things can be pulled out from under you at any moment."

"Oh, I know," he said. "I've felt that way many times in my life. Why do you think I was out here chain-smoking after your father died?"

"Because you're human. You can't always be sensible."

"See, you understand that because I'm your uncle. I'm just a man to you. Parishioners assume my collar barricades me from shock, from pain. Since I'm a priest, they assume I never suffer from the same crippling confusion as others when life unfolds the way it does. The same crippling confusion that would cause you to scream 'fuck' through a hospital."

"Sorry about that."

"Don't be. Your reaction tells me you're not dead inside. After enough of these things occur in a man's life, that's what can happen. Numbness. Apathy."

"I'm not numb," I said. "Just reeling."

"When you get punched in the stomach like this, that happens. When your father died, do you remember me hurting my right hand? How I said I accidentally slammed it in my car door?"

"Sure I do. You had a cast on at the funeral. Why?"

"I lied. I never slammed my hand in any door. After I administered the last rites to your father, I walked out here and lit a cigarette before heading to the edge of Caz Creek down there," he said, pointing ahead in the distance. "I looked over the water and started praying, asking God what possible reason he could have for taking your father right after he took my sister.

But the more I prayed, the angrier I became. Eventually, I flicked my third cigarette in the creek and started screaming at the stars, yelling 'why' over and over again."

"And the hand?"

"While screaming, I needed something to whack, and the nearest thing I could punch was a metal parking sign. I wound up and smacked it three times before I felt my hand cave. You remember how cold it was that day? Imagine hitting a thick, cold piece of metal in that weather—with a bare fist. That's what happened to my hand."

After that sentence, there was silence, whether for recognition or recollection. We rocked back and forth on the balls and heels of our feet, trying to stay warm amid the lakefront chill.

"Why are you telling me this now?" I said.

"Because I want you to understand that I know what it feels like when the lights go out, when all hope is sapped and you have no reason to believe that any God-given explanation exists for what's happened to you. Lots of people have felt like this when faced with a situation like yours. But over time, they start to feel and deal differently."

"So how did your feelings change after my father died?"

"I came to an eventual understanding that God wanted to unite him with your mother," he said. "Those two belonged together since the day they became a couple, so to have them on separate planes of existence would have been more tragic than having them both absent from this one."

I flicked my cigarette to the pavement.

"So how should I deal with this? How should I move forward?"

"That's for you to find out. Maybe you'll come to an optimistic understanding that you've lost a child, not the opportunity to have another. Settle on some conclusion, have faith in that realization, and you'll get through this darkness. You'll find the light again."

"That's it?"

"I'd tell you to go give a parking sign a few whacks, but we both know how that will turn out," he said with a grin. "Relief is temporary; the repercussions of such stupidity are permanent. My right hand still aches every time the temperature dips under thirty degrees. Didn't help my piano playing, either."

I nodded, then filled my bare hands with hot breath before stuffing them into my pockets.

"You going back inside?"

"Yeah," he said. "I know some of the Sisters of Mercy who work in the building, so I'll make sure they keep Dana comfortable while she's here. You?"

"I need to run out, but I'll be back in a bit to stay the night."

"You want me to come with you?"

"No, I'll be fine," I said. "Just need to take care of something downtown."

The lights outside the White Room were shining on brittle, frozen pavement. There were no cars parked out front, no people outside clasping cigarettes between fingers. It was dead, but the interior lights and quiet hum of blues guitar slipped out its doors and onto the street. I knew Luther had to be inside.

When I walked in, I found four men at the bar, sipping pints of beer and talking underneath the jukebox's Rolling Stones. They paused their conversation to stare me down in the doorway. I looked past them and to the bartender.

"Luther around?"

"Not sure," he said. "He was supposed to leave for his winter place in Florida at some point, but he might still be in back. Can I tell him who's calling?"

"John Nolan."

He stood tall, folded his arms across his chest.

"Johnny Nolan?" he said. "What you want to talk to Luther about?"

"It's about my wife, Dana."

He dropped his head before looking back to me.

"Oh shit," he said. "Right, right, Dana's your wife. I'm real sorry, man. How's she doing?"

"She's going to be fine."

"That's good, man. She gave all of us a real scare in here tonight."

"I'll bet she did," I said. "So you think you could go back and see if Luther's around? I need to talk with him for a minute."

He finally relaxed and uncrossed his arms. He had to see the sadness in my stance, the weariness of even discussing the situation; I could tell. With a polite nod, he headed to the back room and returned with Luther trailing behind him in jeans and a white T-shirt. Even with reading glasses covering his eyes, he looked exhausted. When he removed the glasses, his eyes appeared rubbed and red.

"Johnny," he said. "How's she doing, baby?"

"She's going to be fine. She's sleeping right now, and they're going to keep her at Mercy for a few days this week. Guess that's the usual protocol for women who suffer miscarriages."

Luther put his head down for a second or two, took a deep breath.

"They didn't give me too much information when I was there, but I assumed that was the case. It's some tough stuff, man. Tough stuff."

"Hey, can we step outside for a minute? Maybe have a smoke?"

"Yeah, yeah," he said. "I got to catch an early flight in the morning, but I can spare a few minutes. Whatever you need."

I led him out the front door, lit up and offered him a smoke. He had his own, so we inhaled and exhaled together on the desolate block, vacant of traffic, lit only by flickering street lights and the glow of tavern interiors. I took a drag amid the shadows and looked up to Luther.

"So I'm not going to waste your time," I said. "I'm not going to stand here and pretend you and I have some newfound connection. We have our history, and we both know it isn't exactly what anyone would consider smooth."

He crooked his head and took a drag. After he exhaled, he let out a laugh and shook his head.

"History, huh? Your wife just lost a baby and you come down here to talk about some motherfucking history? You got to be kidding me," he said. "Your wife's at Mercy, and you come on down here to stand in the fucking cold, to bring up some tired, old bullshit? Johnny, I don't know how many ways to say it. It wasn't me, and it wasn't anyone I know. I can't believe you still think I'd send thugs down the street to whip your white ass for supposedly stealing my thunder. You got to let that fantasy shit go, baby."

"Look, I'm not standing out here to rehash old times, alright? I came down here to bury that shit for good." I took another long drag. "I have bigger problems these days, like my wife in a hospital bed. But if it wasn't for your help, she might be in the morgue. That's why I'm down here, goddammit. I came down to say thanks and let the past be the past."

He looked to me, raised his eyebrow and took a long drag.

"You want to bury the past, huh? Just like that? No more making up stories? No more of you coming in here, accusing me of trying to steal your girl?"

"That's right," I said. "After tonight, that past shit's not important to me anymore. All that matters is that Dana's okay. You were there to help when I wasn't, and I owe you for that."

He crossed his arms across his white T-shirt. Outside in short sleeves, he wasn't even shivering.

"You don't owe me nothing, baby. And you know why you don't owe me nothing?"

"Why?"

"Because I don't give a fuck about you."

I took a step back.

"Luther, I don't know what—"

"Save your breath. Let's not let what happened tonight be interpreted as me doing you some motherfucking favor. You think I give a shit about you? I'm Luther White," he said. "I was backing Joe Cocker at Shea's while you were picking Deep Purple licks in your garage. I was jamming with Clapton at the Aud when you were shitting your diapers."

He took another drag, stared ahead and continued.

"I'm an institution in this city, son. And who the fuck are you? Just another kid with a dusty guitar, another motherfucker with stories. If you think we have some history, some friction because you used to outdraw my bar for Friday night drunks years back, that's your beef, baby. I care about Dana, my employee. I helped her, not you, so I don't give a shit if you want to squash whatever problems you have with me or not. You got that?"

He flicked his smoke to the pavement and turned to face me. I stood speechless, expressionless. I took my own final drag and dropped the butt to the sidewalk.

"Whatever you say, man. If this is the way you want to play it, that's fine. I just came to say thank you."

"Well, you did," he said, then walked toward the door. Before opening it, he turned back. "Now get your ass out of here, Johnny. I got to fly down to the beach, get myself a drink and some sun. You should get back to that hospital, you hear? Get back to Mercy and take care of our girl."

12

Before that first day dawned
The day I'd see your eyes
We stood apart alone
Said our first and last goodbyes
-"Gone Too Soon" by J. Nolan

Another few days and things could've been much worse. Another few days and Dana's pregnancy would've reached its twentieth week, the cutoff point between determining our loss a miscarriage or a stillbirth. If we'd endured a stillbirth, we'd have received a birth certificate and had the option to have a burial service for our child. One day, I sat with Dana in her hospital room and watched an overweight nurse callously present such stillbirth paperwork to a grieving mother who was recovering across the hall.

"Miss, I know your baby died prematurely, but you still have to fill out this birth information."

Holding the clipboard, the mother stared intently up at the nurse, searching behind the woman's eyes to possibly wonder whether her job had rendered her this cold, this numb to disregard maternal emotions. The nurse never blinked; she only held out a pen, tapping her foot against the linoleum before she looked out the window and exhaled.

"Is it too much to ask for a break from this goddamn snow? Every freaking hour more and more dumps down to ruin my day."

The mother took the clipboard and pen before staring out the window and into that same snow. She let tears fall to her gown as she bit her lower lip and took deep breaths. She never even glanced at the paperwork or put the pen anywhere close to it. She just kept staring out her window, let whatever thoughts of her lost child float about as white fell to the streets of South Buffalo. I assumed this entire contemplation from across the hall. The nurse couldn't see it from a few feet away.

"I guess I can give you a few minutes with that," she said, then turned and left the room. "I'm going to jump down to the cafeteria and grab a pop. Be back in a few minutes to collect it, okay?"

A few more days and our baby would've had a name and an official listing in the state of New York Records Office. A few more days and we would've had the option to make funeral arrangements for our child, to bury the baby in the same plot where my parents lay. That nurse would've marched into our room with that stillbirth paperwork and offered it like she was dropping a restaurant check. If I encountered that presentation, the same type I watched, I couldn't have been restrained from grasping that nurse's uniform top and tossing her fat ass out the door.

After understanding how close that moment was, I tried to appreciate things I previously found relatively intolerable. My cold steel City Hall desktop was suddenly not so cold. My chair, the surrounding concrete walls and incessant phone calls from city residents, ones rambling on about faulty spark plugs or expired milk were not as oppressive. If a consumer walked in from Niagara Square, wound up and punched wrinkled knuckles into my jaw, it wouldn't have been that bad. I never had to fill out that stillbirth paperwork. I didn't have to lay a tiny infant to rest at Holy Cross Cemetery before it ever took its first breath. That's why a seat at my desk was suddenly so tolerable two weeks after I brought Dana home from Mercy Hospital.

"Are you sure you want to be back here so soon?" said Pete, leaning over my cubicle wall. "Maybe you should take a few more days off. You seem edgy."

"I'm not edgy. At least no more than I've ever been in this seat before," I said. "And why should I take more time off? So I can barricade myself in my apartment and relive this whole ordeal over and over again?"

"What about Dana? You don't think she'd like you around for support? For comfort?"

"Pete, she was practically pushing me out the door this morning. I resisted a bit, but I'd be lying if I said I didn't want some breathing room—even if it's here. Plus, when I lay next to her, I see that vacancy."

"Vacancy?"

"Every minute I've spent with her since the miscarriage, I've been trying not to look at her stomach," I said. "When I do, it's like a punch to my gut. Just a glance down and what we've been through comes flying at my face again."

We let some quiet seconds pass and digested our exchange.

"You know this isn't the end, right? My sister's first pregnancy ended in a miscarriage and she's had three healthy kids since. Actually, all three of 'em are closer to damn wild animals than talking, walking children," he said, laughing. "Trust me Nolan, as bad as this is, it's only a setback before you really get going."

"I appreciate your optimism, but you haven't sat with Dana since she's left the hospital," I said, leaning back in my chair to scratch my stubble-covered face. "You haven't seen the empty look in her eyes or listened to how casually she's talked about this whole thing. Honestly, I'm not even sure she has any interest in having another child."

"Jesus, John, this all happened, what, a few weeks ago? She's probably still in a bit of shock. You have to give the girl at least a few months of recovery time."

"But there's this remorselessness about her. I just can't explain it. Of the two of us, I've been the more emotional one. She seems more concerned with the therapy classes she's missed than the lost pregnancy. The other day, she talked about going to stay with her parents in Florida. The next, she seemed intent on getting back on the White Room's waitress schedule."

Pete stepped back and folded him arms across his chest.

"Maybe that's her way of dealing with this. Christ, you're back at work, aren't you? Who's to say that Dana's not looking for the same kind of professional distraction?"

"I'm not an idiot, okay? I understand a need to distract from this inconvenient truth we're dealing with. It's something else. I mean, have you ever sat with Tracy when she seemed to stare right through you?"

"Tracy's never had a miscarriage."

"There's apparently a glazed stare that goes with one. That's what I'm dealing with right now. When I'm in the room with her, it's like I'm not even there. Like she's dazed, looking past me and toward some other existence. Some other life."

"Give her time. The girl needs time."

After going out for lunch, I was back at my desk, sifting through some of the old files that had piled up while I'd been home with Dana. A woman on Bailey Avenue bought a used Lexus that turned out to be a lemon. A man on Grant Street claims he was forced to leave a downtown bar after two beers because of his color. A Buffalo State student needs to get his rental deposit back from his deadbeat landlord. Residents were already receiving their tax return checks, deliveries that kicked off an irrational spending season. People would blow their refunds on giant plasma televisions and elaborate stereo systems they had no clue how to operate; they'd find questionable cars or motorcycles in local circulars, buy them with straight cash. Complaints from these purchases had already started to roll in, both by mail and off the street. Flipping through the manila folders on my desk, I heard fingers rhythmically tapping on the front counter, then stood to see another complaint to contend with the fifty on my desk.

"Can I help you?"

"Yeah, um, I'm here to see a John Nolan," said the young man, standing tall and twirling a car key ring on his index finger. "I filed a consumer complaint with this office and was notified by mail that he's handling my case."

"I'm John Nolan. And you are?"

"Jamie Bethford. I have a complaint against a bar, the White Room."

"Buffalo's home of the blues, huh? Would've remembered that one if I'd seen it. Give me a second to find it, okay?" I said. "Got a bit of a manila mountain forming over here."

"Sure thing," he said. "I'll just grab a seat over here."

My desk phone began to ring.

"Consumer Affairs, this is John."

"Do you have your apartment keys?" said Dana.

"And hello to you, too. How are you feeling?"

A moment of silence passed.

"Fine, um, just fine. Do you have your keys or not?"

"Sure I do, but why? Where are you going?"

Another moment.

"Out. I have to run some errands."

"Some errands? Like what?"

"School work, some other stuff," she said. "I don't really want to get into it. I just wanted to make sure you can get in when you get home."

"So this mysterious stuff you're doing is going take until after five to finish? Where exactly are you going?"

"I got to go, okay?"

"What? Wait, Dana, talk to me. What is—"

A dead sound, then a dial tone. I took a deep breath while clutching the phone. I wanted to slam it down, but instead placed it lightly into its cradle before sifting through the pile of files on my desk. When I found Jamie Bethford vs. The White Room near the bottom, I pulled it out and flipped through vague details, with only mere generalities like "refund desired" penned across the form. I emerged from my cubicle with the file to find Jamie seated and waiting.

"Sorry about that call," I said. "The wife."

"No worries. And I appreciate you taking the time to help me out."

"That's what we do here, right?" I took a seat next to him. "To get started with this, I'm going to need some more information. You didn't give me much to work with here on your paperwork, so it's a good thing you came in. You mind walking me through the specifics of the complaint?"

"Yeah, no problem," he said, then leaned forward in his chair and scratched the back of his high-and-tight haircut. "I was in there for Monday Night Football a month ago with some of my buddies, having a few pitchers and plates of wings, and we had a problem with the service. It wasn't a huge deal at first, but it became a major issue before we left the place. Actually, we didn't leave as much as the owner threw us out. That's kind of what my complaint's about."

"So Luther threw you out? Luther White?"

"I guess, yeah. He's an old musician or something? One of my buddies told me."

"So why'd he toss you out? Were you guys drunk? Belligerent? What?"

He laughed and scratched the back of his head again.

"Normally, I would say yes. We can get after it pretty good, but not that night. I mean, it wasn't even halftime when we got tossed."

"So what happened?"

"I think I unintentionally insulted that Luther White's girlfriend. She was our waitress, and she kept disappearing for, like, twenty minutes at a time."

I shifted in my seat.

"That place can get pretty crazy on Monday nights."

"I know," he said. "That's one of the reasons we were giving this waitress the benefit of the doubt until one of my buddies mistook a back office for a bathroom. When he opened the door, he caught a glimpse of her in this room, fooling around with Mr. White. And honestly, if the owner wants to get with his pregnant girlfriend in his office, that's his—"

"Pregnant?"

"Yeah," he said. "That's the other reason we were giving her some extra time to get to us. I mean, working in that joint pregnant can't be an easy gig, right?"

I nodded my head, swallowed and breathed.

"Anyway, we didn't want to make a huge deal about it. Like I said, if the owner wants to make time with one of his waitresses, that's his business. We still went to the manager and told him of the situation, told him how this waitress was spending her time. We were just hoping for a free round or something. Instead, we got two bouncers at our table. They walked us to the side door, tossed us out and roughed us up a bit outside. We didn't get to finish the pitchers or food we paid for, so I'd like to get a refund."

His words were noise, mere popping and buzzing sounds. Staring at the office floor, I folded my hands together in front of my face.

"Like I said, I really didn't want to make a big deal about it, but—"

I looked up to interrupt him, to stop his sentence cold. He must have seen the anger stretching my eyelids, the tension stiffening my shoulders before the question stormed from my mouth.

"Then why are you here?"

He paused and shifted in his seat.

"What? Well I—"

I stood to look down at him.

"I said, then why the fuck are you here?"

"Whoa, um," he said, now abundantly aware of my demeanor. "I'm not sure what I said wrong. I just don't think my buddies and I should have been handled like that. It's not our fault we caught some waitress going down on the owner in his office."

"Say one more thing about Luther White and my wife and I'll knock your fucking teeth in."

"Your wife? Oh shit, man, um—"

"Say it, dammit," I yelled, loud enough to reach Pete in back. "Just give me the chance to put my fist in your mouth."

He stood up from his chair and slowly backpedaled toward the door.

"All right, um, you know what? Forget the complaint. Actually, forget I was ever in here and, uh, have a good day, okay?"

He got hold of the handle, swung the door open and slipped uncomfortably out of the office. I could only stare at the cold, concrete wall in front of me, unable to move until I heard Pete's voice behind me.

"John, what the hell is going on?" he said. "What was all the screaming about?"

I hit the ground of Niagara Square and started up Elmwood, my heartbeat thumping heavier than my strides against the cold concrete. I reached Allen and walked to my front door to see my mailbox to the left, with Dana's name blacked-out with Sharpie. I kicked through the entrance, jumped up the stairs and opened the door to our apartment. The living room looked as it always did, as did the hallway and the kitchen. Pictures still hung, appliances were plugged in. When I stepped into our bedroom, I found Dana's dresser drawers empty, her closet clean of sundresses and shirts and sweaters. Her body pillow was gone from the bed, as was all her make-up from the bureau top. In the bathroom, my soap sat idle amid the absence of shampoos and conditioners that once lay strewn about the tub.

I walked down the hallway and back into the living room. To the side was the spindled baby crib, fully constructed and empty. The mantle over the fireplace hosted two framed pictures: one of Dana and me at Niagara Falls on our one-year anniversary, and another of us inside the Nighthawk after one of my Friday shows. Happy times. Resting in between those two moments was an isolated white envelope, my name written on the outside. I scooped the envelope off the mantle, ripped it open and pulled out the paper inside. In the fading sunlight of the front windows, I read the first two words: Dear John.

13

When your life falls to pieces
Falls down around your feet
Kick those pieces to the side
And walk on up the street
-"Life After Death" by J. Nolan

My apartment's kitchen had fantastic acoustics, better than either the bathroom or living room. When I sat within its confines and plucked Deirdre's E string, the sound would dance through the room and bounce off the walls and windows, off canisters filled with coffee and sugar. I could sit in a wooden chair, strum A and D chords and stomp my right boot on the floor to replicate a bass drum beat. I could sing lyrics I'd scribbled on napkins or sections of scrap paper, and I could devise transitions between the verses I'd create. When Dana worked nights, I sometimes filled the kitchen with these sounds and enjoyed a cold Budweiser or three while strumming rhythm over the nine minutes and forty six seconds of Van Morrison's "Madam George." The kitchen was a loner's refuge, a place for a solo act. Dana never sat and listened to me play, never asked me to play "American Woman" or any other Guess Who song. She stopped enjoying any music that snuck from my lungs and fingertips years ago.

The only times I took my guitar to the Buffalo streets were on Tuesday nights, when I holed up in a McGinty's booth with Butch Strombone to pick Tragically Hip songs. I'd show

Butch chords and he'd yell things like "fuck yeah" over pitchers of Molson Canadian and sensational stories about his roadie
father, T-Bone. But McGinty's could never hold Deirdre's sound
like my kitchen could; it could never send chord reverberations
bounding off refrigerator doors and floor tiles. The moments
I spent picking my six-string in our kitchen with Dana around
were rare.

But Dana left me a letter. That letter gave me my kitchen
back.

Her absence allowed me to sit in my favorite room and
bask in its solitude. My middle finger found A strings on the second fret, my ring finger on the second fret's D and index on the
first's G. I could hammer down power chords through acoustic
versions of early Ramones songs. I could run my hand over my
Nolan family crest sticker, enjoy the nicks in Deirdre's neck and
faded brown finish over her body. I could stroll into McGinty's,
ask Butch if he wanted to intensify our lessons to cover anything
outside the Hip catalogue. I wasn't going to be a father anytime
soon. I wasn't going to be a husband anymore, either. I could do
whatever the fuck I wanted.

That's why I sat in the kitchen of my empty apartment,
listening to Bon Iver's *For Emma, Forever Ago*, strumming my
guitar strings along with his crackling vocals on "Skinny Love."
Streams of steam floated off the top of my coffee and into the
chill of the Sunday morning around me. I lit a cigarette, exhaled
the smoke through the coffee's steam and pulled the needle back
to the album's first groove. I wanted to play along with every
song; I wanted to spend my Sunday picking and humming. I took
another drag and heard a knock on my door. It wasn't locked, so
I didn't get up; I just yelled.

"Open."

"Hello?"

Meg.

"Come on back," I said. "I'm in the kitchen."

She was alone, without the boys. I kept smoking.

"You want some coffee?" I said. "I made a whole pot earlier this morning."

She looked to me, then surveyed the scene surrounding me: the sink full of dishes, the ashtray overflowing with butts and the scraps of paper with scribbled lyrics strewn about the floor.

"What time did you brew the pot? Two? Three?" She grabbed a coffee cup from the cupboard. "You never met us for Mass this morning, so I thought I should swing by. Have you been to bed since yesterday?"

"Not really, no," I said before another drag. "Been sitting up in the kitchen here, going through some albums, some songs I've written. Where are the boys?"

"Playing hockey with Finn at St. Stephen's," she said, pouring herself some coffee. "You have any milk?"

"Check the fridge."

She walked over to the fridge, found the milk and checked its date.

"Jesus, John, this expired three weeks ago." She walked the carton over to the sink and dumped it down the drain. "Would you please turn off the music and put the guitar down? Just put it down so we can talk."

I leaned the instrument against an empty chair and turned down the stereo's volume with its remote. Meg stirred two teaspoons of sugar into her coffee and pulled up a chair. Seated across from me, she looked up from her coffee.

"You can't do this. You can't let your life go down like

this."

"Down like what? I'm not allowed to sit in my kitchen and play guitar on a Sunday morning?"

"C'mon, don't bullshit me. You don't think I know how you're feeling?" she said. "I've been abandoned and fucked over. I've spent lots of time sitting in the dark, spinning sad, painful records while crying myself to sleep."

I took a final drag, stubbed my cigarette in the ashtray's pile.

"These songs are acoustic," I said. "That's why I'm listening to them, so I can play along. I'm fine."

She let out a pop of a laugh.

"You're fine? That's why you're chain smoking in your kitchen, drinking black coffee and listening to maybe the most depressing album recorded in the last ten years? Christ, the heart-broken guy had to isolate himself in a log cabin just to compose something this sad."

"I haven't been listening to the lyrics."

"Again, bullshit. I know the past few months have been hell. Every time I think about what's happened to you, I get short of breath. I'm hurting for you; Finn's hurting for you. Even the boys know that things aren't going well for their uncle. You should hear Mickey every night, praying out loud before bed, praying to God that his Uncle John starts to feel better." She inhaled to hold back tears. "You can't continue on like this, isolated and away from the ones who love and care about you. We want to help you through this rough patch."

"Are you honestly lecturing me about the negatives of isolation? You turned off your phone for weeks after Billy disappeared, remember? Finn and I had to camp out on your front porch just to get a glimpse of you or Brendan."

"And that was a mistake. Back then, I wanted to shield everyone from the pain I was feeling. But when I did that, I felt worse. I felt even more alone."

"And that's you. That's how you felt, and that's how you dealt."

"So how do you feel?"

"I said I'm fine."

"So you're not going to be honest with me?"

"You want honesty? Straight, inconvenient honesty?"

She leaned back in her chair and smirked.

"No, I'd like you to lie," she said. "Yes, of course I want the honest-to-God truth."

I looked back to her for a brief moment, took in her concern before I got up from my chair and walked to the coffee pot. It was still hot, so I poured its thick mud into my used mug. Meg stayed in her seat, sitting silent and waiting until I fell back into my chair again. After I put my full steaming cup down on the table, I connected with her empathetic gaze.

"I feel like the last time anything made sense to me was when I was attached to this guitar," I said, then grabbed Deirdre's neck and set her on my lap. "I felt free, alive. When my fingers walked around on these strings, I felt satisfied. I didn't feel depressed or lonely or black inside. I didn't feel like a dark cloud was following me around Buffalo. I didn't feel like a section of my stomach had been carved out by a dull knife."

"A dull knife?"

"That's what it feels like." I ran my left fingers down the strings. "That's what it feels like when your wife leaves you a fucking letter to say she's left you, that she's disappeared to Florida and wants a divorce. That's what it feels like when you read she doesn't love you, that she's relieved she had a miscarriage.

That she wasn't even sure if the baby she miscarried was yours."

I sat back and lit another cigarette.

"That's what it feels like when pieces of paper reveal four wasted years."

I glanced down to Deirdre's strings before I raised my dry, irritated eyes to meet Meg's. I took another sip of my coffee, enjoyed the bitter taste while her watery gaze was wandering through the silence. After she stared at the floor for a few seconds, she looked up and wiped away her tears. She took a deep breath, exhaled and reached across the table to gently grab my free hand.

"Well," she said, then paused for a moment. "At least you got a letter."

Two weeks later, I took the Metrorail to the Seneca Street stop and walked my guitar case to McGinty's. I hadn't met up with Butch Strombone for a Tuesday night guitar lesson in months, so I decided to get down to the bar for an evening of free Canadian pitchers, instructional picking—and an escape from my apartment.

Everyone from Pete to Finn to Meg said I needed to get out of the goddamn place, if only for a night or two. The apartment provided me shelter, but no comfort. Everywhere I turned, I saw Dana, on our couch, chairs and bed. In a feverish cleaning spree, I'd taken the stray items she'd left in the place, bagged them and walked them as trash to the Allen Street curb. Her presence still lingered, not only on furniture and finished flooring, but in memory. The only respite I could find was to walk down our stairwell and close the front door behind me, leave it all upstairs and go find a distraction. Hauling Deirdre down into the comfort of McGinty's to accompany Butch on Hip tunes was an adequate distraction.

When I stepped through McGinty's front door, I found the barroom mostly empty. Butch was behind the bar, hair parted and feathered, his studded dog collar secured around his neck to match his studded leather wristbands. His T-shirt of the evening was a navy blue number that featured "Chuck Norris for President" in white lettering around a picture of Norris's face. Modeling this pitch, he was leaning against McGinty's shelves of whiskey and gin, listening to a customer talk about Rick Martin and the Sabres' French Connection line of the 1970s. When he noticed me at the entrance, he stood upright to loudly clap and hoot and interrupt his conversation with the bar's lone boozer.

"Johnny Nolan is back in the saddle! Excuse me, buddy," he said to the patron, who popped a quick shot of brown liquor. "What the fuck, dude? I didn't think you were ever gonna show up again."

"Sorry, man. Had some shit going on."

Vague and simple. No reason to burden the Bone with specifics.

"Some shit, huh? Well, you missed some serious shit around here. Check this out, dude. From a Saturday up at Chestnut Ridge two months back."

Butch picked up a framed picture from behind the bar and handed it to me. It featured him on a dirt bike in front of a snowdrift, dressed only in a pair of white briefs and bike helmet, sucking beer through a funnel. I smiled and let out a small laugh. It felt good to laugh.

"Sorry I missed it."

"But you're here tonight, right? Let's fucking grab the guitars and get at it," he said, then slapped the bartop as I pulled out a stool. "And you couldn't have picked a better week to show up. Need your help."

"Why?"

He leaned forward, relaxing his shoulders.

"Met this bike hag at Touch of Class pool hall in Blasdell last weekend. Chick was decked out in black leather pants, Harley T-shirt, the works. And you should have seen the pair on this one." He paused to mimic giant breasts with his hands over his own chest. "Anyway, anyway, when we went outside to smoke a butt, I told her I played a killer version of 'Wheat Kings.'"

"I've never taught you that song," I said of the Hip's acoustic classic. "Why didn't you tell her about a song you can actually play, like 'Scared'?"

"Fuck, I don't know. Was fifteen beers deep and the chick said she dug that song. Plus, the jugs. My God, you should've seen 'em spilling out of this little black tee. You know the Bone's a breast man."

I did know.

"I can teach you that one tonight. Shouldn't be too hard for you to get a handle on. When are you going to see this woman again?"

"Friday night," he said. "That badass AC-DC tribute band Big Balls is playing at the Nighthawk. We're gonna meet up here and hammer down a few Long Islands before the show. After a few hours of face-melting covers, figure I'll walk her back to my place and strum a few chords of 'Wheat Kings' before two handfuls of hooter."

"Another notch added to the Bone belt."

He took a step back to gaze off dreamily through Mc-Ginty's aroma before he returned.

"Who knows? This one could be a keeper. Ol' Butch ain't getting any younger. Time comes when a man needs to nest."

I absorbed Butch's comment for a few seconds, then took a heavy slug of my beer and responded.

"Just don't rush it. Sometimes, when you try to get somewhere fast, shit unravels and you'll have nothing but a wreck of a life lying at your goddamned feet."

I leaned forward to stare into the bottles of Jameson and Jack lining the wall. I looked to Butch, silent and scratching the front of his T-shirt, considering what I'd said before he replied.

"You know what, Johnny?" he said. "It's a fucking Tuesday—and your shit's too heavy for a Tuesday. It's a simple day, and the Bone's a simple man, so let's focus on the task at hand: teach me this song and help me get laid. Real fucking simple. I'll worry about shit unraveling after I handle this hag topless. Deal?"

"I envy your attitude, man. And that's why you're the Bone."

Butch let my statement float as he walked over to the line of taps and found the Canadian. He stood watching the beer fall and foam into the plastic before he released the handle, looked up and grinned.

"Fucking A right."

He grabbed some glasses and the full pitcher, left his lone barfly to be handled by the night waitress and led me over to the back booth where his old, chipped hand-me-down acoustic Epiphone was resting. The weathered, black-bodied instrument had a hole cracked into the front body and a green Poison sticker plastered next to the hole. Butch's father collected a bunch of used guitars from his roadie days, and this beauty was the best of the bunch. His son made it his own with the Poison sticker.

Over the next few hours, we went over the chord progressions of the song together, repetitiously following a G chord with a C as we inhaled cool pints of Canadian. Of all the songs Butch could've chosen to lie about being able to execute as an expert ax man, this was a good one to pick. It largely consists of only the G and C, with a B tossed in late in the song and an E minor on the bridge. By eleven o'clock, we'd plowed through five pitchers, but he was getting a handle on the action. After he toiled through his first mistake-free rendition, Butch stood up on the booth's bench to pick and belt out the tune's lyrics for the whole bar to hear. Surprisingly, there were fifteen or so drinkers in attendance. He was strumming and singing about rusty breezes and weathervane Jesus. I backed him up, handling the eventual brief and twanging solo behind his rhythm. In front of us, patrons were murmuring the lyrics to themselves or rhythmically clapping between chords. After Butch clipped his last note, they stood to cheer and hoist their bottles and glasses toward the two of us. We climbed from the booth to accept hoots, pats on the back and the shots of Crown Royal waiting for us at the bar.

With the unusually brisk Tuesday night business, Butch had to hop back behind the bar and pour pints between shots of Crown and Black Velvet. I found a stool and another pint while McGinty's was buzzing with laughing customers and jukebox junkies, ones who usually pumped in dollars to hear numbers from Seeger and Springsteen. With my head swimming and sight wandering across Smirnoff bottles, juke selections washed over me, accentuating my alcohol high. I was simply existing away from my sister and uncle. Away from God and nephews, from consumers and coffee shops. Away from fatherhood and fidelity. Unfortunately, such independence is always interrupted.

"Excuse me," said a male voice behind me. "Are you Johnny Nolan?"

I turned around in my seat to see a young man and woman, maybe in their early thirties.

"That's me."

"The same Johnny Nolan who used to pack the Nighthawk?" he said.

"You got him," I said, raising my pint in acknowledgement.

"I'm sorry to bother you, man. We saw you playing back there and thought it was you."

"The hair's shorter and the face is shaved, but it's still me."

"The two of us met at one of your shows five years back, and we just got married last year. My name's Kevin, and this is Kelly."

"Kevin and Kelly. Glad to be of help."

"Hey thanks," he said. "We used to go to the Nighthawk every Friday night when we were first dating. Man, those nights were an absolute drunken mess. I'll never forget how you'd get the whole crowd to join in on singing that Beatles' song, 'You've Got To Hide Your Love Away.' Just a bunch of strangers, arms draped over each other's shoulders swaying, drinking and singing. That's how the two of us met. I threw my arm over Kelly's shoulder for that song and bought her a beer afterward."

I laughed.

"Ah, another Buffalo love story," I said. "Boy buys beer, boy drinks beer. Boy buys seven more, drinks seven more, then finds girl for a barroom sing-along."

"True, true," he said. "And we're not the only ones. Lots of couples we know met at those Nighthawk shows. When you stopped playing on Fridays, we stopped going. A lot of people did."

"That's what I've heard."

"Think I remember them adding a karaoke night in your place. Guess people can only listen to so many secondhand Rush songs before they find somewhere else to drink."

I laughed again, then slipped off my stool and onto the empty one next to it. "Whoa, sorry about that, guys," I said. "Been here a while."

"Don't worry about it," he said. His wife stood next to him, smiling and agreeing. "So why don't you play anymore? Judging by tonight's cameo, you obviously can still wail."

I grinned at him and took another pull off my pint.

"I'm sure you could still pack the Nighthawk. We loved those nights you plowed through Neil Young albums, front to back. And the shows with your original stuff? Loved those, too. You were a big draw around here. Still could be."

I raised my pint to their beer bottles and connected.

"That's real nice of you to say," I said. "And who knows? Maybe it's time I end my retirement. Maybe it's time for a Nighthawk comeback."

"You should seriously think about it. There are a lot of good musicians floating around here these days, but none like you."

The jukebox switched discs after the final syllable of his sentence. A silver circle lowered to spin and emanate its tormenting content through the barroom. Three boot stomps echoed before a roots-blues riff escaped like a midnight exhale of Marlboro smoke. Luther White's moans followed, and "Beer For Blues" began to serenade patrons who perked with realization and delight. Kevin loved it; so did Kelly.

"Fucking Luther! Wow, good timing," he said, smiling. "This is what I'm talking about. You and Luther White? We don't have enough musicians like you guys playing these days. With his performance career on its current when-I-feel-like-it basis, we need you, man. This city needs the both of you to do your thing and represent us."

My pint glass was half empty in my hand. Staring down at McGinty's grime-laden bar floor, I overheard Butch laughing as he slapped high-fives, poured another line of shots and yelled, "Everybody's getting ripped to the tits tonight, baby! Oh yeah!" After a few seconds passed, I turned to Kevin and Kelly, bit down on the inside of my cheek and tried to conjure up a grin.

"Please don't mention my name in the same sentence with Luther White's. I'm from Buffalo, and I don't need him to represent me. I don't need him to do anything for me."

"C'mon, man," Kevin said. "Everybody likes Luther White, right?"

I pushed up off my stool to stand with lifeless legs and finish the end of my beer. Another Crown shot from Butch was waiting on the bar, so I picked it up and hoisted it down. The liquor chased the beer down my throat and burned, lit up my chest like a fireball before it landed softly in my stomach. After I set the shot glass down, I took the empty pint glass in my right hand as Luther's vocals covered McGinty's like a fleece blanket. I glanced at the jukebox, its yellow fluorescent lights taunting alongside grease-coated tabletops and framed hockey photographs. In one swift motion, I wound up and flung my pint glass at the box's glass exterior. It hit square, smashed through the front to rattle the plastic flip pages and send shards of glass around its position. It also stopped the song from playing, relieving me to the point that I didn't even notice the startled silence from the remaining customers. In the hush, I looked at my poor fan again and answered his question.

"Fuck Luther White."

14

If we can find the right chords, girl
The right lyrics to follow
Maybe the days we stumble through
Won't feel so damn hollow
-"Nights of You & Me #15" by J. Nolan

I've sat on the benches in Lafayette Square before. Some days I would step out of City Hall, walk to the park, find an open seat and eat a sandwich. Back in my playing days, I'd grab a quick nap on a bench before summer shows. But I'd never woken on one while covered with my navy overcoat, my face stuck to the damp wood and no recollection of how I got there. I'd never felt faint early morning sunlight slip through the Square's trees and touch my face. And through all my wild times, I'd never woken on one of those benches with the moist touch of a dog's slobbering tongue on my face. This is how I welcomed the morning after my meltdown at McGinty's: cold and confused, with a friendly black Labrador sniffing and licking my face until his owner yelled from the distance.

"Otis, dammit! Would you get away from that man? Otis!"

When I heard the voice, I slowly sat up and crossed my arms, shivering and aching as I became aware of my surroundings. I turned and squinted to see her jogging toward me, with Otis's red leash jingling from her hand. When recognition settled in, she slowed to a walk before coming to a halt a few feet from the bench.

"John? Jeezus, is that you?"

Just Sam.

"Um, I think," I said. "But don't really have a good explanation for *why* it's me."

She looked me up and down, standing in front of me as she grabbed Otis's collar and snapped the leash on.

"The way you look and smell, that bench suits you," she said. "Are you okay?"

I rubbed the right side of my face and squinted at the sunlight.

"I'm incredibly hung over and cold. Other than that, I think I'll make it."

"Should I even ask what you're doing out here, at this hour?"

"Last I remember, I was tossed out the front door of McGinty's and smashed my face against the side of a parked car. After that, I got nothing. Don't remember a thing."

"My God. Well, does anyone know you're here? What about your wife? She's gotta be worried sick about you."

"Yeah," I said as I slowly sat up. "I'm pretty sure my wife doesn't give a shit whether I'm dead or alive."

"C'mon, why would you say something like that?"

I took a deep breath, rubbed my temples and looked back to her again.

"Because she left me about four months ago."

She sighed, covered her mouth with her hand and stood for another few seconds of uncomfortable silence.

"My God, John, I'm so sorry. I just, um, I—"

I waved off her concern.

"It's okay," I said. "How were you supposed to know? Should you've assumed I was passed out on a park bench because my wife left me?"

"If I was abnormally perceptive, sure."

"That would be something," I said, smiled. "Honestly, though, I'd trade such perceptive abilities for a strong cup of coffee. Interested?"

"Right now?"

"Sure. Why not?"

"What about work?"

"I'm far too hung over for work, even by City Hall standards," I said while rubbing my temples again. "Besides, I'm sure Pete will cover for me. What do you say?"

"Okay, sure," she said. "Would you mind taking a walk to Cigarettes & Coffee? I know it's a hike, but it might do you some good to stretch your legs a bit."

"You read my mind."

We walked down to Main Street and up the sidewalk parallel to the Metrorail tracks, past the towering Buffalo marquee at Shea's. As we passed its doors, we exchanged different stories about the nights we'd seen a rock show, movie or play within its theater walls. Sam told me about the Saturday afternoon with her parents and a special showing of *The Wizard of Oz*; I countered with the night my dad and I watched a manic Joe Cocker sweat through "The Letter." With Otis leading us up Main, we let our conversation flow through the quiet morning, its hazy calm only interrupted by the rumble of subway cars and pickup trucks. With every step I took, I felt revived, my legs no longer cramped. With every sentence I spoke, I felt my headache dissipate, the throbbing less severe. With every smile I caught from Sam, every look of interest peeking through those dark, tortoise shell-rimmed rectangular frames, I felt more at ease as we found the front door of our destination.

Once inside, I surveyed the red interior, walls lined with framed record sleeves from artists like Wilson Pickett and Solomon Burke, Otis Redding and Sam Cooke. The back wall accommodated a huge black-and-white photo of Otis Redding from his performance at the 1967 Monterey Pop Festival. It stretched to all corners of the wall, filling the space with a sweaty and crouched Redding wailing into a microphone. Sam and I grabbed an empty table in front of this photo, and her dog settled on the floor next to us.

"Do you want just a coffee?" she said. "I think I might have them toast me a bagel, too."

"Just the coffee, but you're not buying. I asked you to join me, so I'm paying."

"Why would I let you buy me a coffee in my own coffee shop?"

"You own this place?"

"My father does, so I guess you could call me a part owner," she said. "That's why I pick up the entertainment licenses. Also, the Saturday Serenade was my idea. My father agreed I could run it on the condition I took care of the licensing process. He hates politics, so he despises walking within ten yards of City Hall."

"Understandable," I said, then leaned back in my chair and watched her grab two coffees and a bagel. When she returned, she pushed my coffee toward me, dropped a dog treat down to Otis and took a bite of her breakfast.

"So how long have you been involved with this place?" I said. "I live right down the street and pop in all the time. I've never seen you in here."

"When do you come in?" she said, chewing her bagel. "Saturday and Sunday mornings?"

"Exactly."

"I volunteer both of those days. At the St. Jude's Community Center off Delaware."

"Really? My Uncle Finn used to be involved there. Father Finn Leary."

"The famous Father Finn?"

"So you've heard of him."

"Heard of him? The guy's a legend at St. Jude's. I'm surprised there's not a statue of him at the main entrance."

"That's where he started out way back, before he became a priest. The center led him into the clergy. Where's it leading you?"

"Not to the convent. Not yet, anyway," she laughed. "I'm just a volunteer who sits with about twelve to fifteen kids, ages nine to thirteen and mostly from single-parent homes. We hang out and play music."

"Play? What instrument do you play?"

"Oh no, I'm not the one playing. I wish I could play something, but I can't. I spin different records, stuff they haven't heard before. Most of these kids can't afford to buy CDs, so I bring mine and we listen, talk about the songs, and even do a little dancing. I really like to dance."

"Sounds like a blast."

"It is," she said, then sipped her coffee. "I do it in conjunction with the coffee shop, so we listen to a lot of soul, rhythm and blues; maybe some Parliament funk every now and then. The kids get a kick out of how many of their favorite hip hop songs sample parts of the tunes I play. You should see their faces when they recognize a James Brown bass line from a Kanye West or Lil' Wayne song."

"Somebody's got to teach these kids the origins, right?" I

said. "So have you always been this into music?"

"Oh yeah, definitely. Wednesday through Saturday, I used to live at local joints like Nietzsche's and Sportsmen's, soaking up whatever live act performed." She paused to pour two packets of sugar into her coffee and stir. She let the contents dissolve and looked across the table. "Years ago, I'd even swing into the Nighthawk on Fridays to see this guy kill on acoustic. What was his name again?"

I let some reaction time pass between us while flashing a "you got me" grin. Eventually, I put my coffee down, leaned back and engaged.

"So you've known who I am this whole time and never said anything?"

"Does it really matter? You're obviously not that guy anymore, right? Not the same guy in torn jeans and T-shirts who'd rip through that crazy cover of 'Astral Weeks.' Am I wrong?"

"No, but you still could've said something; you could've asked. You asked me for my name, didn't you?"

"I had to," she said. "In my defense, the first time I came into your office, I really didn't know if it was you. With your shorter hair and clean shave, I wasn't sure. It took me a few more trips to feel confident enough to ask for your name to confirm that, yes, the Nighthawk's Johnny Nolan was now handing out entertainment licenses in City Hall."

"Not the most rock and roll position?"

She smiled and leaned forward.

"Why don't you play anymore? My god, you *owned* that place on Fridays. I remember some nights you could look across the room and see everyone from Motorhead metalheads to Ani DiFranco's feminist army dancing and singing. If I'm being too nosy, just say so."

"You're not being nosy."

"Then what was it? Did the scene wear you down? Those hazy late nights soaked in beer, blow and casual hook-ups?"

"That's part of it, yeah," I said, then sipped my coffee. "What about you? Is the strain of the scene why you're now spinning discs for kids instead of pounding OV splits on Fridays?"

"Sure, it wore me down. You can only keep up with the shots of Crown and sunrise closings for so long. I still love the music; still love that nostalgic chill a good tune can send down my spine. I could never walk away from that."

"Neither could I, but I needed to leave that stage, those nights. See, after my parents died—"

"Oh, I'm so sorry."

"It was years ago, but thanks," I said. "After they died, playing guitar for the cheers of drunken Journey fans yelling for a cover of 'Don't Stop Believin'' wasn't fun anymore. It felt empty. And ridiculous."

"What about your own songs? I mean, when you slipped those in, people liked those, too."

"Those songs didn't fill the room. Crowds wanted covers. They wanted to hear me play other bands' shit. After a while, I just got sick of it. And I couldn't ignore the likelihood of disappointed parents looking down on me, watching their only son waste his life as a rip-off musician. So I walked away. I left it behind and tried to pursue something more fulfilling."

"Like marriage."

I glanced across the table, then back down to my coffee.

"God, I'm sorry," she said. "Sometimes, I blurt things

out without thinking. It's not my place."

"It's fine, really."

"Okay, but please know I didn't suggest that to salt a ripe wound. I'm only mentioning it because I've been there. I know."

"Divorced?"

"No. Just through a serious relationship that went south. Marriage was our next step before I caught him stepping out. Caught him with this young blonde in the side room of the Nighthawk, actually," she said. "The whole thing made me feel so vacant, so lost. The only things that seemed to help were those stacks of vinyl in my bedroom. Music eased the pain as I moved on."

"My guitar has done the same for me." I took a deep breath. "I've been spending a lot of recent nights in my kitchen, strumming along with records until I can't keep my eyes open. It's the only way I can push the thoughts of her away, the only way I can incinerate the memory of years I wasted on her. On us."

"So why not try to incinerate that memory in front of a crowd of people? I mean, where would we be as audiophiles without the pain of others oozing out of tape decks and turntables? For instance, look at this man's face right here." She pointed to the wallpapered picture of Otis Redding behind us. "Do you think he's summoning humor or heartbreak for the emotion he's displaying here? The man's crying like his world's been smashed to pieces."

"True, but I don't think I'm ready to sing about my pieces," I said. "They're all too raw. Christ, I don't even think I'm ready to talk about this with you."

"Yet here we are."

"Because you were nosy."

"You just said I wasn't being nosy."

I leaned back and crossed my arms.

"Guess I changed my mind."

"I'm sorry about that, but can I make one last point? After, I won't say another word, I swear."

"One point. After all, you did pay for the coffee."

"I guess, yeah," she laughed, then sat up straight and focused her blue eyes at me. "So I don't know you very well. At all, really. But after our morning together, you seem like a good guy who's recently had a bad run."

"Understated, but true."

"I also know you're a talented musician who no longer plays music. A talented musician, I might add, who I found this morning passed out on a park bench."

"Your point?"

"My point is that this bad stretch of yours has left a gaping hole in your existence. Without artistic expression, the void won't be filled," she said. "You're an artist, right?"

"I was."

"Well, artists fill their voids with their art, with a talent of expression most people don't possess. If you suppress this ability, the void could grow and slowly eat away at you."

I took another sip of coffee and looked across the table again.

"And if I play?"

"You'll start to heal," she said. "I promise."

15

I once drank beers with St. Stephen
Ripped some shots with his gold crown
Ol' Stephen winked and raised a drink
To the path we'd wander down
-"Saint Somewhere" by J. Nolan

From the time I was a young kid, I spent May's last Saturday in St. Stephen's gymnasium, taking in the annual "St. Stephen's Green" fundraiser for the elementary school. When I was a student, I went with my parents, who let my sister and me sing and kick with Irish step-dancing troupes as bands like The Blarney Bunch cranked out Celtic classics on the gym's small stage. My mother would adorn us in green sweaters and Irish-themed pins, with sayings like *Kiss me, I'm Irish* inside a shamrock. She'd let us drink green-dyed ginger ale while my father and Finn raised pints of Guinness. After Finn became a priest, he would stand on the stage and give an Irish blessing over all in attendance, then return later to play piano or guitar for whatever band called on him. It was a happy tradition, one Meg, Finn and I continued with Brendan and Mickey. They became the little ones who danced and sang while I sat with Meg and Finn, raising pints of stout to my lips. On that night, I needed tradition and family. I needed music. I needed a few pints.

Meg and Finn knew my sordid story's intimate details. We'd spent multiple dinners together, nights I recounted moments of the previous weeks and months with Dana. I told them about her erratic behavior, about her state of mind in the aftermath of the miscarriage. I told them about the White Room, about Luther. I told them both about the letter Dana left, about the sentences that introduced the collapse of my last four years, of the life I'd transitioned into after my parents' death. There was no sense in hiding details from them, no point in keeping inconvenient truths to myself. I was broken. Sitting with me through the sounds of whistles and fiddles and pipes, Meg and Finn were there to make repairs.

"So what happens now?" said Meg. "What do you need to do next?"

"Sign the divorce papers," I said before a long slug off my plastic cup of Guinness. "They arrived at the apartment yesterday, but I haven't opened the envelope. Just don't have the stomach for it."

"Then find your appetite tomorrow," said Finn. "Scribble your name on the lines and get them in the mail to Dana's attorney on Monday morning."

I leaned back in my chair to look across the table at Finn.

"I know, and I will. It's just—"

"It's just what?"

"Well, of all people who have an opinion about this, shouldn't you be the one suggesting a reconciliation or some other solution for this situation?"

"Because I'm a priest?"

"Yeah," I said. "Guess I expected you to be the one to take a hard stand against divorce, at least initially."

He pushed his pint to the side and folded his hands near his mouth, like he was collecting his thoughts. He flipped a glance at Meg, a little one to get her attention. She looked back at him to match his apprehension.

"I guess I'm not really sure how to wade into this one.

It's just, well—"

"Finn, if there's something you need to say, say it."

"You're sure?"

"Yeah, go," I said. "Whatever you're tripping over can't be any worse than the last few months."

"I guess there are two reasons I'm not taking a stand against this divorce," he said, then leaned back in his chair and crossed his arms. "One, Dana left. She split. She made her choice, and she doesn't seem to be giving you an opportunity to change her mind. She's made her decision abundantly clear, so what am I supposed to say to you? Wait for her to come around? Row your boat with one oar? Hell no. Despite your intentions, she quit on you, so it's not about whether I'm for divorce or against it; it's about what other choice you have. Seems like the only one is to sign those papers, let her loose and go on your way."

"And two?"

He hoisted his pint to his lips for a hearty drink, then lowered the stout, took a deep breath and looked back to me.

"I think you loved the role Dana filled more than you actually loved Dana."

His statement sat awkwardly between us, like an unexpected guest no one knew how to talk to. I was even more surprised when my response didn't stammer.

"Excuse me?"

"You told me to tell you, so there you go. That is what's on my mind. Our minds," he said, nodding to Meg. "You're crushed about your *wife* leaving, not about Dana leaving."

"And we understand that. We do," said Meg. She reached across the table and grabbed my hand. "We know where you were when Mom and Dad died. We know what you needed, what you wanted in life. And Dana was right there to lean on. We get it."

I pulled my hand away from her.

"You get it?" I said. "So you honestly think that's all there was to it? A goddamn shoulder to cry on? You think I didn't love Dana?"

"Of course you did," said Finn. "We've listened to you for months, seen you torn up. I don't doubt that you cared for the girl, that you loved her. But ask yourself what you loved more: who Dana was, or who you wanted her to be."

"What does it matter?"

"What does it matter?" said Finn. "Well, your answer could end this conversation with either reluctant acceptance or an apology. As for Dana, her answer took her to Florida."

"Translation?"

"Who she is unfortunately is not who you want her to be," he said. "If she were that woman, she'd be here, toasting this day with us."

We let Finn's line usher in a silence between us. Seconds dragged ahead. I could only let my sight roam across the gymnasium full of smiling young couples and laughing children. Pipes were squealing; bass drums were thumping. The family accusation rumbled and settled in a head gently dazed by stout. Visions of Dana's face were attached to my months of anger and loss and pain. But what was at the root of the pain? An absence or her absence? I could only consider and sip while looking across the table to Meg and Finn.

"So what if you're right?" I said. "I'm not saying you are, but what if it's true? What the hell am I supposed to do? Accept this hiccup, sign those papers and move ahead? Just like that?"

"Of course not, but this is happening," said Finn. "Those papers are on your kitchen table whether you want them there or not. You can leave that envelope sealed for a month. It's not going to turn Dana into whoever you wanted her to become. It's not going to ease this truth, and it's certainly not going to erase Luther White's role in this. I'm sorry to even mention his name. Just when I thought that guy couldn't stoop any lower—"

When he spoke Luther's name, it stormed from his mouth, ratcheting up his aggravated tone even above where it was when he spoke of Dana. His eyes seemed so full of concentrated anger it was as if he were trying to release a bit of it through an elongated stare. Before he burned this fury through my forehead, he unclenched his jaw, released three syllables and re-clenched after they'd escaped.

Finn always kept his history with Luther as just that: history. He never spoke of their shows together, those hours when his keys joined Luther's moans to occupy the center of Buffalo's blues universe. When I was a teenager, I'd asked about those nights, asked about what it was like to play beside the great Luther White. He would only respond with a half-hearted smile before a generic comment like, "Yeah, it was something." Even in the thick of my Nighthawk days, when I unintentionally became a Luther White adversary, Finn never commented or intervened with a history lesson. As time passed, I stopped asking for one.

After his quick outburst, Finn sat straight up in his chair and took a deep breath. He had his moment, and he needed to calm down. He placed his palms on the tabletop, looked down toward his lap and gathered himself. Once settled, he took another sip of Guinness and continued.

"I'm sorry about that, kid. Don't mean to be so fired up, but it's one thing to see these marital problems happen with parishioners. It's another to see them in your own family. As for Luther's involvement, well—"

"Well what? What exactly happened with you and Luther back when you were playing together?"

"That's my problem. Let's just leave it there."

"Why?" I said. "If there were any time to talk about this, I think we can agree it's now."

"Now's not about me. It's about you, so let's let my past with Luther remain where it is, okay?"

"So you're not going to talk about it? Not even a word?"

"You want a word on the guy? One word and we can move on?"

"Sure."

He raised his pint to his lips, took a nice slug and left remnants of the stout's head on his upper lip. After he brushed it off, he looked to me again.

"Commitment," he said. "The man doesn't know the meaning of it, so I guess that explains his involvement in this mess."

I let my remaining questions rest as we existed though an uncomfortable silence, taking jittery sips off our pints. If Finn were a weaker man, he would've let his resentment step forward to share the stage. That wasn't his style. Finn Leary was conciliatory and selfless. Despite the resuscitation of personal gripes, he held them down and, instead, helped me.

"It's hard to wear this collar with you two," he said. "It's tough to give faith-based advice when there's this fire in my gut, an anger that makes me want to ignore every vow of peace and, instead, pick a fight for the both of you. But I can't. I can't throw punches, can't settle scores. All I can do is offer simple, rational recommendations."

"And that's for me to start over."

"Or slowly adapt to this divergence, yeah," he said before he finished his pint. "You didn't ask for it, but here it is: an opportunity. That's all Dana's giving you, all your life is giving you, so take it. And lucky for you, you have an experienced confidant here to help you in this redirection."

"I've already told him that," said Meg. "John, if you want to sit in your kitchen and listen to sad records, that's your call. Remember how down I was after Billy? I survived, and so will you."

"Great, I get it. More of the same shit about moving on, about accepting what's happened."

"That's not what I—"

"Stop," I interrupted. "I know you're trying to help, but I'm the one who has to move on. I'm the one who has to live with these events, these mistakes. You can both clap your hands together and be done with them. For me, it's going to take some time. I'll get there. Just not today, and not tomorrow."

We let this statement land, listening to the surrounding sounds, to the throaty vocals and rhythmic claps floating around us. When the performing musicians came to an end of their first set, Finn used their break to begin with me again.

"Can I suggest another idea for you? Another way to work through these things?"

"Sure."

"Deirdre," he said. "You need to grab that guitar and get back out there, back on stage somewhere."

"You don't think I've considered this?" I said. "You're the fourth person in the last week to bring this up."

"Then maybe you should start listening," said Meg. "You said as much in your kitchen, how things haven't made sense since you put down your guitar."

"I know, but—"

"But what?" she said. "Give me one good reason why you shouldn't get back out there."

"You know why."

She looked to me until her face embraced recognition.

"So it's still about Mom and Dad? You honestly believe that if they were sitting here right now, they wouldn't be urging you to get back up there, to do what you were born to do?"

"You think I was born to cover Van Morrison songs?"

"Is that really how you see yourself?" she said. "Dad used to talk about how his son was a musician, how his son scribbled lyrics on bar napkins and fell asleep with his guitar. He didn't care what songs you played, as long as you were playing. I'll never forget the sparkle in his eyes when he watched you up on that Nighthawk stage."

"Me neither," said Finn. "Your old man was so proud of you. Maybe even a tad envious, too. Poor guy couldn't even play power chords."

This comment took me away for a few moments and let me picture my father in the corner of the Nighthawk, rhythmically tapping his wedding band against a bottle of Genesee. Those memories were always painful, evidence of times I'd never recover. Now, they were igniting recollection of a time of possibilities, a time when life wasn't dismantled and scattered into jagged pieces. My parents would never be subjected to this mess in their life on Earth. For this, I was appreciative.

What I had told Meg about the last time my life made sense was true. I needed that brown Martin body on my thigh, its scuffed neck clutched in my left hand. I needed to look up through the glare of fluorescent stage lights and find my parents, feel the touch of their spirit. I needed my life to make sense again. With this thought, I inhaled the last of my beer and lowered my empty cup to join Finn's. It was his turn to grab the next round.

"So let me give you something to think about while I go grab a few more beers," said Finn. "My band has a gig at the Nighthawk next Friday, playing again with that goofy band Mustache Tango. How about doing a walk on?"

"To play Kings songs?"

"Kings, Van Morrison, whatever you want to pick. I'm not saying one show will straighten your life out, but it might get you moving in the right direction. Just think about it."

He walked to a table lined with pints of stout, then gathered three into his cupped hands. As I watched him, thoughts of Dana, the miscarriage, and my last four years were interrupted by a vision of the Nighthawk's interior. I remembered the lights, the crowd and the communion. I thought about renewal, and I knew what I needed to do. When Finn arrived back at our table, he set our pints down in a triangular formation.

"I'm in," I said, "but would you be down to do some original stuff? I have some songs I've been writing, some simple acoustic tunes I taped on a little four-track."

"Whatever you want to do," said Finn.

"And this is what you need to do," said Meg. "You've got to move toward shaking the mud off the things you love. For instance, look at the boys over there. When I see them, I don't think about their father. I don't see a speck of that terrible past in their faces. All I see are those beauties, two little gifts that I love and need."

She stared over my shoulder at Brendan and Mickey. I turned around to see them sitting at a table across the hall, laughing with some of their classmates from St. Stephen's. One of their skinny friends jumped out of his seat to perform a little Irish jig, tapping his Nikes on the concrete floor as the band played fiddles and banjos behind him. Brendan was rhythmically slapping his fingertips on the table, mimicking the thump of the bass drum as the boy continued dancing. Mickey left his chair to stand near the boy, arms crossed as he studied him up and down. Meg reached across the table and grabbed my arm.

"Watch him, Johnny. He's got that fighting glint in his eye. Have you seen that look before, guys?"

"Um, yeah, I think we've seen it," said Finn. "Right, John?"

"I'm on him," I said and slowly rose from my seat.

Before I could take a step toward Mickey, he started clapping and stomping his foot to the music. The St. Stephen students joined him, all slapping their hands together as this kid tore up the joint. Finally, Mickey stopped clapping and started his own jig. The soles of his black Chuck Taylors were clicking against the floor as his arms stayed crossed, locked across his navy and green sweater. The kids crowded around him, laughing and clapping and singing as the band was rolling through their session instrumental, providing the ambiance for our annual Irish bash, our own Nolan hooley.

16

If you want a resurrection
Try to rescue who you are
Walk right down these tattered streets
And find yourself a bar
-"First Second Chance" by J. Nolan

I found Butch behind the bar at McGinty's and handed him a bottle of Black Velvet Canadian whiskey. That was the simplest apology I could offer for the jukebox. I knew how far a bottle of booze—accompanied by sincerity and an honest explanation—would go with the Bone. Plus, I was his music teacher. He needed his guitar lessons and me as much as I needed him and a few beers before my return to the Nighthawk. After I gave him the bottle, he put it under the bar and put a free pint of Molson Canadian in front of me.

"The owner was fucking pissed about that juke," said Butch, wearing a tight, light blue T-shirt with the advertisement 'Mustache Rides, 5 cents' emblazoned across the front. "You're lucky you only broke the glass. If you'd have broken the machine, I wouldn't have covered for you."

"I appreciate that you did. Really am sorry about the whole thing."

"Sorry or not, dude, if you'd have busted that thing, left me to work here without my tunes, I would've taken you out to Swan Street and pulled out my Chuck Norris shit." He took a fighting stance and karate chopped the air. "Not saying I'd do it, but if I had to, I could kill a man with one kick. Heel of my boot right to the throat. Lights out."

I took a sip of my pint.

"Thanks for sparing me," I said. "I should have told you about Dana and everything before, so you knew what you were dealing with that night."

"Yeah, what the fuck, man?" He threw his frayed and stained bar towel over his shoulder. "I know I don't seem the sensitive type, but I'm here, man. The Bone is ready if you need to talk about your pain."

"I know you are, but sometimes, it's hard to remember that when you're wearing a shirt that hawks free mustache rides."

He stepped back to cross his arms and shield the front of his tee.

"Don't judge a book by its cover, my friend. You think I'm empty inside? Think the Bone doesn't hurt?"

"I didn't say that—"

"No, no, I understand what people might think of me, with the shirts, dog collar and sexy haircut. But I get stung like anyone else, man. Remember that bike hag I was telling you about? One with the huge cans?"

"Sure."

"So I go down to the Nighthawk a few days ago to catch this one-man tribute to Eddie Money, and there she is, way up in the front corner with some other dude. She's kissing his neck, dancing behind him. Instead of confronting her, I just turned around and walked out—right while the fucking singer was busting into 'Gimme Some Water.' You believe that shit?"

"The stuff about the girl, or that fake Eddie Money has that song on his set list?"

"The fucking girl. Although—" He stepped back,

paused. "I do love that fucking song. It's a rarity. Even Eddie never plays it."

"Sorry about the girl, but look at it this way: You're a good dude, and you're getting to be a decent guitar player. Add those qualities to your general machismo and you'll be ready to roll for the next girl."

"What the fuck is 'machismo'?"

"It means you're manly," I said. "Macho."

"Oh," he said. Butch grabbed two shot glasses, lined them up on the bar and filled them with Southern Comfort. "So let's do a manly shot, eh? To your new start."

"And to yours."

"And to my fucking machismo, right?"

"Sure, Butch."

We raised the shot glasses and clanked them together before hoisting the liquor down our throats. Butch exhaled and slapped the bar three times.

"That's a good burn, Johnny. Lights up the chest like a fucking Zippo."

"I might need another one of those in a bit," I said. "Keep this to yourself: I'm playing with Finn's band over at the Nighthawk tonight."

I sipped my pint, then noticed Butch smiling back at me.

"I know."

"What do you mean you know?"

"People have been talking, man. I didn't want to say anything until we hashed out our shit here," he said. "Not sure who put the rumor out there, but it's been rumbling around for a few days. So it's true?"

"Yeah, it's true."

"About fucking time."

"Thanks, and who are these people you mentioned? Who's been talking?"

"The Bone's people, here in the bar," he said. "There's some excitement, I can tell you that. I don't think you realize how packed the Nighthawk was when the two of us were still over there. You were a big draw, man. Way bigger than that Eddie Money cover fuck."

"So you're going?"

"Now that we're square I am. I'll just shut this place early, kick out the regulars and head over. No one's gonna cry about a lost night of drinking here."

"What about the owner?"

"Fuck him," he said. "The Bone makes the rules around here."

He stepped back to lean against the worn wooden shelves featuring Irish whiskeys, tequilas and Tanqueray. He ran his fingers through his feathered mullet while standing underneath a framed picture of himself, half-naked and straddling a dirt bike. He lorded over the empty barstools and omnipresent odor of congealed chicken grease and secondhand smoke; over the nights of spilled vodka and strummed Zeppelin. Sipping a pint in his confident presence, I knew Butch needed McGinty's as much as the bar needed him. It was an odd codependency between undervalued dance partners. When circumstances rendered one weak, the other could lead. On those nights, Buffalo bartender Butch Strombone made the rules.

"To the Bone," I said, raising my glass.

He cracked open a bottle of Bud and clanked it against my pint.

"Fucking A right."

I left McGinty's at nine o'clock and drove my Outback into the garage across from the Nighthawk. The start of June joined cool evening breezes with the remnants of spring drizzle, floating and twisting off the lake and through open-air downtown garages. I pulled my guitar case out of the back seat and walked to the garage exit, then stopped and lit a cigarette underneath an overhang of concrete. From where I was standing, I could see the Nighthawk's front door, the yellowed weather-beaten entrance and the dim lights that hung over it. People were lined up at the door to show IDs and pay the five-dollar cover. Others stood off to the side in smoking circles, their leather coat collars up and baseball caps pulled down to shield them from light raindrops. I'd walked through that old door so many times, shaken hands with bouncers like Butch and taken down whatever shot Sues poured at the corner of the bar. Now I was back, tentative and nervous. What if the magic was gone, with the moments in my head merely memories existing as revisionist history? What if I found the stage, but couldn't find the place I once owned on it?

Watching visitors pay and smokers smoke, I realized I didn't give a solitary shit about such creeping worries. Whatever glory I jangled and strummed amid was in the past, left to exist as subjectively recalled moments. At that moment, I only wanted another chance, just one more shot to walk through the Nighthawk door and perform. That chance was waiting, right across the street. After one last drag of my cigarette, I threw it to the wet pavement, clutched my guitar case handle and walked past the revelers to find the bar's front door.

With my woolen Irish cap pulled low, I entered and approached a shadowed corner of the bar. Sues had the 20/20 vision to see a discreet sniff of coke from thirty feet away. Even hustling behind the taps, pulling pints of Guinness and cracking open tallboys of Genesee for leathered punk rockers and jean jacket-clad alt country disciples, she still noticed my entrance. When she did, she didn't open those mascara-lined eyelids wide, didn't run over for a huge hug or kiss. She was casual, cool. She simply stopped what she was doing, grabbed the bottle of Jameson and a shot glass, and walked to my corner. She filled the glass, pushed it toward me and looked up.

"Welcome home, Johnny Nolan."

An infusing chill danced down my back before I inhaled the hot whiskey. After it slipped down my throat, I left my discreet spot to find Finn, standing with Patty Vee on the secluded landing next to the stage. When they saw me, they both raised their beers. Finn slapped me on the shoulder when I reached them.

"So?" he said to me. "You ready?"

"I will be. Just need to get up on that stage and hit the first chord. When do you think you'll call me up?"

Finn and Patty looked at each other.

"Do you want to tell him or should I?" said Patty.

"I'll do it," said Finn. "So we have some good news and some bad news. What do you want first?"

"The bad, I guess."

"Well," he said, "the bad news is that we're not calling you up on stage with us. We can't do that anymore."

"What do you mean? Why not?"

He put his hand on my shoulder.

"Kind of mentioned to Sues a few days ago that you'd be playing with us. Turns out she told some people who told some people and—"

"And what?"

"The crew in this bar, the ones packed elbow to elbow,

paying the cover and drinking the beers? They're not here to see us. They're here to see you, and they don't want a walk on. They want to see you play the whole set."

I looked at the both of them as they stood before me, grinning.

"So you guys are okay with this? Patty?"

"Johnny, we're not rock stars," he said. "We're beer-drinking musicians, man, here to have a good time. As long as I'm up there jamming, getting people singing and dancing, I don't give a shit what I play. Tonight, it's your lead. We play what you want to play, whether covers, Kings tunes or even some of those new songs you've been working on."

"So Finn played my tape for you? The songs I recorded in my kitchen?"

"He did, and we liked them," he said. "We ran through a couple this week, so we could probably bang 'em out. Might stumble a bit, but we'll drive through."

I looked to the both of them again, then peered out to the crowd stirring below.

"You know what?" I said. "Not tonight. Let's just go up there and cover some classics from back in the day. Let's have a little fun."

"Like I said, it's your lead; it's your night. Let's make it a memorable one."

"That's all I want to do."

"And you're gonna do fine up there, trust me," said Finn. "I'll be right behind you the whole time."

"As usual," I said.

"You got it, kid. Now go set your guitar next to the stage and relax. We go on in an hour."

After I put my case to the left of the stage, I came back

up to Finn and Patty, against the high top with them while the opener, Mustache Tango, found the stage. The ska act had refused to evolve past the nineties, as most of the band was fashioning the plaids and sunglasses and cabana hats groups wore during the decade's brass-infused heyday. The lead singer was wearing lime green sunglasses and shouted deep, throaty vocals reminiscent of the Mighty Mighty Bosstones' Dicky Barrett. The band even had their own plaid-suited Bosstone-ish dancer, solely on stage to kick and flail his arms and legs next to the lead guitarist and singer. It was good party music, and gave the twenty or thirty who paid attention to the band a chance to jump and dance. The rest of the packed bar was simply shouting conversation over trumpet squealing and ska chords, trying to wave down Sues for another Genesee while waiting for the cacophony to end.

When the band finished, there was a spattering of applause and sarcastic hoots from customers already several beers in. As I watched the members of Mustache Tango empty the stage, I felt Finn's slap to my back.

"Want to step outside with me for a minute, out the side door over there?"

"Sure."

Finn walked outside, looked up to the sky and held his palm out. It had stopped raining, so I lit a cigarette for us to share. After my first drags, he took the smoke from me, held it between his fingers and watched the slow burn.

"So," he said, "I wanted a minute alone with you before we get up there."

"For what?"

"To tell you how proud I am of you."

"I know you are," I said. "And no matter how this goes,

thanks for tonight. Thanks for getting me back in here."

"You don't need to thank me for a damn thing. You're the one standing here, trying to move forward." He passed me our cigarette. "You remember that talk we had at Mercy Hospital, about how important it is for a man to fight through the darkness when the lights go out? When his life is sapped of hope?"

"Of course I do."

"Well, look what you're doing. You could've curled up in a ball and succumbed to the events in your life, let them destroy you. You didn't. Sure, you're down, but at least you're ready to fight. That's why I'm so damn proud of you. Even though you're hurting, you're moving forward. God, I wish I could see the look on your parents' faces, watching how tough you've become."

I passed him the smoke for the last drags.

"I wish they could see me on this stage tonight, Finn. I wish they could see us playing together."

"They'll be watching, right at the corner of the bar where your dad used to drink those Gennys."

"You think there's beer in heaven?"

He smiled, took the final drag and dropped the cigarette to the pavement.

"Absolutely," he said. "Wouldn't be heaven otherwise."

He headed back inside and I followed him to the stage steps. Patty Vee and the guys were already on stage, plugging into amps and tuning up. Before I could pull my scuffed guitar from its case, I felt a tug on my shirttail from behind. I turned to see Mickey, wearing a black Beatles T-shirt and smiling in front of Brendan and Meg.

"Hey, Uncle John. They let me into the bar," he said. "I didn't think kids my age could get into bars."

"I think there's a few on Allen Street I could get you into, Mick," I said, smiling.

"They wanted to see you play, even if it's only a few songs," said Meg.

"You're going to get more than that. I'm playing the whole set, so get comfortable. Go grab that corner table up on the landing, the one we just left. Not sure what this crowd on the floor's going to be like."

"We can't stay down here and dance?" said Mickey.

"You can, but that table up there is the V.I.P. section. It's reserved for special individuals, like nephews of guys in the band."

"Oh." He looked up at the table. "Guess I'll go be a V.I.P. Good luck, Uncle John."

I gave him a fist bump, then gave another to Brendan before watching them climb the stairs and find the table. Once they were settled, Meg looked down to me, gave me a wink before I grabbed my guitar and headed up the stage steps. Between Patty Vee and Finn's piano was a wooden stool, waiting in front of the microphone at center stage. I remembered my last time at that spot, the last time I'd moved across the Nighthawk stage and found a seat. One more deep breath before I walked to the stool under the bar's eruption of hoots and cheers and whistles. The chant started, the one that used to soothe me like a shot of Irish whiskey. The rhythmic shouts of "JOHN-NEE NO-LAN" preceded the five claps, *CLAP, CLAP, CLAP-CLAP-CLAP*. My heart was thumping, fast and hard. I glared through the hot lights, through the red, blue and yellow bulbs. I turned to the stool, picked it up and set it aside. I needed to stand. I pulled the mic up, adjusted it accordingly, took another deep breath and exhaled.

"What's up," I said through the cheers and screams. "I'm Johnny Nolan, and these are the Nickel City Kings. Tonight, we are once again kings of the Nickel City."

I turned to Finn as the thickening barroom roars intensified.

"I'd kind of like to warm up a bit," I said. "You want to do Saint Dominic's Preview?"

"Ambitious start. I like it," he said of the Van Morrison classic, then yelled "Saint D's" to the rest of the band and counted it off.

"One, two, three, four."

He started in on piano for a few notes before Patty Vee joined his progression with a quick electric riff. George jumped in with light percussion and Neko followed with a pick of his bass strings. I started to strum on rhythm acoustic and stepped to the mic. Vocals eased forth about chamois cleaning windows, Edith Piaf's soul and the Cathedral Notre Dame. I worked to the second verse, about San Francisco and a jagged story block. I stepped back for the first bit of the third, the line that brought beers into the air and pulled everyone in for a sing-a-long. Looking out at the crowd, I could see their faces eagerly waiting, so I leaned into the microphone and led the serenade.

"And it's a long way, to Buffalo."

After the line, cheers showered the stage as the band started circling to give the noise a chance to die down before we continued. When we did, I sang about Belfast City, about a Safeway supermarket in the rain. Strumming gently to guide the band, I could see men and women singing and handling beer bottles as they affectionately held each other, swaying side to side. When I strummed the last note, the crowd erupted, stomping and clapping and chanting again. Surveying the bar, I let my sight cut through the cheers and the chants and the guttural adulation, and I didn't look for who was missing. I didn't see Dana. I didn't even try to imagine her on a barstool, calling out a request. There were too many people wild with excitement, too many wide blues and browns and greens bright with relief for the night and the music that filled it. Sure, I knew some of them. There was a delirious and whistling Butch, as well as a few friends and acquaintances scattered about. But there were strangers, too, men and women I'd never met in my life dancing and singing because they wanted to, not because they had to. This satisfaction blocked the absence of Dana and injected me with such internal satisfaction that I didn't envision her emeralds floating anywhere around the Nighthawk. I thought about those eyes every day, thought about the various suspicions their hue coerced me to ignore. For that night, those eyes were gone.

The applause continued as a vision of my father slipped forth, one of him smiling at the bar's corner where he used to stand. I remembered the nights my mother stood with Meg, backed up against a sound booth covered in Anvil and Plaster Sandals band stickers. I looked to the landing to see Meg and the boys, clapping, yelling and smiling. She knew what I was thinking, knew the parental memories that were racing through my head and chest. The boys were excited, joyously joining the chant that rattled Nighthawk's stained glass windows and yellowed photographs from shows past.

And this was enough. This was how a wandering man needed to be embraced. This was how a tired soul needed to be awakened.

I looked through the faces and found a familiar woman, one with dark brown shoulder-length hair. Wearing tortoise shell-rimmed glasses, she was leaning against the bar and clapping as vigorously as the rest, yelling just as loud. When my gaze found hers, she reacted. Sam could feel the look from forty feet away.

"Thanks," I mouthed.

I read her lips to say "You're welcome" before she added, "good song."

I replied with an "I know" and winked before I turned back to the band. They were waiting and ready amid the burning lights, howls and hoisted beers. Gathering with them aside the drum kit, I felt an overwhelming relief rifling through me, one that released beads of sweat to gleefully slide down my face. The band had to know the night's truth after one look at me. They had to know I didn't care what song we jammed through next, just as long as I could tend to the herded masses before us, the exiled patrons who'd returned to the Nighthawk for dance and drink. Whatever Finn cued up with the tinkle of keys would be another note of the soundtrack for this communal homecoming, soothing the frustrations of displaced souls or those growing old. Some had returned in search of a time when a guitar chord cured, when a four-line verse could save. Some were yearning for the undervalued simplicity of recollection, the truth that a song can recover a romantic past that's faded away. Others came for it all, to down it like a shot of Crown. Together as one, we were unleashed, free to feel something we wish we could bottle, uncork and inhale. In the midst of it all, I didn't wonder how I ever let this feeling slip away. I simply grasped it again, stuffed it in my denim pocket as renewal and approached the microphone.

"Man, it's good to be here," I said. "It's good to be back home, back at the Nighthawk."

17

When you've found the things you've lost
Paid the price you had to pay
You'll find the things that once were gone
Are now around to stay
-"Bring It All Back" by J. Nolan

The Nighthawk was nearly empty. The delirious drinkers who packed the joint had finally exited, leaving me to sit at the bar with Sam and sip comped bottles of Bud. Sues was standing behind the bar to fetch the beers, but she didn't seem to mind. She was relaxed and smiling, leaning against the worn liquor shelf and banding loose dollar bills piled in two metal buckets. After tending to the voracious drinking habits of the night's attendees, she'd easily made a week's pay in one shift.

"It was just like old times in here tonight," she said. "I saw faces I haven't seen in years, people emerging from their suburban abyss to brave downtown and see you up there again."

"It was a good time," I said. "Just what I needed."

"You're welcome. Again," said Sam, who raised her beer to me for cheers.

Sues looked to Sam and smiled.

"You see? This is one of the people I'm talking about. When was the last time you were in here, Sara?"

"Sara?" I said. "This is Sam. Samantha."

"Sara's my middle name," said Sam. "People used to call me that name years ago, back when I was a semi-regular fixture in here."

"A blondie back then, too. I don't forget a face," said Sues. "See what happens when you play, Johnny? People return for a piece of their past, if only for a few hours."

"Not me," said Sam. "I'm happy to leave those old days right where they belong. Tonight was good enough on its own."

"Finn said it was the best show the band's ever played," I said. "Did you see the bear hug Neko gave me before he left? For once, the poor guy didn't have to worry about some degenerate flinging a boot at him. Seemed pretty grateful."

After I took a long drink, I noticed Sues stop counting her cash and place it in a pile on the liquor shelf behind her. She leaned back against the shelf, crossed her arms and flickered her eyelashes in my direction.

"So are you ready for the obvious question?"

"What? When am I going to play again?"

"Of course," she said. "You know the owner was here tonight, right? Standing by the door with a big fucking smile on his face. I wouldn't be surprised if he asks you to play next Friday. Actually, I wouldn't be surprised if he asks you to pick up your residency again. Do you know how much we rang tonight?"

"No idea."

"About as much as we typically rake for that AC-DC cover band Big Balls' insane Black Wednesday show the night before Thanksgiving."

"And that's good?"

"It's our busiest night of the year," she said. "Like I said, you're gonna get a call after he sees the register totals."

I gave her a nod and finished my beer.

"We'll see," I said. "All I know is tonight was amazing. Just let me enjoy it."

I got up from my stool and pulled on my coat, and Sam

did the same. Sues began banding her dollar bills together again, then stopped to lean over the bar and hug us. Sam walked outside in front of me, but Sues's voice stopped me at the exit.

"Hey Johnny, you think you could incorporate a fire-breather into your act?"

"Excuse me?"

"Big Balls' drummer has this bit where he breathes fire before the band busts into 'Highway to Hell.' Drives everyone in the joint fucking bananas. If you could bring something like that into your next show, I bet you'd top their register numbers."

"Incorporate fire into act. Got it," I said. "I'm sure Finn will be all over that idea."

When I found the sidewalk, I met Sam and let out a laugh.

"What's so funny?" she said, leading me up the street toward Washington.

"Nothing, nothing. It's Sues. She said I should incorporate some pyrotechnics into my next performance to really push it over the top."

"That's ridiculous."

"Of course it is, but it made me think of this one night back when I was still playing the Nighthawk every Friday. A night when I met this crazy blonde after a show."

"What, was she some sort of pyromaniac?"

"Close. She juggled fire. We went up to the square and she tossed these flaming ropes around. Nearly set the park on fire. There's still this huge bare spot in the branches of a tree over there."

"That's crazy," she said. "Whatever happened to the girl?"

"We fled the scene before the fire department arrived,

then went back to my place. Woke up the next morning and she was gone. Never saw her again," I said. "Crazy times."

"For everyone," she said. "You know, that was the last time I performed that fire dance. Let my dark hair grow out in the following months, too."

I stopped walking. I stood still with Lafayette Square two blocks in front of me, then turned to Sam. Sara. Blonde. The Nighthawk. Fire. Sara the Fire Dancer?

"You've got to be fucking kidding me," I said. "That was you? But what—"

"I know, I know. I'm not the stick figure I used to be. Plus, my hair's longer and a different color. Oh, and I wear the glasses. Just like in the movies, right? When characters want to hide in plain sight, they slap on glasses like a mask. Just like that," she said, snapped her fingers. "Tricky, huh?"

"All the times you came into City Hall, the few times we talked. Why? Why didn't you ever say anything?"

"What was the point?" she said. "Like we talked about the other day, you're not that guy anymore. You're not the same dude who brings home random, flame-juggling chicks."

"And that's who you are? Still some random rock chick in fire-retardant pants?"

"Look at me. Do I look like that girl anymore? Do I act like her, talk like her?"

"Of course not. That's why I'm so confused here," I said. "People change. You've obviously changed, but why should that prevent you from fondly recalling any piece of your past?"

She glanced at the pavement, scuffed her rubber sole against the sidewalk surface.

"I don't know. Guess a clean break from the past made more sense than a fragmented one. I loved going to see local bands or some up-and-comer who rolled into town. You remember that night My Morning Jacket played the Nighthawk?"

"Of course," I said. "Show is legendary."

"That night was awesome, but it was another night of booze or pills or whatever the night flung at me, and I had to walk away from that. I had to start fresh and move in a new direction. I couldn't figure out a way to pull the positive experiences out of the pile without the negative ones still clinging."

"So that night with me was a clinger?"

"Not at all," she said. "That was a fun night."

"So why'd you split in the morning? No number, no note. Nothing."

"You were the Nighthawk's Johnny Nolan," she said. "I knew it was just another night for you, so I left it at that. No reason to drag it out."

"And now it's just another night you've erased."

"Until tonight. Secrets revealed on the streets of Buffalo. Wahlah," she said, then waved her arms like at the end a magic trick.

We kept walking down Washington to Lafayette Square, toward the site of our infamous evening. Thoughts of the night replayed in my head as I lit a cigarette and found an open bench to lean against. The night was dark and still, with only the rattling sound of a shopping cart being pushed down Main Street disturbing the silence.

"You really think it's impossible to separate the positive and negative aspects of your past?"

"I don't know anymore," she said. "Until I started talking with you, this really wasn't an issue. Not a whole lot from those days comes into my path anymore."

"Remember when we were talking the other day in Cigarettes & Coffee? When you talked about separating the music from the scene?"

"Sure."

"Well isn't that a separation between positive and negative? You can't consider leaving a rock club to seek musical refuge in a soul-themed coffee shop a clean break. You can't consider fleeing the Nighthawk to teach kids about music at a youth center a complete separation."

"What's your point?"

"My point is that, tonight, I got back on that stage and performed again after denying it for years. Denying it because of its association with the negative, with the death of my parents. If I even grazed an E string in the months after they died, I'd think of them and start to cry."

Sam peered across the park, up to the Liberty Building's rooftop statues and off to the illuminated exterior of City Hall. When she turned back to me, her lenses reflected the dull glow of surrounding street lamps.

"So what changed?"

"The miscarriage. Dana leaving," I said. "After walking around in that darkness, I could only find comfort in the days I held my guitar, days everything seemed to make sense. I never understood Deirdre's importance until I picked her up amid all this shit. I thought she was something I played for fun. For my family, for girls. I didn't realize how she guided me, how the instrument was a part of me."

"Like your parents."

"Exactly," I said. "When I was up there tonight, I felt like they were watching somewhere, happy and not giving a shit that I was down here strumming cover tunes."

"And what about the rest of it? Did you feel like any of

the old urges of the scene were creeping back?"

"There were all kinds of accompaniments that joined those old performances, whether booze or drugs or—"

"Crazy blonde Ramones fans."

"I think we've covered that," I said. "I'm not that guy anymore. I'm just John Nolan, and I'm not interested in jumping into a goddamn scene. I'm only interested in the music, the way it makes me feel. I need it. I know that now. How about you?"

She pushed her brown hair behind her ears, let the moonlight find her cheekbones.

"I'm just Sam, and I love a good Van Morrison cover. Always have."

"And there you go. That's one positive thing we've each retained from our wild past. Now if you wanted to start juggling those flaming ropes again—"

"Oh not to worry, sir," she said. "My pyromania has officially been retired, but this isn't a bad way to spend a late night moment in Lafayette Square."

"No sirens or fire trucks. I'll take it."

She stood from the bench and held out her hand for me to shake.

"So we start anew from here, okay?" she said. "No more surprise revelations."

I raised an eyebrow and met her waiting hand.

"You sure about that? Last chance to empty the chamber."

"I'm all clear, ready to build on the present."

"And I can help with that?"

"Absolutely, Mr. Nolan," she said. "Absolutely."

On the Monday following my Nighthawk comeback, I was back

at my desk in City Hall, sipping a Tim Horton's coffee and sifting through my never-ending pile of consumer files. I was slowly sifting through a complaint against Time Warner Cable when I turned to see Pete patting a beat on my cubicle's gray exterior.

"Have any smokes, Nolan? I feel like climbing up to the observation deck to enjoy the sun. The goddamn winter months around here earn us mornings like this."

I confirmed the existence of two cigarettes in my crumpled pack of Camel Lights and joined Pete in search of welcoming Lake Erie breezes. We found the observation deck empty, though the afternoon would welcome a litany of city drones, escaping their offices to find solace under our meteorological payback. After we each lit up, Pete reached into his back pocket. He pulled out a section of the day's *Buffalo Gazette*, slapped me in the chest with it and handed it over.

"We're recommending reading today?" I said. "Save it. I know why the Sabres' season ended. I don't need to read the alternative theories."

"I'm not handing over the Sports section, pal. Flip open to page five."

I flipped the paper's pages through the breeze. Right at the top, occupying nearly half of the page, the headline stared back at me. *Nighthawk Nolan: Local Favorite Stirs Frenzy With Surprise Return.*

"I take my wife and daughter to Toronto for the weekend and this is what I return to?" he said. "C'mon, Nolan. Are you fucking kidding me? You couldn't tell me about these plans last week?"

I rolled up and stuffed the paper into my back pocket.

"I had no clue what this was going to turn into. Honestly thought I was going to pop on stage for a song or two. I'm real sorry, man."

"Even if it were only a song, I should've been there. Shit, after reading that write-up, I'm pretty pissed I wasn't. Reporter said you were really clicking, almost like you never left."

"That might be a bit of an overstatement, but I'll take it."

"So is this a return?"

I looked to Pete, took a drag and exhaled.

"To what? The stage or life?"

"It's kind of the same thing for you, isn't it?" he said. "I mean, by the description in this article, it appears you finally figured that out."

I nodded in agreement and stood silent for a few seconds, enjoying my last drags amid the pleasant aroma of Cocoa Puffs from the nearby General Mills smokestacks. When Pete finished the last bit of his cigarette, he interrupted the silence.

"So we've known each other a pretty long time, right?"

"Since high school."

"So can I be straight with you about something? Something I've never told you about before?"

"Sure."

"So here it is," he said. "When you came in here to ask for a job a few years back, to ask for my help, I really didn't want to put in a word for you. I didn't want the office to hire you."

"Why?"

Pete walked forward to lean against the plexiglass, pensive as he looked across the lake to Canada.

"Because this fucking building eats souls, man," he said. "It hollows people out. A passionate guy like you, guy who breathed so freely in life and on stage? I thought once you decided to stash your guitar for a desk that you were as good as dead. I honestly didn't think you'd last a month."

"Then why did you help me out?"

"I knew your parents' death shook you up. I knew you were trying to do the right thing with Dana. And as a friend, I needed to pick you up. But this place? This place is for guys like me, not guys like you."

"And who are you? What makes you so different from me?"

"I'm a goddamn Polak who loves beer, hockey and my family. I wasn't blessed with the ability to play a song on guitar five minutes after hearing it on the fucking radio. I fill a seat in this building. I'm not saving the world, and I'm cool with that. I get paid, my daughter eats, and I can maintain a nice little life in this city. I don't need anything else," he said. "You do."

I leaned back against the bricks and looked out to the Canadian shoreline.

"So what are you saying? You want me to quit working here? Not sure if that article detailed my Friday night cash take, but it wasn't much. I still need a paycheck, pal."

"And you can get that here—as long as you keep playing. If you do that, you can plant your ass in that seat downstairs and flip through complaints about coffee and cat dicks. You can advocate away until you cut a record, tour or die. Up to you."

"And what if I don't play again? I don't know if the Nighthawk wants me back."

"Then you'll play on a fucking street corner. At Elmwood and Allen, right in front of your apartment building. You can play out in Niagara Square during lunch for all I care, just as long as that guitar's in your hands. This is how your life will continue from this point forward," he said. "Am I really telling you anything you don't already know?"

"Not really, no."

"So why are you being a prick about this?"

I flicked my cigarette to the deck, took one more look at the waterfront and turned to Pete.

"I just want you to feel important for a minute or two," I said. "Christ, that 'just a Polak' line of yours was really depressing."

"Oh, fuck off." He slapped my arm and grabbed the paper from my back pocket. "I'm framing this article, pal. Going right up on my office wall."

We walked back into the office to find a woman fashioning a gray knit ski cap, short-sleeved tee and tattooed arms while rapping a drum beat on the front counter. Sues.

"So, Johnny Nolan," she said. "What do you have planned for Friday night?"

"This Friday?"

"How about every Friday, starting next week and right through the end of July—to start."

Pete smiled and wrapped his right arm around my shoulder. Before I could respond, he intervened with my answer.

"Sign him up," he said. "He's in."

18

Come with me tonight, girl
I'll bring this old guitar
We can find a little love
Maybe take things too far
-"Nights of You & Me #44" by J. Nolan

I pressed down my Outback's horn for the second time. Parked in Meg's driveway on a Saturday morning in June, I was waiting for Brendan and Mickey to kick open their house's front door and barrel down their porch steps, just like they did on every one of our spontaneous Saturday adventures. I did it to give Meg a break, to give her a chance to relax on her couch or go for a jog through Cazenovia Park after a stressful week of work. Sometimes, I did it because I simply needed an excuse to go on excursions I wouldn't otherwise attempt alone. That morning was one of those times, albeit masked as a charitable act. After Brendan and Mickey finally stormed down their steps and into my car's seats, they didn't seem to care about my reasons. When you're a kid, you just like to be going *somewhere*. With this understood, we buckled in and coasted out of South Buffalo to find our Saturday somewhere.

"So where are we going again?" said Brendan, seated in shotgun.

"First, we're going to St. Jude's Community Center's music appreciation group for kids."

"Why?"

"Thought you guys would enjoy it," I said. "There'll be a bunch of kids sitting around, listening and learning about different kinds of music. A friend of mine runs the group."

"Mr. Konarski?" said Mickey. "I like him."

"No, not Pete. It's a new friend."

"Who?" said Brendan. "Have we met him?"

"It's not a him. It's a she, named Sam. Samantha."

"Is it the woman from your show the other night?" he said. "The one you were talking to when we left?"

"Yeah, that's her. You guys will like her, I promise. She'll play some good music at St. Jude's, and afterwards, we'll go down to Rudy's Red Hots for a few dogs."

"Is she coming with us?" said Brendan.

"She might. Is that okay, detective?"

"I guess," he said, then sighed and turned away to stare out the window.

While navigating through the endless orange construction cones along the waterfront, I glanced at Brendan, silent as he watched us pass the dilapidated factories along the Buffalo River. I couldn't tell whether he was tired, upset or both.

"So what's the deal, Bren? Are you deep in thought over there or what?"

He shifted his gaze forward through the windshield, off into the distance at Seneca Tower and the grand steeple of St. Joseph's Cathedral.

"Is this Sam going to be your new girlfriend?"

"What? No," I said, rattled a bit by his boldness. "Why would you ask that?"

"Aunt Dana's gone, right?"

"She is, yeah," I said. "And you don't have to call her your aunt anymore. She's just a woman named Dana."

"Dana the whore," yelled Mickey.

"Whoa, Mickey." I looked into the rearview mirror. "Where did you hear that?"

"That's what Mommy calls her. Dana the whore. I heard her on the telephone."

"That may be, but you can't call her that. Kids don't use that word."

"Sorry, Uncle John."

I bit the inside of my mouth while coasting down to the foot of Delaware Avenue, then turned to Brendan after the light moment passed.

"Look, sometimes in life, you lose things. And when you lose these things, it can make you really upset."

"Like with the baby. When we didn't see you for a while?"

"Right," I said. "That was a rough time for me. But we Nolans don't panic when things get rough."

"Like when my dad left."

"Exactly. Your mother stood strong and made it through. Now it's my turn. I'll make it through, so don't worry about it."

I reached over and patted him on the chest as we rolled toward the McKinley Monument. He glanced out his passenger side window again for a block or so, then turned back to me.

"But what if this Sam wants to be your girlfriend?" he said. "She *is* pretty hot."

I laughed as we circled around the Niagara Square rotary, through the swallowing shadows of City Hall and the Statler Hotel.

"Hot, huh? You sure you're not asking these questions because you want to make a move on her yourself? Try to control yourself today, slick."

We found a parking spot in front of St. Jude's, with scattered city youth trickling into the community center's front door. When that door swung open, faint sounds of piano, strings and snare drum hits slipped out to us and stopped Brendan in his tracks.

"Are you taking us to listen to hip hop?" he said. "This is a Kanye West song."

"Just wait until we get in there. You'll see."

I led them through the doors and down a short, vacant hallway. Lining the pale walls were faded pictures from years past, shots featuring kids tossing a football outside or sitting in a classroom, smiling for the camera. In the middle of them all was a large, framed photo of Finn. With thick dark hair and a patchy, scraggily beard, he strummed his guitar and sang surrounded by a group of laughing tweens. He hadn't worked there in years, but Finn was still claimed by St. Jude's. He was still theirs.

A little further down the hallway, we arrived at the source of the sounds. In a little open classroom, we found Sam, sitting on a teacher's wooden desktop with a small CD player as a group of kids sat attentively on folding chairs in a semi-circle in front of her. When she saw us standing in the doorway, she paused the song and hopped off the desk.

"Everyone, I'd like you to meet our special guests today. This is Brendan and Mickey, and this is their uncle, Mr. Nolan. Mr. Nolan is a musician here in Buffalo."

Brendan sheepishly raised his hand, while Mickey waved wildly, like he'd become a contestant on a game show. I smiled and said hello while they checked me out, seemingly wondering whether they'd seen me before or ever heard me on the radio. Unless they'd listened outside the Nighthawk's cracked windows, I was fairly certain they hadn't. With this assurance, I led the boys through the seated children to find three open spots.

"Okay, since our three guests are first timers here, who wants to tell them what we're doing this morning?" said Sam. "Yes, Marcus."

"We're listening to how rappers use parts of old songs to make new songs," said Marcus, a young boy sitting up straight in an oversized royal blue Bills football jersey.

"That's right," she said. "Every one of you has probably sung along to a song and never realized that the beat, rhythm or lyrics to that tune were inspired or even borrowed from another older song, one your parents or even grandparents probably like. Who here thinks their parents' music stinks?"

Nearly every hand in the place immediately went up, save for Brendan's or Mickey's. I appreciated their loyalty—or timidity.

"Well, after today, you're all going to think your parents and grandparents are way cooler than you ever did before. After today, you'll want to borrow their records or CDs and burn them onto your iPods. So are we ready to start the first song again?"

With the kids stirring and mumbling in front of her, Sam went over to the little desktop stereo and pressed play, releasing the same intro piano tinkling we heard echo on our way into the building. Bass and snare drums joined the keys in a repetitious stream. Some of the kids began bopping their heads to the beat, obviously familiar with the song even before Kanye West's vocals came thumping out of the speakers, spitting words about a sweater and a sweet brother, about diamonds and Ruby Tuesday's. Brendan poked me when the strings and heavier bass entered the fray around us.

"I have heard this song," he said. "One of the kids on my

hockey team plays it all the time."

"You like it?"

"Not really," he said, then quickly reconsidered. "But I like the piano and backing vocals with the drums. It's catchy."

"Those vocals are smoother in their original version."

"Whose voice is it?"

"Wait and see," I said. "The point of this class is for you to learn something."

Kanye's vocals bounced around the room for a little longer before Sam faded out the song and scanned the class.

"So who knows the name of the song?" She looked right to Brendan even as multiple hands rose into the air. "Brendan, what do you think? Ever heard it?"

"Um, I think it's called 'Gone.' By Kanye West."

"Absolutely correct. Off his *Late Registration* album a few years back. Has anyone else heard this song before?"

After she watched most of the kids nod, yell or even tap out the enduring beat repetitiously on their thighs and chests, Sam reached into her red messenger bag, pulled out another disc and set it into the player.

"Now that we have the easy part out of the way, who wants to tell me the name of the legendary singer at the beginning of the song? The voice backing Kanye."

I turned to see the collection of tweens look confusedly at one another as Brendan and Mickey looked to me.

"Do you know?" said Brendan.

"Of course I know, but I feel like a failure as an uncle because you don't. Remind me to lend you some of his music this week."

"So who is it?"

I raised my hand.

"Yes, Mr. Nolan."

"It's Otis Redding, and the sample is from one of his older tunes, 'It's Too Late.'"

"That's correct," she said, then popped *The Great Otis Redding Sings Soul Ballads* into the stereo and skipped ahead to the aforementioned track. It was absent of Kanye's added snare hits and strings and, instead, slipped along with Redding's sampled vocals and tapped keys, as well as a subtle bass and saxophone. The song didn't really interest the kids. They stared out the surrounding windows or up toward the hundreds of dots embedded in the ceiling as the piano and saxophone notes drifted past their faces. A few mumbled jokes passed through the silky rhythm before a frustrated Marcus stood up from his chair.

"C'mon, Sam," he said. "Nobody's ever heard of this old dude, and this song is mad boring. Can you put that Kanye joint back on?"

"This old dude?" Sam hopped off her desk again. "The old dude is a soul legend, my young friend. And if his song is so *mad* boring, why'd Kanye decide to sample it for his own work?"

"I don't know. Maybe he felt bad for the dude's boring song."

This brought on some laughs and pats to Marcus's back as he sat back down. Sam intervened once the commotion simmered down.

"No. The reason Kanye used the sample is because he was inspired by it. He was inspired by Redding's original song, and used that inspiration to create something entirely different. That's the way artistic inspiration works. Sometimes, it can come from unlikely places."

She looked at me and winked. I smiled and nodded,

then scanned the room to see most of the kids listening to her as she paced about and moved her hands around, talking about the connection between Otis and soul and hip-hop. She was their teacher, one they actually wanted to listen to. Inspiration can be found through influence. Other times, the desire to have an influence can be inspiration. Would the information she relayed help some of them find their own inspiration to create something unique or complex or Yeezy-esque someday? Maybe. But as I was listening to Sam laugh and speak over the low-tone smoke of Redding vocals, I turned to Brendan and Mickey. They were sitting attentive, inhaling everything she said. And as I looked down, I noticed Brendan's foot tapping to the soft, surrounding beat.

We arrived at Rudy's Red Hots to find its patio packed with families, young couples and tattooed Allentown hipsters, all eating mustard-soaked hot dogs or sipping frosty beers under beams of afternoon sunshine. The place brought eclectic crews together because of its grilled lunches and waterfront locale, both ideal for the inception of Buffalo's summer. After we found a table, we took our seats, ready to feel the touch of smooth Erie breezes between bites of Sahlen's hot dogs and salty curly fries.

"So do you guys come here a lot?" said Sam.

"When it's warm," I said. "Plus, these two really like the curly fries. Combine that with the view of the lake and it's pretty solid."

"I had my last birthday here," said Mickey. "We had an ice cream cake shaped like a football."

"No Cookie Puss or Humpy the Whale?" she said.

"Who are they?"

"You know, the ice cream cakes from Carvel."

"What's Carvel? Is that another hot dog place?"

"Wow, did you just date yourself," I said to her. "I think the last Carvel around here closed when I was in high school."

She let out a pop of a laugh and smiled.

"Not a good day for me, I guess," she said. "First, the kids have never heard of Otis Redding. Now, Cookie Puss is dead. God, I'm slowly turning into a relic, huh?"

"Somebody has to teach these kids music history. And I'd bet a few of those kids went home and asked their parents about Otis. You had their attention, right guys?"

Both Mickey and Brendan nodded before they turned to greet our young waitress. They ordered hot dogs, curly fries and Aunt Rosie's loganberries, while Sam and I ordered burgers, fries and Cherry Cokes. Our waitress walked off with our order, then returned moments later with our drinks. I watched Brendan and Mickey unwrap straws and sink them into their maroon-filled cups before they moved onto elementary school business. I looked across the table at Sam, who sat dreamily gazing out over the lake. She took a deep breath and turned back to glance over her Cherry Coke, like she felt my sight grazing her pale cheek.

"I'm glad everyone enjoyed themselves today. Not sure how many more Saturdays we'll be able to have like it."

"How many more? What are you talking about?"

"Some of the volunteers have been hearing whispers about a shortage of operating funds," she said. "Donations to both the church and center have been down, and with Buffalo's incomes not exactly skyrocketing, I can't imagine we'll be getting generous handouts any time soon."

"So what's the plan? You think St. Jude's will shut down its center?"

"Nothing's definite yet, but they are going to end some programs at the end of the summer. That's all I know," she said. "Since I volunteer and donate money from the coffee shop, I imagine they'll keep my groups around through cutbacks. But if they decide to shut the whole place down—"

"Has anyone contacted Finn about this?"

"I don't know," she said. "Just caught wind of the news this morning."

"Someone needs to drop him a line. Guy's a fundraising machine, so I imagine he could come up with something. You've heard of the annual St. Stephen's Green fundraiser?"

"Sure. They always show clips of the performances on the news every year."

"Finn created the whole event. Actually came up with the idea while he was still working at St. Jude's."

"Do you think you could mention something to him? You can give him my contact info and I'll fill him on the few details I have."

"I'll call him tonight," I said. "Knowing what that place means to him, I'd bet he'll do everything he can to keep it going. Hell, I will, too. Have a lot of good memories there."

"So do I," she said. "And I'd like to have some more."

Our waitress arrived at our table, holding the plates of hot dogs and hamburgers and fries. She placed the lunch items in front of us, just as the overhead patio speakers emitted seaside sounds of gentle waves. A two-chord dance of acoustic picking was followed by an introduction of delicate snare hits and light piano notes, soon joined by a familiar, soothing vocal about sitting in the morning sun. With his hot dog and curly fries waiting in front of him, Brendan looked up to the speakers and listened for a brief moment.

"Hey Uncle John, is this another Otis Redding song? Voice sounds like his."

I smiled and nodded to him, then turned to Sam.

"You see how important one person's words can be? How easily they can influence?"

"Oh, so now *you're* encouraging *me*? Just like that?"

I smiled.

"Funny how quickly things can change."

19

Standing on your front porch
You long to be inside
Walk through that door to home
You'll find some things to hide
-"Front Porch" by J. Nolan

Finn and I were leaning against a secluded high top on the raised landing to the right of the Nighthawk stage, looking out at yet another packed barroom floor. Since we'd taken over the Nighthawk's Friday night slot in early June, we'd been welcomed by this crammed scene every weekend. Young men in tight tees with poor shaving habits stood among wiry young women in form-fitting plaid button-downs. Older guys in faded baseball caps draped their arms around dates and reclaimed spots from days long surrendered. All were gathered as one, holding bottles of Old Vienna and cans of Genesee, laughing and talking as the house stereo blared pounding piano notes and snare hits of an old Elvis Costello song. Costello's vocals spoke of an amateur hour, fidelity and changing a channel, an upbeat soundtrack for finger tapping and ale sipping. Finn and I engaged in both under the floating rhythms. We were at ease, talking about St. Jude's while waiting for the night's opener to take the stage.

"So I've talked to some people at the center and they've confirmed what your friend Sam said. Guess their status is pretty bleak," said Finn, standing up straight with palms flat on the high top. "First and foremost, though, they're concerned with the church itself. With all the parish closings in the area, I think they'd accept the center shutting down if it meant the church could stay open."

"And you don't think they can have both?"

"In an ideal environment, sure. But where's the money for it in *this* environment? From a thinning congregation? A cynical community?"

"What about devising an annual fundraiser like St. Stephen's Green?"

"Fine idea, but St. Jude's needs an influx of funds yesterday, not tomorrow. It took St. Stephen's Green a few years to get its legs and become the successful event it is now. I'm not sure the center has that much time. It's already working at half the strength it did in my days there."

"What if we played a fundraising show here? We could line up some sponsors and donate the door's take to the center."

He took a pull off his bottle of Bud.

"Not a bad start, but I don't think we have the firepower to carry a show like that alone. Not yet, anyway."

"So we get a few other local acts on the bill. Drop a line to the guys of Mustache Tango. I'm sure they'll get in on it."

"You think Mustache Tango has the star power to get Buffalonians to empty their wallets?" he said, smiling. "If we want this to hit on the first try, we'll need a bill that generates some serious buzz."

"So what local music legends do you have in mind? Ani? Willie Nile? The Goos are in L.A., Rick James is dead, and—"

"And Luther White," he said. "Who might as well be dead."

"Right."

I sucked the scarce remains of beer from my bottle.

Since I'd found my place on stage again, I'd found it easier to deal with even the mention of Luther. Hearing his name didn't make me grit my teeth or hurl pint glasses at jukeboxes. He wasn't someone I spent much time thinking about anymore. Maybe he was out of sight, out of mind. Or maybe my anger toward him had been replaced by the empowerment I reclaimed on stage. Whatever the case, his mere existence didn't sting the way it once did. It merely elicited a sip and an exhale.

"You ready for another one?" I said to Finn.

"Sure, but let me go up and get a round. I need to say hello to Sues."

I watched Finn walk through the masses before they got rowdy, stomping the dusty Nighthawk floorboards as Wolfhorse took the stage. Every member of the band seemed to be donning an unofficial uniform. Scraggly beards were teamed with plastic-rimmed glasses, tight jeans, and multi-colored novelty tees that seemed better sized for the tiny torsos of St. Stephen's elementary students. Each bandmate raised their can of Pabst to the crowd before plugging in, which elicited typical Nighthawk enthusiasm, the kind of encouragement that, back in the old days, beckoned me to hoist half a beer down my throat in three seconds. But these guys were new; it was their Nighthawk debut. They knifed their first chords through the bar's Absolut-tinged fervor and Cream Ale aroma, inhaling an atmosphere they'd never forget. One look at their faces and I knew this to be true. Behind their Costello frames sparkled the same fascination I first felt years ago. One glance and I could see it all.

And maybe this is what others couldn't see. This is what people considering the discontinuation of community center programs needed to understand. Maybe they'd never picked up a Gibson or a Fender, or even tapped on the ivory keys of an ebony-colored Yamaha. They needed to feel the electricity of performance; they needed to know how an artist's words can touch a population yearning for inspiration. In turn, they needed to learn how the responsibility of plucking a string, hitting a snare or exhaling syllables into a microphone instills even the meekest person with a sense of invincibility. How could this opportunity of empowerment be treated as disposable? Without instruments in their hands and lyrics in their heads, the members of Wolfhorse were simply four bespectacled hipsters stuffed into children's clothing. With their melded fusion of acoustic strumming, keyboard tinkling and harmonious yowling, they could become agents of encouragement for a sect of Buffalo's aimless youth. Maybe.

When Finn came back with the beers, he stood next to me as the crowd below pushed toward the stage. Wolfhorse twanged their way through one mountaintop howl before transitioning into another, holding the attention of nodding men in Black Keys gear, of women in vintage gray Patti Smith tees. Finn and I stood listening, occasionally nodding approval to each other during impressive solos or lyrics. If we hadn't had such a solid set planned for the night, those exchanged nods might've erred envious.

After the crowd clapped and screamed through the end of Wolfhorse's set, they roamed around the bar in different directions. Some went to the bar for shots of Crown Royal; others cut out the front door to rip a quick Camel Light before our set kicked off. Their collective relocation gave Finn and me the room we needed to step off the landing and find Patty Vee and the rest of the Nickel City Kings at stage left. The house stereo welcomed us across the barroom floor with the Cookie Monster growl of Tom Waits, his scratchy, impassioned vocals about traveling and monkeys and rain joining a stomping backbeat and jangling tambourine. The crowd reclaimed standing spots against the Nighthawk's brick walls or load-bearing pillars to watch us ascend the stage steps and grab instruments. Neko strapped on his shiny black bass and plugged in while Finn and George found their respective stools. Patty Vee swung his cream-colored Les Paul over his neck and picked at the strings.

When I found my spot at the center of the stage, I took Deirdre from her case and leaned her near George's drum kit. I picked up Patty Vee's back-up electric guitar, a scuffed and yellowed Fender Esquire. After I plugged it in, strapped it on and tickled its strings for a tune, I looked out to the bar, once again packed from the front door to stagefront. Slowly, the requisite Johnny Nolan chant spread from one end of the bar to the other with its emphatic syllables, claps and thumps. I exchanged nods with the soundboard tech before I turned to the band.

"'Everybody Knows' on four, okay? I'll take lead, Patty's on rhythm," I said. "Ready?"

They each nodded before George counted it off with taps of his drumsticks. After his fourth tap, I ripped into the song's opening like I was kicking in a creaky screen door. With my fingers effortlessly shifting between a G and a C, my body furiously shook like it was being electrocuted. I picked Patty Vee's Fender with such violence that the smile on my face must have seemed maniacal. I was ripping chords with raw emotion. I was summoning the unborn child of Keith Richards and Creedence Clearwater Revival. I was clawing my way toward a Southern-spiced sound before exhaling Neil Young lyrics to the Nighthawk house. This is how it had to be done, and the reckless enthusiasm of the crowd seemed to agree with me.

Patty Vee and I stood together at the stage's center

microphone to sing about back home and taking it easy. The crowd soon joined us, shouting out lines about passing time and a girl living somewhere. Some swayed and spilled their cans of Genny down royal blue Sabres tees; others were flicking air guitar strings, ignoring the actual chords and, instead, letting their skinny fingers find imaginary frets of their own invisible Fenders. They stood together, bouncing and dancing and singing until their movements turned into the same clapping and chanting that greeted the end of every song the new Nickel City Kings performed. All night, the cycle continued through the music of Dylan, Morrison and Springsteen; through the lyrics of Waits and Young; through the hometown anthems of the Nickel City Kings. All night, the communion was preserved.

Toward the end of the evening's set, I felt sweat rolling down my brown bangs. I walked back to my amp and finished the last remnants of my bottle of Bud before Finn's hand found my arm.

"Have you looked toward the back of the bar?" he asked. "By the front door?"

"No. Why?"

"Take a look now, but don't be obvious about it. Real quick."

With one casual motion, I glanced at the door to see two large black men in black leather jackets. One seemed familiar; the other I'd never seen before.

"Where do I know the one on the left from?"

"The White Room," said Finn. "He's a bartender there. The other is one of the bar's bouncers. Their presence here can only mean one thing."

"Luther's back in town."

"Probably," he said. "Assuming these gentlemen are here

for you, what do you want to do?"

I looked down at my brown boots until an idea flashed forth.

"Maybe we should play them a song they've heard before."

"What'd you have in mind?"

I grinned.

"How about 'Beer for Blues'? You remember the piano notes?"

"Of course I do, but are you sure you want to do this? Sure you want to stir things?"

"Stir things? If things weren't already stirring, then why are Luther's goons standing at that exit? Something's going to happen, so we might as well come out swinging."

Finn cracked a smile and nodded, then slid back over to his keys to situate himself. I walked to each member of the band and told them of the plan, grabbed a stool and Patty Vee's scuffed Esquire propped against the amps. After I plugged in, I placed the stool at center stage and took a seat. I reset the microphone stand to reach my settled position, then smiled at the crowd as they waited for our last song of the night.

"So we have one more for you," I said. "You think you can handle another one?"

Hoots and shouts and screams showered the stage, accompanied by hoisted bottles of Bud, Molson and Old Vienna.

"All right, all right. We hear you," I laughed. "Now, how many of you out there have heard of the great Luther White?"

This elicited a few claps amid a house full of boos and shouted expletives. The Nighthawk never worshipped at the altar of Luther White. Its staff or inhabitants would never treat him with the reverence the rest of the city bestowed upon him. My known past and rumored present with him probably had something to do with their stance. Barstool whispers about Luther and Dana had likely made their way around the scene. But there was more to it than these floating tales; it was bigger than that. Over all his years spent earning his place at the top of Buffalo's performance pyramid, Luther had never earned his Nighthawk keep. He'd never clipped a string on their stage, never echoed his distinctive howl through the bar's ambiance; he'd never knocked back a shot of Crown with Sues. Within the subversive community of the Nighthawk, Luther White wasn't a legend. He was irrelevant.

"I know," I said. "I've never heard of him, either."

An explosion of raucous cheers and boot stomps followed my sentence, then converted itself into the traditional Johnny Nolan clap chant. I looked to Luther's associates as this commotion cascaded over the bar. The bartender slugged off his bottle of Bud Light and dismissively laughed; the bouncer stood with his leathered arms crossed, angrily glaring at me. After I connected with his stare for a moment, I continued.

"But before ol' Luther was some guy we've never heard of, he was a man who cranked out some of the best blues Buffalo's ever heard. Tonight, we're going to steal one of 'em. And if that fucker has a problem with it, he can walk his fat ass up Washington Street and try to take it back."

This reignited the crowd's rebellious enthusiasm. I counted off the song's opening with four Doc Marten boot stomps on stage planks before I began to shred the E and A strings between the seventh and ninth frets. It was a token blues riff, but one that belonged distinctively to whoever picked it, whenever he picked it. As I aggressively made it mine, I heard Finn's fingers dancing across his keys, finding the right notes to complement my direction. George ditched the understated skin work of Luther's original version and, instead, became unhinged, smashing snares and cymbals to match our pace. Neko and Patty Vee fell in line as well, backing the stolen words that stormed from my mouth, vocals about old guitars, cars and dirty blues bars. Together, we ignited an audio explosion, playing with a fury flammable enough to set a Queen City block ablaze, an authority powerful enough to march down the street and shake Luther off his White Room barstool.

We hit our last notes and kept our stage spots before the controlled riot we instigated. Patrons stood shouting and saluting, roaring and raising toasts. We waved our thanks, found our way to the steps at stage left and began gathering our gear. When the crowd thinned around us, Finn and I walked to the nearest corner of the bar to get a round for the band. But even with the post-show electricity still flowing through our fingertips, we hadn't forgotten about the problem at the Nighthawk's front door.

"Stand behind me, dammit," said Finn, holding the back of my sweat-soaked white T-shirt. "Stay back so they have to go through me to get to you."

"Why?"

"Because they're less likely to hit a priest, that's why. Just stay where you are and don't move. Can you still see them?"

"No," I said, looking at the exit. "Maybe they left to report us to Luther."

I felt a huge paw on my left shoulder at the end of my last syllable. I turned around to see Luther's men, both smiling with their arms crossed. Finn quickly grabbed the back of my shirt again and pulled me behind him.

"Problem guys?"

They turned to each other and laughed.

"Let me guess," the bouncer said. "You the priest, right? Father Finn? Yeah, Luther warned us about you."

"So he's back from Florida?" I said.

"He is," the bartender said, "Wants to meet with you, clear up some shit. Doesn't want no trouble. Just wants to talk."

"He obviously knows where to find me. Why isn't he here?"

"C'mon, man," the bartender said, laughing. "After hearing this angry mob tonight, I think we both know why he ain't here."

"So where is he?"

"Down at the White Room," he said. "Wants you to come down for a drink."

"Now?"

"Yeah. Bring the whole band if you want. Like I said, he doesn't want no trouble."

After we exchanged nods, they took a few steps back to talk to each other. I took advantage of the space and turned to Finn.

"What do you think?"

"What do I think? I think I'll go tell the band that you and I are headed to the White Room."

"You and I? So you trust this?"

"Of course I don't," he said. "That's why I'm going with you."

20

Remember old man trouble?
When he walked across your floor?
He sat and stayed, made you pay
'Til you pushed him out the door
-"Old Man Trouble" by J. Nolan

The White Room was scarcely populated. A few tables were full of boisterous biker couples, with men dressed in weathered leather jackets or vests that showed off biceps and forearms covered in faded outlines of flaming skulls and snarling dragons. Their women flanked them in tight tees or snug white tank tops, with hair teased and make-up caked in a fashion two decades past their heyday. At the bar leaned three older men, dressed in casual polos and deck shorts, yelling animated conversation under the electric guitar riffs of Stevie Ray Vaughn. Finn and I walked into the bar with Luther's men behind us, just as they had been on our walk from the Nighthawk. They followed us through the White Room door and nodded to the night's bartender, a pale, goateed and tattooed gentleman in a white Affliction T-shirt with its sleeves torn off. He got their signal, nodded and walked off.

Finn and I waited in wooden chairs at an open table near the White Room's empty stage. Vaughn's transcendent licks were followed by Howlin' Wolf words about a highwayman, red lights and a Cadillac. Minutes later, I looked toward Luther's open office door to see him emerge. He was dressed in a bright red golf shirt, shiny black slacks and red wingtips, and his footsteps clicked over to our table before he pulled up a chair. He didn't pause and wait for a greeting; he didn't make eye contact with either of us. He didn't try to shake our hands, and he didn't say hello. Luther was perceptive enough to know that if he offered any of these things, he wouldn't have gotten anything positive in return.

He set his big paws down on the table. He crossed his arms across his bright red chest before looking across the table. I met his stare and held it, like I wanted to pin it to the ground. Before the tension ramped up between us, Luther turned from me to talk to Finn.

"Long time, Finn." He let a sly grin emerge. "Long time."

"Hasn't been long enough," said Finn. "But let's stash the math and get to why you sent your boys out to fetch us."

"Old fiery Finn. Looks like the priesthood hasn't chilled you out none, huh?"

"If you mean it hasn't given me amnesia, then no. It hasn't, but I assume our little trip down here has nothing to do with you and me. It has to do with Johnny, so let's get to it."

"Whatever you say, Father Finn." He mockingly bowed his head and smiled, then turned back to shout to his bartender. Seconds later, the slender man slinked over to our table with a bottle of Jameson and three shot glasses, set the goods on the table and let us be. Luther handled the whiskey bottle and poured shots into the empty glasses.

"I usually don't drink this shit. But on account of you two Irish motherfuckers coming down here, guess a little taste won't hurt."

"So what are we drinking to?" I said. "Happiness? Success? Fidelity?"

After he topped off the last shot glass, he placed the
bottle down at the center of the table and looked to me again.
This time, his stare was softer; almost apologetic. With this, he
crossed his hands under his chin and delivered.

"Forgiveness," he said. "I wanted you to come down
here tonight so I could make things right. So I could apologize."

I leaned back in my chair before folding my arms across
my chest.

"Just like that, huh?" I said. "Man, you are drunk on
your own legend, aren't you?"

"Now what the hell is that supposed to mean?"

"The great Luther White privileges me with his presence
and a free drink, and I'm supposed to forget the past? Forget
about you and Dana? By the way, how's she doing?"

"That stuff with Dana just happened," he said. "I thought
it was a little fling, just another go-round with one of my waitresses. I never thought she'd pick up and leave you, and I most
definitely didn't think she'd try to follow me down to Florida.
Truth is, I haven't seen or talked to her in months. I cut her crazy
ass loose right after she showed up at my door with suitcases."

Looking across the table, I thought about Dana. In a
splash of seconds, thoughts of her and Luther stormed forth and
flashed scenes that may or may not have ever happened. But as
quickly as those visions appeared, they were interrupted and
quelled by the reality in front of me. Here was Luther White,
a worn-down blues lothario living on inflated reputation and
echoes of old applause, a guy waddling around tattered barbeque tables and clutching faded glories. Such dwindling power
could still hook him a lady now and then, and Dana was one of
those ladies. Maybe she'd turned into just that, or maybe she was
always such a woman, waiting to break free of the version of her

I'd created. Maybe I'd simply ignored this spontaneous, reckless Dana, the one who'd leave a boyfriend, job or husband with a shift in the breeze. She made her own decisions; she chose her own direction. She followed her own impulsive instincts, and those instincts led her toward the crowded arms of a rusted icon. In that moment, I wasn't upset about Dana. I simply felt sorry for her.

"So what now? What is it you want me to say to you?" I said. "That we're cool? That I understand why you fooled around with my wife? That I have any clue how imbalanced she had to be to chase after an old, broken-down fucker like you?"

This drew Luther's glare, wide-eyed and intense across the table. After he let this land and penetrate, he eased back with a deep breath and collected himself.

"You know what, Johnny? I can't make you understand what happened. I just want you to know that I'm sorry about it, about everything. And I'd like the chance to make it up to you."

"There you go again. You honestly think there's something you could do for me to make this right?"

"That's not for me to decide, baby. Like I said, I can't make you feel any other way than you're going to feel. I can only offer you an opportunity. I can offer you a chance at something you've never had before. That's the best I can do to make amends."

"What are you talking about?"

"Been getting some calls about you over the last few weeks, since you decided to dust off that Martin of yours and return to the Nighthawk. Some of my old New York label contacts have been reading about you in the *Gazette*. Some even saw footage from one of your shows on that YouTube and wanted to know if I'd ever heard of you."

"And what'd you tell them?"

"I told them you used to be a hell of a picker, one of the best in the city. But shit, I didn't know you were back out there until my phone started ringing."

"Had some shit going on that I needed to work through," I said. "Did you tell your industry buddies about your role in that?"

He leaned back in his chair again, annoyed and flustered.

"Ah hell, I should've known how this thing was going to go down. Sheep don't stray far from the flock, eh Finn?"

"Can you cut through the crap, Luther?" said Finn. "Skip the bullshit build-up and get to what you want to tell us."

"All right, fine." Luther sat up straight again, folded his hands on the table. "What I have is a real simple proposition, straight up. I want you guys to come in here and play a show. With me."

I looked to Finn, then back to Luther.

"Excuse me?"

"I'm talking about a one-night only event that will get these industry folks in here and get Buffalo chattering. If we team up, we could give this city one of the best shows they've ever seen."

"Jesus, that Florida sun must've melted your perception of reality," I said. "What alternate universe are you living in?"

"A universe where golden opportunities are scarce, baby. In a world where it's harder to find success than bury a grudge," he said, employing his soft, empathetic gaze again. "Look, I get it. You both think I'm shit, and that's cool. That's your right, and you wouldn't be dead wrong in thinking it. I'd still like to try and make things straight by giving you a shot at something brighter. To give you a chance at the ticket I could never cash."

"And what's in this for you?" said Finn. "Pardon me for not swallowing this selfless offering whole, but what are you getting out of this?"

"C'mon, Father Finn. You should know why I'm doing this. After a man sins, he repents. This is my attempt at atonement, baby. Nothing more."

"Nothing more?" said Finn. "Not the chance to stuff your bar with customers, fill your pockets with cash? Not the chance to score a little exposure at our expense? To shine under Johnny's light before your bulb burns out?"

Luther laughed.

"So you think I'm trying to hitch a ride? Me? If anything, I'm giving your boy here a shot to shine under my light, baby. Whether I'm on top or not, I'm still Luther White. This is *my* city. People still come into this joint to see me do my thing, to see me under that spotlight while I deliver Buffalo's blues. That shit ain't never gonna change. This shit between the three of us? It can change if you let me make things right."

"I wish I could believe your word. I do," said Finn. "I wish our history didn't prevent me from believing anything you say."

"And I can't make you believe. I know that, but I can still try. I can offer you this show, this one night in front of folks who can take your boy to the next level. If it goes down the way I think it can, it'll be a step in the right direction. Maybe a step past some of our old shit, too. What do you think?"

"Luther, I'm a forgiving man. I am, but it doesn't mean that—"

"Wait," I interrupted, putting my hand on Finn's shoulder before looking across the table. "We'll do it."

"What?" said Finn. "Johnny, you don't know what—"

"We'll do it, but with two conditions in place."

"Okay," said Luther. "Name 'em."

"One, our night's take, as well as all the money from the door and the bar, go to St. Jude's Community Center. We'll play it as a benefit show."

"And the other?"

"You make a personal donation to the center on behalf of the White Room, to sponsor the creation of future music programs."

"A donation? How much we talking?"

"Somewhere in the ballpark of five grand."

He sat up tall, opened his eyes wide and let out a hearty, booming laugh.

"Shit," he said. "So that's how much forgiveness is going to cost me?"

"I didn't say anything about forgiveness. But this price will buy you one thing."

"And what's that?"

"A cleaner conscience," I said. "Like you said, you can't make us feel anything. By doing these things with this show, you can at least feel better about yourself. You can feel like you've done something right."

I sat up straight and locked in on Luther as he considered my proposition. At the same time, I could feel Finn seething next to me, staring red-hot anger into the sweat-drenched side of my scalp. He had things to say, objections to shout so loud they'd startle biker couples and drown out juke tunes from Vaughn or Wolf or Muddy Waters. With Luther settled, staring and considering, Finn sat silent. He swallowed his resentment and, instead, waited with me for something positive to ease from Luther's legendary lungs. After seconds passed like hours, something finally slipped forth.

"Okay, baby," said Luther. "If this is what it's going to take, this is what it's going to take. You and old man Leary here have got yourselves a deal. As for the show's date, how does next Saturday night sound? Too soon?"

"Nope," I said. "That night sounds fine."

"Good. I can have my people here start to get the word out on Monday, call the local radio stations and get some flyers up in here and around town. But there's still one more thing we have to do."

"And what's that?" I said.

Luther leaned forward, grabbed one of the waiting whiskeys and held it up in front of his face.

"We still got to have this drink. What do you say?"

I looked to his raised shot and the Jameson bottle at the center of the table. Flanking its green glass were two shots of whiskey, simmering, teasing and tempting. Instead of reaching for one of them, I noticed to Finn, slumped in his chair and staring at the White Room's dusty wooden floor planks beneath him. When I glanced back at Luther, I saw him still holding his shot, raised and waiting. I pushed away from the table, arose from my chair and left him in that position.

"Save it," I said. "If the show's a success, if we make a little money for St. Jude's, then maybe we'll have something to toast. This? This little back-and-forth we just had? I wouldn't toast it with a sip of fucking birch beer."

"Suit yourselves," said Luther. He hoisted the hot, stinging booze, gulped it down, winced, gritted his teeth and slapped the tabletop three times to rattle the bottle and remaining shots. When Finn stood from his seat to join me, we turned our backs on Luther and walked toward the door. As I pulled the handle and held the door open for Finn, I heard Luther's booming voice fill the bar behind us.

"Johnny Nolan and Luther White. Together in the White Room on Saturday night!"

I didn't turn around to acknowledge the rhyme. I simply nodded to myself and followed Finn out the door.

21

When we were young and running
We'd race beneath blue skies
Never thinking 'bout the days
When worry'd fill our eyes
-"On The Run" by J. Nolan

July Mondays are a relaxing time in Niagara Square. City Hall workers and downtown attorneys use their summer months to take extended vacations, to find their quaint lake cottages at nearby Sunset Bay or Crystal Beach. This massive vacancy benefits guys like Pete and me, guys around for the majority of the summer months to bask in the warm temperatures and peaceful work environment. On the days leading up to the fourth of July, Niagara Square could resemble a lakefront ghost town, as car and foot traffic relocates to beaches and suburbs for nights of hot dogs, Budweisers and bottle rockets. On one of these weekdays, Pete and I could've easily split a lunchtime chill of Canadian in the shadows of City Hall. Instead we found ham sandwiches, cigarettes, a Monday *Gazette*, and a McKinley Monument bench to enjoy one of these sun-soaked pre-Independence Day afternoons.

"Can I ask you a question?" Pete was chewing on a bite of his sandwich and wagging the *Gazette*'s Sports section at me. "Do you think it's wrong that I don't want to raise my Mia to be a Buffalo sports fan?"

"Why?"

"Why?" He accidentally spit some of his sandwich onto the pavement. "Because I don't want her to go through the same excruciating pain I've been trudging through my entire life. I mean, look at this shit." He smacked the paper with the back of his hand. "Right after the Sabres tank another season, we're about to welcome another pile of shit Bills team. Christ, I haven't heard of half these fucking guys on their training camp roster."

I took a bite of my sandwich and chewed.

"C'mon, man," I said. "You know you can't do that. We were born into this, so we have to stick it out and hope they discover some of their old magic. Besides, who you gonna have her back? The Flyers? The Patriots? You'd never be able to side with something you hate."

Pete wasn't looking at me. He was glaring at another newspaper section he'd flipped to as I sat preaching loyalty and inconvenient commitment. After a moment of silence passed, he looked up to me and disappointedly shook his head. He pulled out the Entertainment section, rolled it up and held it in front of me.

"Can't side with something you hate, eh? And why not?" He tossed the section into my lap. "Looks like you are."

"What are you talking about?"

I picked up the paper from my lap and opened it to read the article's headline at the page's right sidebar. *Nighthawk Nolan To Unite With White: Dynamic Duo Team For Saturday Benefit Show.*

"So I have to read about this shit in the goddamn *Gazette* again?" he said. "I'm not expecting you to tell me about every one of your shows, but this? A show with Luther? Have you lost your fucking mind?"

"It's for St. Jude's," I said. "They're in desperate need of money, and Luther's the only guy in town who can help me deliver the donations they need. I was going to tell you about it."

"When, Nolan? When were you going to tell me? Next Monday, after this deal with the devil's done? Christ, you should be down at the White Room beating this guy's ass, not backing him on guitar."

"You think I'm happy about this? I'm not, but what other choice do I have? Do you have another way I can raise about twenty grand by playing my guitar for three hours? That's what I can take to St. Jude's from this deal. That's how I can keep the center running."

"At what cost? Your dignity? Your pride? Your shame? The minute you step on stage with that fucker, you flush it all down the toilet. You can't do that, man."

"He's right, Johnny."

Pete and I turned from our bench seats to see Sam, wearing a white tank, khaki shorts and low-top black Chuck Taylors, walking toward us with Otis. His tongue was wagging under the bright sun as he found a spot on the ground next to our bench. Sam pulled a dish from her backpack, filled it bottled water and watched Otis lap up it up before she unclipped his leash so he could settle and rest. She walked to stand in front of us, holding the dangling leash in her right hand.

"Hey," I said. "You know Pete, right?"

"Sure. You're not feeling sneezy today, are you? If so, I'll keep my distance."

His shook his head while his mouth held bits of his sandwich.

"No, no," he said. "But let me swallow this bit of food, just in case. I don't want to accidentally cover you in ham."

They both laughed before Sam looked to me.

"So, you have some lunchtime left? Enough time to take a walk with me and Otis?"

"Is this about the Luther show?"

"What do you think?" She pulled her own *Gazette* Entertainment section from her backpack and held it up.

"Yeah, let's take that walk."

Sam stuffed the water bowl and newspaper into her backpack, and we took Otis for a walk up to Lafayette Square. Once we crossed over Main Street's Metrorail tracks, she unleashed her dog, pulled a tennis ball from her backpack and tossed it across the square for him to fetch. I stood next to her, watching Otis dart around trash barrels and fallen tree branches to retrieve the fuzzy ball and return it, dripping with slobber. Over and over again, he found every toss and returned it to where we stood. And right after he dropped the slimy ball in Sam's hand, he'd ready himself for the next throw. After she hurled him his ninth toss, she turned to me.

"Can I ask you something?"

"Sure."

"You ever wish you were a dog? Even for a moment?"

"I don't think so," I said. "You?"

"Oh, sure. Sometimes, I look at Otis and wish we could switch places, if only for a day."

"Why?"

"Well," she said, "take this little game of fetch we're playing here. Otis seems to be *really* enjoying the repetitious act of finding the ball and returning it to me. He's not wondering why he enjoys the act; he doesn't even seem to be considering it. He's just gearing up and doing it. He loves it, and anyone who walks by can see that."

"Like the joy you feel as a little kid."

"Right," she said. "But when you grow up, doing those things you enjoy grows more and more complicated. You think about why you do these things and whether you even have the time to devote to them. You think about the money, people and repercussions associated with these things. Eventually, the analysis can wear you down and—"

"Diminish the things you once loved so much."

"Exactly."

"I get it, sure," I said. "So if you were Otis for a day, you would—"

"Bask in the pure, unbridled joy he feels every day, without the complications or concessions usually associated with achieving that enjoyment. Understand?"

"So this is about the Luther show, right? In order to feel the joy of helping children enjoy music, I have to sacrifice my dignity by sharing a stage with the guy. That's what you're driving at?"

"I am, but I'm also talking about me," she said. "In order for me to keep feeling that joy of working at St. Jude's, I have to let you do this. I have to watch you endure something you hate while doing what you love, and I don't want you to do that. I don't want you to have to make this sacrifice."

"Sometimes people make sacrifices to get to where they want to be, to do what they want to do," I said. "Look at the tree over there."

I pointed to the bare spot amid the crisp, leafy branches of our infamous oak tree, the one Sam accidentally set ablaze on that summer night over four years back. It would always stand as an emblem of our past recklessness, of the nights when the music and the scene were one and the same. Now the music and the scene were separate, with one multifaceted and the other left behind.

"Do you know what music was to us back then? It was a vehicle," I said. "It got you out to the Nighthawk for a scene. It put me on a stage and gave me a status. Sure, it inspired and entertained us, but more than anything, it classified us. It gave us an identity, and we needed that. Now? Now we've matured past that point, and we both need the music for more. It runs through our veins and fuels our lives, our souls. Whether I pluck a string on my guitar or hear Springsteen sing about the skeleton frames of burned out Chevrolets, I feel that simple joy you're talking about. I feel that intrinsic warmth rip through my body and numb my scalp. Four years ago, I didn't understand the ability I have to pass this feeling on to others. Four years ago, you probably didn't realize that you could do the same for those kids at St. Jude's, did you?"

"No. And honestly, the way I lived my life four years ago, you're lucky I didn't set you on fire."

"Fair enough," I said. "But here we are, with the chance to keep growing in this new, safer direction. Wouldn't you like to continue on this path?"

"Sure I would, but—"

"Then let me do this. Let me deal with this because, in the end, it'll be worth it."

"And you're sure there's not another way?"

"I don't think so."

A full moon illuminated the downtown waterfront's Canalside corner on the fourth of July. Thousands of mothers, fathers, children and young couples filled spread quilts across grass expanses and sat waiting for Buffalo's annual Independence Day fireworks. Food vendors lined the area's sidewalks, selling hot dogs, fried dough and draft beer. Local bands filled the warm lake breezes with music, singing soul standards and Bob Seger covers from a stage set at the edge of the excavated commercial slip of the Erie Canal. Most of the collected crowd relaxed amid the festivities. Others spent their night letting loose, rhythmically clacking flip-flop soles atop cobblestone streets and boardwalk planks.

  Meg and I were sitting in canvas camping chairs atop a blue blanket, sipping draft beers as Mickey and Brendan gathered elsewhere with members of their St. Stephen's gang. Since we could see they were safely having their own fun, eating fried dough with their group near the stage, we could be at peace with the sights and sounds of another waterfront holiday. And in the midst of this rare relaxation and privacy, I was free to discuss things with Meg she wouldn't freely talk about around the boys—like the recent run of good fortune in her dating life.

  "So at the risk of jinxing things, how's it going with Ray?"

  "Things are going well, though I appreciate your superstition," she said. "I'm constantly knocking on wood when talking about this relationship."

  "How long are you guys going on now?"

  "Steady? About six months." She mockingly knocked on the side of her head. "Actually, we're planning on going out for dinner this week to celebrate. I was going to ask you to sit with the boys, if you don't mind."

  "I don't mind at all. As long as your date's not Saturday night, we're good."

  This triggered a pause, a moment for the conversations of strangers and sounds of Seger to fill our shared space. Meg and I had talked about the upcoming show throughout the week. We'd weighed the show's opportunities against its negatives and, every time, the opportunities won. St. Jude's would get some financial breathing room; that was certain. There would also be the chance to impress an independent label rep or two. If I did, maybe some original Johnny Nolan material could find a place on Record Theater shelves. Maybe the lyrics I scribbled down in my kitchen could eventually emanate from coffee shop speakers on Allen Street. Maybe. Possibly.

Aside from helping St. Jude's, the only guarantee I had was Finn's reluctant participation. We hadn't talked much since I made the deal with Luther, since we walked out of the White Room in silence. I knew he wasn't happy about it, but I also knew he wouldn't derail the show. He was too selfless to let his own objections stand in the way of aid for St. Jude's, a place that laid the foundation for his vocational path. And as our uncle, he always put Meg and me first. He always watched our backs as we walked forward, and this time wouldn't be any different.

"You know Finn's trying to protect you, right?" said Meg. "He's protecting you the way he always has, the way he always will."

"I know, but who's he protecting me from? Luther? You think I need to be reminded of why I shouldn't trust the guy? After all the shit he's pulled over on me, I think I've seen it all."

She leaned back in her chair, took a short sip of her draft and looked to the moon.

"That's just it," she said. "You haven't."

"What are you talking about?"

"Guess you still don't know what happened with those two."

"No. Do you?"

"A little bit, yeah. Mom told me about it a while back, but she told me to never tell you. She was afraid you'd be upset."

"So what happened?"

"Back when Finn was working at St. Jude's, he was playing with Luther pretty regularly. During the day, Finn would teach kids how to play the guitar or piano over at the center. At night, he'd back Luther around town, at whatever blues hole he was headlining. And back then, most of the kids who hung around at St. Jude's were huge Luther White fans, remember?"

"Of course I remember," I said. "I was one of them."

"Since Finn and Luther were pretty tight, he asked him to show up at the center one Saturday and perform for the kids. Finn's idea was that Luther could show up, play a few tunes, and maybe teach the kids a thing or two on the guitar. After he promised to be there, the day was all set to happen."

"Yeah, I remember that Saturday. Luther never showed up because he was really sick."

"That's the thing," she said. "He wasn't sick. Finn just told everyone that to cover for him. What really happened was Luther went on a crazy bender and simply blew off the day at St. Jude's. And he never even called Finn; he just didn't show. Later that day, after all these disappointed kids left the center, Finn went over to Luther's apartment to get an explanation. Instead, he was met at the door by a cloud of pot smoke and two half-naked women."

"What did Finn say?"

"He walked in and found Luther drunk and smoking a joint on his couch with another woman. When Finn tried to get answers, Luther just sat there and laughed it off, acted as if the day planned for these kids was no big deal. Instead of apologizing, he bragged about himself as these women surrounded him on the couch."

"And Finn just stood there?"

"For a minute or so, yeah—until he eventually hauled off and decked him. Sent Luther crashing through his coffee table. Then Finn walked out and found another existence."

"Another existence?"

"Father Finn," she said. "That was the event that pushed him into the seminary. That was the moment he decided he wanted to become a priest, and Luther was involved in that moment. That's what happened between them."

"So why wouldn't Finn tell me about this? I think we can agree that if there was ever a time to tell me, *now* is that time."

"We can agree, but I can't tell you why he's kept this from you. Like I said before, Finn's always protected us; it's what he does. And sometimes, family members keep things to themselves in order to protect each other."

"And you're saying this from experience?"

"As of this week, yes. I am."

She reached into her purse and pulled out a folded and crumpled obituary section from the *Gazette*.

"Why are you giving me this?"

"Scan down the last names and look at the D's."

When I found the name in bold type, it stared back at me. DOYLE, William. Former South Buffalo resident, deceased at age thirty-seven. No mention of his two children.

"Jesus, Meg. How did you find out about this? Who called you?"

"No one," she said. "I just happened to be flipping through the paper and it jumped out at me. I was going to wait until later to tell you about it, but—"

"So you haven't told the boys?"

She looked down at the stitched blanket beneath her brown sandals.

"Tell them what? That they'll never have the father they've never had? For all intents and purposes, their father's been dead for six years. Brendan knows him as the past and Mickey knows him as a myth. They're not looking for him, so why would I tell them he can't be found?"

"And what do you know him as?"

She paused for a moment, looked out over the Buffalo River and toward the outer harbor.

"A ghost," she said. "One who gave me my children and faded away. Everybody deals with break-ups differently, and that's how I eventually dealt with Billy leaving. I turned him into a goddamn ghost. The fact that he's now gone for good doesn't really change anything. Once someone's gone for long enough, they might as well be dead. If they're never coming back, what's the difference?"

"I'm starting to get that," I said. "Day by day."

"Out of sight, out of mind and, eventually, out of your life."

We let the surrounding sounds fill the space between us again as we took sips of our beers. I inhaled the thin froth in my cup and sat thinking about what Meg said, considering when even the mere recollection of Dana would cease. When would she simply turn into a memory that'd fade away with time? She was gone for good, but there were still those nights she'd haunt my dreams. She'd creep into scenarios I had no control over and startle me awake with her appearance. I'd envision her gaze or feel her touch, then lay wide-eyed, confused and sweat-drenched as I stared into darkness and thought about wasted days, days I'd never have back. She was gone, though the memory of her could still torture the scattered minutes of morning and leave me with questions. After another sip of beer, I turned back to Meg.

"So when did you stop thinking about Billy?"

"Stop?" she said. "I still think about him, but not *actually* him."

"I don't understand."

"I think about the guy I thought he was, the guy I wanted him to be. I think about the guy who took me to hockey games, the guy who burned Grateful Dead discs for me. The guy I thought would be my husband. I'll probably always think about that guy, the idea of him. But that guy died years ago, way before the name Doyle showed up in the goddamn *Gazette*. You know what I mean?"

I only needed a brief moment to consider the question.

"I do."

Meg smiled and turned to see Brendan and Mickey walking up the nearby cobblestone path to claim spots around our blanket and chairs that overlooked the harbor. As soon as the patriotic anthems began storming from large speakers on the performance stage, the darkened skies above were illuminated with green, red and blue explosions, with dancing particles darting high above docked fishing boats and shuttered grain elevators. Each eruption elicited expressions of awe on the faces of young children, happily looking heavenward for the next sparkling design, the next succession of pops and cracks. Huddled families sat clapping together, cheering together, laughing together. They took turns pointing and shouting and singing until the night's sky returned to its dark origins, void of bright colors and cacophony, only sprinkled with Queen City starlight and the shine of the moon. Another night's dramatic celebration of independence was in the books, and memory of it would exist until a greater event took its place.

I gathered our chairs as Meg pulled up our blanket, folded it and tossed it over her shoulder. We began walking with the dispersing crowd in a gang of four, over the narrow canal bridge and herded together as Meg nudged me in the arm.

"Hey, what do you have planned for the rest of the night? Do you have anywhere to be?"

"No. Do you want me to sit with the boys?"

"Would you mind? Since it's only ten, I thought I'd pop over to Ray's house and surprise him and his girls. They were planning on hanging out in their backyard to watch some neighborhood fireworks. What do you think?"

"Go. I'll take these two back in my car. Hey guys," I said to Brendan and Mickey, a few steps in front of us. "You're coming with me, okay?"

They looked back, nodded and kept shuffling along with the crowd. I patted Meg on the back before I waved goodbye and watched her veer toward her car parked off Perry Street. The boys and I broke through the masses, talking about the night's highlights of fireworks and music until we were in my Outback and headed toward South Buffalo. When I finally reached their driveway, I turned to see Brendan in the front seat and Mickey in the back, both asleep. I shook them both awake, led them into the house and up to their bedrooms. The night had worn them down, filled them with so much excitement and spectacular imagery that it drained them. Like uncle like nephews, I guessed. Worn down from my week, I stood in their bedroom's doorway, watching them as they found their beds and collapsed into their covers. They were so tired; they couldn't wait to find rest. I loved those summer nights as a kid, those evenings when your days whipped you into exhausted submission. Back then, I was tired from un-questionable joy. Adulthood introduced a new kind of fatigue.

I flopped onto Meg's living room couch and flipped on ESPN. Slowly but surely, my eyelids fluttered shut and I slipped into sleep as the television beamed baseball highlights. In that rest, what seemed like three minutes was actually three hours. What seemed like a head nod was deep, relaxed slumber, the kind that disoriented; the kind that elicited confusion once a hand nudged you awake. Awakened from such a snooze, you're initial-ly startled, frightened. When I awoke at two in the morning with Finn hovering over me, I experienced all of these feelings once he said my name.

"Johnny, Johnny. Wake up, kid."

I flinched and jumped back.

"What's going on? What are you doing here? What time is it?"

"It's a little after two. You have to wake up the boys and get them dressed."

I sat up straight and confused.

"Get them dressed? For what?"

"We have to take them with us, down to Mercy Hospi-tal," he said. "Meg's been in an accident."

22

As I played on that cracked sidewalk
Watched you dancing on our lawn
I never dreamed there'd be a day
When your dancing feet were gone
-"For Meg" by J. Nolan

There were only a few open chairs in Mercy Hospital's fourth floor waiting room. In the early morning hours after the fourth of July, the room's seats were filled with husbands and wives, girlfriends and boyfriends, sisters and brothers. Some were waiting for updates on patients who arrived at Mercy's doors because of careless accidents involving fireworks, alcohol, fists—or a combination of all three. Others awaited word on those brought to the hospital by non-Independence Day circumstances, victims of such occurrences as heart attacks or car accidents. I left this group to pace the adjoining hallway's linoleum and stare at the sprinkled dirt flecks embedded in its finish between sips of thin, Styrofoam-cupped coffee. Brendan and Mickey sat leaning against each other on the carpet in the waiting room's corner, sound asleep and covered with the royal blue Sabres blanket we brought with us. When my sight dizzied from staring at the floor, I'd look back to the waiting room to see if they were still asleep. At that hour, there was no way they'd start stirring.

Hours earlier, when Finn and I woke them up in their beds and dressed them for the hospital, we told them Meg had been in a little accident, but not to worry. She'd be fine, and we just needed to be at Mercy so we could bring her home once she was released. We had no idea if she was going to be okay. We only knew what the hospital's nurse told Finn over the phone. Meg had been in a two-car accident, broken her left arm and leg, and suffered severe head trauma, which triggered a seizure when she first arrived at the emergency room. Since then, she'd been stabilized and was responsive, two points that gave us both sighs of relief.

  The nurse couldn't tell us how the accident happened, and she had no idea why Meg was driving around alone at the time of the crash. These were just two of the questions Finn and I wanted answers to as we emerged from the elevator and approached the fourth floor reception desk. Instead of joining him in tandem to talk with doctors or nurses familiar with the situation, I let him take the lead. He knew some of the hospital staff through St. Stephen's and every one of the hospital's Sisters of Mercy. If he found it necessary, he knew he could name-drop to get the best possible treatment for Meg, and the most complete information for us. Appropriately, a doctor and nurse who he knew greeted him at the receptionist desk. After I watched him speak to them, watched him explain why he was there in the early hours of the fifth of July, I took the boys to the waiting room and settled them in.

  The boys were asleep as I was pacing, still waiting for Finn to return as beams of morning sunlight began to sneak through Mercy's curtains and blinds. I was longing for answers while walking across those goddamn tiles again, smelling those same sterilized scents of hanging plastic and clean sheets, scents that filled the memory of nearly every traumatic event of my life. When thoughts arose of my mother and father's last minutes, that plastic smell rose with them, returned to waft under my nose. When the events surrounding Dana's miscarriage flashed forth, the aroma of detergent, bleach and clean pillow cases rushed with them, initiated an odd dance in which suffering could ignite the senses.

After I took another sip of coffee, I felt a hand on my shoulder. Finn.

"So how is she?"

"It looks like she's going to be okay," he said. "Doctor I talked with said her condition is nothing short of a minor miracle, so we should be thankful for that."

"So this is good news."

"Pretty much, yeah. Aside from a few concessions."

"Concessions?"

"Right," he said. "First, there's her leg. She busted it in multiple places, so she's going to have to go through some extensive rehab if she ever wants to run through Caz Park again."

"What else?"

"The head trauma. Meg doesn't remember the accident, and she doesn't remember getting rushed to the hospital. She's responsive and coherent now, but with that memory loss, and with the seizure she suffered so soon after the accident, the doctor thinks it's likely she'll develop epilepsy."

"How soon?"

"Could be weeks, could be months. Depends how her medication and treatment takes."

"So what does this mean for Meg? What does this mean for the boys?"

"It means they're going to need our help. She's going to need her family, and those boys need you to be what Billy Doyle never lived to be."

"So you know?"

"One of my parishioners told me about it yesterday," he said. "Guess he died in a car wreck on the 90 just east of Syracuse. I always thought it was clichéd to say God works in mysterious ways, yet here we are. One parent gets taken in a car wreck while the other is spared in a separate accident."

"More eerie than mysterious."

"Maybe. Either way, I'm thankful he answered my prayers, grateful he didn't take Meghan from us."

"Where is she now? Is she awake?"

"She is, with a nurse monitoring her. Down in room four twenty six."

I walked down to Meg's room as Finn headed back to the waiting room to sit with the boys. When I arrived at the room, I looked past the open door to see the back of a husky nurse, her long braided ponytail hanging over her whites while checking Meg's blood pressure. Though the nurse blocked most of my sister from view, she didn't block her broken right leg, raised and stabilized above the bed. When she finished with Meg's blood pressure, the nurse walked from the bedside to reveal the full picture of my sister. There she was, right arm in a sling; bandages wrapped around her head; reddened bruises and scrapes across her face; a thin bandage across the bridge of her nose. A brown plush blanket was pulled up under her arms, keeping her warm even as South Buffalo's summer sun crept through her window and across her tiled floor. After I rapped lightly on her door, she turned her head slowly to the left and let a smile slip.

"Looks like you're still a terrible driver."

"Please don't make any jokes," she said. "If I laugh, it might feel like a migraine."

I walked to Meg's bedside and sat in an empty chair. I reached to grab her left hand and hold it. Looking at her for a few seconds brought about thoughts of what could've been, what might've happened. It would have been too cruel; too much to handle, too much to lose her. I knew it so certainly, so deeply, that a chill ripped from my stomach through my chest, down both my arms and into my eyes. Holding her hand and looking at her battered face, I couldn't stop the tears from slipping down my face and dropping off my chin as I gritted my teeth.

"Hey, hey, c'mon. Stop it," she hushed, patting my hand. "You're going to make me start bawling again. That's what got me in here in the first place."

"What are you talking about?"

"My eyes were so watered from tears I didn't see the oncoming headlights. That's the last thing I remember."

"You were crying?"

She turned away from the sunlight as she pushed the brown blanket down her chest.

"Let's just say we have another name to add to the Nolan Hall of Shame."

"Ray?"

"Yep. Walked into his backyard and, instead of his daughters, I found him in a lounge chair with another woman. Drove off screaming and crying, cursing. When I was wiping my tears, I saw some headlights swerving toward me and I hit the brakes. That's the last thing I remember before I woke up here."

"My God," I said. "You look okay. How you feeling?"

She mustered a brief smile before letting it fade away.

"Besides my throbbing head, arm and leg? I'm scared. Really scared. Did Finn tell you about the epilepsy?"

"He did."

"So what if it develops? What if I can't drive a car or go to work? And what about the boys?"

"What about them?"

"How the hell am I going to take care of them? How am I going to support them? I mean, I think it's obvious to both of us that finding a man isn't my strong suit, so I'm going to be in this alone."

I leaned forward to touch her arm.

"You're not alone, and you'll never be alone with those two. We'll get through this together, and we'll go forward together. Like we always have."

Meg's tears began dropping to cascade over her scrapes and bruises, to slide down to the cut on her lip. She tried to dry the tears, but when she touched her face, realized it was too painful to wipe. Instead she patted my hand again, smiling and squinting as scattered sunbeams filled the floor space of her room.

When the nurse returned, she said the doctor would be in momentarily to run some more tests, so I let her and Meg be. I headed down the hall to the stairwell that led to the street. I found a spot outside under the sun, pulled out and lit a cigarette in the thick summer breeze. I took the first drag, heard the stairwell door open and felt Finn's hand on my shoulder.

"Can I bum one?"

"Who's with the boys?"

"One of the nuns," he said, then pulled a pack of matches from his pocket and lit the smoke I gave him. "They're still asleep, but she's watching over them. Must be nice to be able to sleep like that. I haven't slept like that in years."

"Me neither."

I took another drag and exhaled the smoke upwards.

Watching the early morning traffic pass on Abbott, I thought about what I said to my sister, how she'd never be alone. It would take more than words to be there, to back up a statement uttered among emotion and pain and relief. It would take more than a bedside hand pat to help her, to raise her boys. Before I sat next to Meg in that hospital bed, I found it easy to accept the nice comments about being a good uncle. It was routine to brush off hyperbolic statements of how I was the only father Brendan and Mickey would ever need. Standing in silence with Finn as we both dragged off Camel Lights, I knew those kind words would no longer be compliments. They would be expectations.

"Can I ask you a question?" I said to Finn.

"Shoot."

"What would you have done if my parents died when Meg and I were younger?"

He took a drag, raised his eyebrow.

"Younger? Like if you were kids?"

"Yeah. Like right when you entered the priesthood?"

"What do you think I would've done? I'd have dropped out to take care of the two of you."

"Just like that?"

"Just like that," he said. "Just like you would step up if Meg needed you to take care of those two boys."

I held a look at Finn, took another drag.

"*Needs*," I said. "This is happening. This is no longer a 'what if' situation."

"And it's not a matter of whether you'll step up. You already have, dammit. Why don't you see this? You're the closest thing to a father those kids are *ever* going to have. You love them, you care for them and you protect them. That's what a father does, and that's what you do for those boys. You always have."

"I was just trying to be a good uncle. You've done a pretty good job at showing me how to do that."

He dropped his Camel to the pavement.

"Pretty good? What haven't I done?"

I glanced up at him, finished my smoke and stepped it into the sidewalk.

"Your incident with Luther," I said. "Why didn't you just tell me?"

He peered at the sky, waiting for words to fall from above and drop into his mouth.

"A kid's hero is a very precious thing. They stand taller than the mere humans they actually are. When all that happened, Luther was your hero. He was your music idol, someone you wanted to emulate. You didn't idolize him as a man. You idolized him as a guitarist, so I had no reason to tell you about the flawed and selfish man he was. Boys need to believe in their heroes, and I didn't want to distort your version of him."

"But that was years ago. Why didn't you tell me during my old stint at the Nighthawk, or even over these past few years when I'd hung things up?"

"I guess I didn't want my grudges to become your grudges, though they came to join each other anyway," he said. "And I hoped that by not telling you, I'd somehow protect you from the truth about him, about what he really stands for. The guy flushed his promise and decided to lean on his musical clout as means for local power. I was close to finally hashing over that past the other night. I swallowed it again for the sake of you and St. Jude's."

"I appreciate you protecting me. I do," I said. "But now that I know this, I wonder whether we're swallowing too much.

I mean, what message are we sending by playing with him on Saturday? What are we saying to those two boys upstairs?"

"That compromise is rarely convenient."

"Sure, but are we compromising too much? Is Luther taking more than he's giving?"

"That's a question you have to answer for yourself," he said. "After I walk off that White Room stage, I'll still be Father Finn Leary. Who will you be?"

He patted me on the shoulder and walked back into the stairwell, back up to the waiting room to sit with Brendan and Mickey. Standing on the sidewalk, I thought about my guitar again, what it felt like in my hands. The polished wood of the neck in my left palm; the raised frets and copper strings on my blistered fingers; the orange pick clenched between my right index finger and thumb. I knew what it meant to be on a stage, to look out at young men and women waiting to be lifted with the flick of a string or exhale of a vocal. Even on those old Night-hawk nights—when one Skynyrd cover could get me two women and three shots of Jameson—I needed Deirdre on my lap or hanging at my waist. I needed the sounds that echoed from her, just like I needed to feel the reciprocated singing and stomping each sound demanded. I could never control such a gift; I could never wield it solely for money or power. From the first time I strummed that scuffed, second-hand Yamaha guitar Finn bought for me as a kid, I never controlled a chord. The chords controlled me.

Later that day, after Finn and I took the boys in to see Meg, we left the hospital and went back to their house. He agreed to sit with them so I could take a drive to the White Room.

I parked my car out front and walked through the bar

doors to find the place dank and empty, with only the hum of a Clapton guitar solo filling the barroom. Standing along with the vacant barstools, I gave a shout to see if anyone was around. Seconds later, I heard the clacking of shoes emerge from the back office and into the barroom.

"Johnny Nolan," he said. "What's happening, baby?"

Dressed in a white T-shirt and black slacks, he walked behind the bar to grab the Jameson bottle and two shot glasses, then thumped them down on the bar.

"After that little taste of Irish whiskey I had the other night, I haven't been able to get enough of this shit. Join me in one?"

"No thanks," I said. "I don't plan on staying long."

"That's the good thing about shots: they pour quick and hit hard," he said, filling the first shot glass. "Last chance."

"I'm good."

"Suit yourself." He ripped the shot back and exhaled loudly. "Woo, that felt good. And that's just a taste of how good tomorrow night's going to feel. You ready or what?"

"Actually, that's why I'm—"

"You been reading the paper? I don't think this city is gonna be able to handle us. They're not going to know what hit 'em, baby. And these label reps? They're not ready for us, either."

"Us?"

"Well, you," he said. "But together? We gonna be some-thing special."

He stood before me, smiling and still clutching the bottle of Jameson. This was the man who was once my hero, more important to me than the President of the United States or Sabres hockey. This was the man whose electric presence put a guitar in my hands and dreams in my head. And there he stood, a victim of his own neglect, a fatality of his own actions. At one time, the music flowed through his veins to pulsate his chest, to fuel his every move. As he stood before me in his stained white tee, with years around his eyes and gray hairs on his head, those times were gone.

"Luther, did I ever tell you about the autographed program you gave me when I was a kid? The one you handed me after you and Finn played a show at LaSalle Park?"

"I don't think so, no."

"I put it in a frame and hung it over my bed. I'd look at that program every night, just stare at your signature and play my guitar until my fingers bled. You were my hero. My idol," I said. "But that was before the night outside the Nighthawk. The night when three of your regulars knocked me around for stealing your thunder."

"Johnny, you know I—"

"I even heard one of them whisper, 'that was for Luther' before they left me lying on the sidewalk. After I dragged myself home that night, you know what I did? I took that frame off my wall and smashed it to pieces. Then I took the program out to the street and set in on fire, just let it burn and curl up on the pavement. And from the minute that program turned to ash until the moment I came in here last weekend, I vowed to hate every last thing about you."

"So what are you saying?" he said. "Why are you telling me this?"

"I'm telling you this because last weekend was a mistake. And as I look at you now, a rusty old man shooting whiskey in an empty bar, I know that. I know who you really are, and I know one thing about me," I said. "As long as I live, I'll never share a stage with a desperate, wasted fuck like you."

I matched his incensed glare as Clapton scored the tension, filled the empty barroom with a series of single-stringed epiphanies. The sporadic chords encircled us until his stare succumbed to reluctant acceptance. He dropped his focus and spun toward the bar's liquor bottles, silent. It was time to head for the exit, to leave the man with his Irish whiskeys and Puerto Rican rums. I walked to the door, pulled the handle and, after one last glance, turned to leave the great Luther White behind.

23

Days went by waiting for a night
When the lights would dim and I'd hold you tight
Right on stage where I knew you'd be
The one big moment that could set me free
-"Night" by J. Nolan

I walked into Cigarettes & Coffee to see Sam, sitting at a table with a cup of coffee and a copy of *Artvoice*. On a Friday afternoon, the place was mostly empty, aside from two white-teed hipsters staring at their silver, colorfully stickered MacBook laptops as Sam Cooke's vocals about birth by the river swallowed the room. At four o'clock, it was too early to entertain the shop's usual, intimate after-work crowd, the quiet, reserved types who skipped the Happy Hour specials on Chippewa and Hertel. And in the middle of summer, it was short on its usual student squatters, those who sipped Americanos and stayed for hours. In the middle of this vacancy was Sam, waiting to be interrupted.

"Mind if I sit?"

"Hey," she said, looking up from her paper. "I thought you were with the boys back at the house?"

"I was. Finn's there now."

"Any news on Meg?"

"She's stable, but they're going to keep her at Mercy for a couple more days. We decided to leave her be for the night and go back tomorrow morning."

"Sounds like good news," she said. "What are you doing

here?"

"Was kind of in the neighborhood. Had to come down-town and take care of some business with Luther."

"Business?"

"About tomorrow night," I said. "I'm not going to do it."

She pushed her paper to the side and cradled her coffee cup above her chest, so the steam drifted up under her chin.

"So what happened?"

"After this morning and today, all that time thinking in the hospital, I decided I couldn't go through with it. I couldn't bring myself to stand with him, no matter what the payoff."

"You're right, and I'm glad you're not doing it," she said. "So what do we do now? What about St. Jude's?"

"Think I have a plan, but it all depends."

"Depends on what?"

"You."

"Me? Why me?"

"You are a decision maker at this coffee shop, right?"

"I am."

"What if I asked you to bump this week's Saturday Serenade to make room for an intimate performance by a certain local musician? Could you do it?"

Looking up at me, she let a grin slip, one that crept up her neck and slowly spread across her face. She took a sip of coffee through that smile and leaned back in her chair.

"That all depends."

"On what?"

"On you."

I sat up straight, decided to play along.

"Okay," I said. "What about me?"

"Do you plan on making this a relocated Nighthawk

show, or do you plan to come out from behind the covers? To take this night and fill it with your songs, your music?"

"I might lead in with a cover or two, but that's it," I said. "I want to drive this night with my own stuff. My own music."

"Really?"

"Really. Will you help me?"

"Johnny," she said, "you know I will."

Sam and I spent the next few hours inhaling coffee, making phone calls and sending out e-mails. First, I called Finn, told him of the new plan and change of venue. While he was pleased, he also stayed reserved; he said we'd talk more later. In the meantime, he'd call the rest of the band with the news. I called the Entertainment desk at the *Gazette* and told them the Luther show was cancelled, but that I was instead holding a solo benefit show for St. Jude's at Cigarettes & Coffee. After I chatted up their in-office reporter for a while, he committed to a mention about the show in Saturday morning's edition. Sam went on the café's website to post news of the show, then continued onto their Facebook and Twitter feeds to post info for their connect-ed friends, handles and associates. Replies to the news began flashing across social media to generate a local trending buzz and gain traction on other local music sites. Just like that, word was everywhere.

I was suddenly getting calls from Pete, Butch Strombone and Sues. News of the show was rolling over the high-top tables of downtown Happy Hours; it was swirling around the patios of Elmwood and through the darkened barrooms down Allen. John-ny Nolan at Cigarettes & Coffee on Saturday night. Ten dollars at the door. Be there.

St. Stephen's four o'clock Saturday Mass was packed, with more people piled into pews than at the Saturday vigils before Sunday Bills games. A soothing summer breeze cycled through the church's open doors and windows to keep parishioners relaxed while sitting in khaki shorts, sundresses and short sleeves. When St. Stephen's windows and doors were open, you felt like you were still outside, part of a late summer afternoon. The smell of bunched grass clippings drifted past pews atop the waft of charcoal-cooked Sahlen's. You didn't feel like you were sacrificing a day's waning minutes, time usually spent in porch swings or swimming pools. This is how Finn wanted his parishioners to feel. He wanted to see their contentment when he stepped off the altar draped in cool whites with another Saturday night homily to deliver. Sitting with Brendan and Mickey in one of the back pews, I looked around the church's sun-kissed interior to see a litany of relaxed shoulders and tanned, freckled skin, all waiting for Finn to speak.

"So I have great news for every one of you who are looking out our windows and doors and waiting to get back outside," he said. "Tonight's homily is going to be short—and sweet. Can I get an Amen?"

Laughs and claps and shouts of "Amen!" jumped from the pews, with even a few rare Catholic hoots tossed in for good measure.

"Now, it's going to be a short one because I'm going to assign some homework to each one of you, a three-part assignment you'll need to perform outside these walls," he said.

"First, as many of you already know, my niece Meg was involved in a serious car accident on the fourth of July. Thankfully, she's doing better today than she was two days ago, and I thank everyone who sent well wishes or asked about her status. But she's not out of the woods yet. She could use all the help she can get, so please keep her and her children in your thoughts and prayers."

I peered down to the boys and patted their shoulders. They were both tough kids, ones who merely glanced up at my touch before turning their attention back to their great uncle.

"Second, if you don't have any plans for this evening, I'd like to invite you to a little fundraising show I'll be performing with my young, talented and better looking nephew in the back there. Johnny Nolan, can you stand up and give a little wave?"

I stood up and embarrassedly raised my hand in the midst of turned heads and interested murmurs. Mickey even let a few claps slip before I looked down and shook him off.

"We'll be playing downtown on Allen at a café called Cigarettes & Coffee. All the money we can raise at the door and with donations will go to help St. Jude's Community Center, which is currently hurting for operating funds. As a lot of you know, I got my start over at St. Jude's, so I'd really appreciate it if you can come out tonight, bring a few friends and spread the word. In turn, you'll be treated to some great music and, in the process, fulfill the second part of your assignment."

Walking up the center aisle, Finn paused to exchange grins as parishioners sat relaxed and attentive.

"Finally, the third part is more of a thinking assignment, one I'd like you to consider over the next week. In that time, I want you to answer the following question: What makes you whole?"

He paused to survey the room, to connect with a few more people before continuing.

"What traits or interests or relationships make you into the person you are, the person who wakes up every day and comes into this church every week? Is it one thing, or is it a collection of things? And after you identify these items, can you say you're doing everything you can to preserve them?"

Tanned faces became pensive while listening to Finn's questions, considering their answers while he continued to speak.

"The reason I'm asking this question is because, sometimes, we tend to overlook the things we need as they're right in front of us. We spend so much of our lives chasing brighter things while ignoring the beautiful opportunities around us. We take our talents, faith or families for granted while not realizing that genuine fulfillment can be found in the complete appreciation and utilization of this trio."

He walked further through the silence and continued.

"Have all of our lives turned out the way we expected them to? Have we simply floated through storybook romances and Super Bowl-like triumphs? Probably not," he said, smiling. "But we're all here today, alive and kicking. We're all healthy and free to feel the sun on our faces. After you leave here today, I want you to think about how you got to where you are in life. Remember the people who have helped you get there, then reach out and tell each of them how much you appreciate them. And finally, cherish the talents that have steered you toward your current place in life. Embrace those gifts every day as you share them with others."

After he said this, he looked at me and winked.

"Every last one of us has only one life on Earth, one chance to touch and feel all the things given to us. When you walk back out into that sunlight, consider all the things that make your days worth living. Identify them, and make sure to keep them sacred. They give you strength. They illuminate your life's path. Understand this, and you'll never feel lost in darkness again."

Finn scanned the surrounding faces to connect a few more times, then swung around in his summer whites to head down the center aisle. When he reached the altar, he turned to face the congregation and raise his arms.

"Let us pray."

On Saturday night, microphones and stools were set up in front of the back wall of the coffee shop, right in front of the wall-size iconic 1967 picture of a sweating, pleading Otis Redding. Tables and chairs surrounded the performance area and lined the shop's red walls, barriers emblazoned with the framed vinyl and faded pictures of soul legends. Sam tucked spare chairs into open spaces and added additional seating on their sidewalk patio, outside the open windows and front door. By keeping everything open, she hoped she could generate interest on Allen Street, with passers-by halting to hear what was stirring inside Cigarettes & Coffee.

At about eight o'clock, people began to pay the ten-dollar cover before filing into the shop. The commotion built as the room filled with regular patrons from the Nighthawk and McGinty's, with parishioners from St. Stephen's and St. Jude's. Standing by the main counter, I watched Pete and his wife Tracy walk in. I watched Sues find a seat, then caught a slap to the back from Butch Strombone. He gave me a hug and told me he brought "the whole fucking bar" with him. While watching customers stream into the shop to fill the tables and chairs, I saw others walk straight to the cash register and drop extra dollars and coins into a large empty water cooler bottle, one Sam labeled with a sign that read "For St. Jude's" on the front of it. Leaning off to the side of the counter, I watched donations fall and bounce, settle and pile.

Standing amid the growing chatter inside and outside on the sidewalk and patio, I was met by Finn, who walked in through the shop's back kitchen door with Brendan and Mickey. Along with the boys, he brought his acoustic Fender, the chipped and scuffed one he now only revealed for special-occasion sermons or private strumming. I asked him to stash his piano expertise for the night and, instead, back me up on the Fender. He would be my band. The venue couldn't accommodate the sound and space necessary for the whole band, so Patty V and the boys agreed to join us as mere fans. It would be just Finn and me, one night only.

Together, we could get through the show. We would navigate through some covers and work through lyrics I scribbled on scraps of torn notebook paper, chords I'd jangled and taped in the privacy of my kitchen. Together, we could strum and pick and sing, bask in the intrinsic chills that regularly straightened the hairs on our forearms. Together, we would use our talents to make government drones dance and tattooed bartenders tap tabletops. We'd make parishioners clap and barflies approvingly grunt, inspire community altruism with blues riffs and rhyming verses. We'd embrace the musical abilities that made us whole, and we'd do it together. Just like before. Just like always.

When I was a kid, I looked up to Finn like a hero. I watched him play piano or guitar, watched him sweat on Buffalo stages while smashing keys or breaking Fender strings. But it wasn't his aura of fame I idolized. It wasn't his place under bright lights that impressed me. It was how he walked away from the lights as if they never shined on him. He never acted like those lights entitled him to anything. He simply treated them as a miraculous opportunity. When those lights dimmed, he'd walk off stage and find me, the little floppy-haired kid fascinated by his every move. We'd slap five and talk about the songs he played, talk about the notes, the chords and the progressions as others vied for his attention. When I grew older, he bought me my first album and first guitar, and sat with me for the first hours I explored every aspect of both. Despite his elevated status as either a local musician or liturgical celebrant, he was always right there to help guide me forward. With an open stool and unexpected responsibilities awaiting me, I turned to see him standing there again. Uncle Finn. Father Finn. Fiery Finn Leary.

"So where are we seating our V.I.P.'s?" he said with his hands on Brendan and Mickey's shoulders.

"To the left of the mixing board. I blocked off a table for the two of them."

"What do you think, men? Go up there and grab your seats."

They looked up to both of us, nodded and headed off.

"So how are they doing?" I said.

"They're okay. Mickey kept asking to see Meg, so we stopped over at Mercy to see her before we came down here. She's feeling a little better, and she said to say good luck."

"I wish she could be here."

"So does she. She asked if we could record the show for her."

"Already taken care of. Guy on the soundboard said he'd burn me a copy of the show, so we'll surprise her with the disc tomorrow."

"Good work," he said. "Also, got a call from St. Jude's earlier. They've been receiving donations through the mail all week, then had a bunch delivered in person today since news of our show ran in this morning's *Gazette*."

"Looks like we're on our way."

"Appears so. With more of those private donations, the door and that water jug over there, we might pull this off."

"Now all we have to do is play," I said. "So you're comfortable with the set list?"

"Sure, sure. We'll lead with that David Gray number to ease 'em in, transition into your songs, then finish off with the ambitious Springsteen cover. You feel like you're ready?"

"I'll get there. In the meantime, thanks for walking through this with me."

"Are you kidding?" He paused to let some silence dance between us for a few moments. "Can I be straight with you? Can I tell you some truth?"

"Sure."

"Before we go up there, before we get on those stools and look out at a night you created, I want you to know something," he said. "I want you to know that you're my hero."

"Thanks, but I—"

"No, no. Don't blow this shit off. Watching you through these past few months has been very special for me. Being part of it has meant even more. It seems like yesterday when I watched you play 'Satisfaction' on that little Yamaha of yours. Tonight, I get to watch you showcase your own words, your own music—and on your own terms. That alone makes you heroic. But watching you set such an example of perseverance in front of those boys up there? That makes you my hero."

He reached out his hand and pulled me in for a hug. My chest and spine tingled as the meaning of Finn's words flowed through both. When we broke apart, we exchanged slaps on the shoulder before composing ourselves as we stood waiting to take our place behind microphones. People were still filing in when

Sam crept up behind me and tapped my shoulder.

"So it's about time," she said. "I'm not sure we can legally accommodate many more bodies in this place, so whenever you're ready, get up there and make this happen."

I smiled, thinking of that old Luther White autograph that hung over my bed. Looking over Cigarettes & Coffee's attendance, seated and standing, hanging inside windows or idling on Allen, I knew it was time to make whatever was going to happen happen. I picked up my guitar case and nodded to Finn before we made our way through the crowd and found our places. When we got to the stools, we were showered with the same claps and cheers and hoots that regularly doused us at the Nighthawk. Casually dressed men and women yelled out my name and shouted for Finn, their voices rattling teaspoons and shaking ceramic mugs that hung near the café's main counter. Sam's quaint little coffee shop was full of more electricity than had ever accompanied a Second Saturday Serenade.

Finn and I acknowledged the crowd before we each sat down and settled in. I pulled Deirdre from her case, set her on my knee before I tuned her strings. Once they were ready to go, I looked to Finn, winked and pulled the mic down to my mouth.

"Wow," I said, scanning the crammed café and out toward the packed patio. "I know the coffee's good here, but this is ridiculous."

Young couples seated in front, back and middle let out laughs.

"Seriously, though, thanks for coming out to support us and, more importantly, St. Jude's. We're going to have a good time tonight so sit back, relax and enjoy. Can you hear me out there, smokers?"

Shouts and hoots returned through the open door and

windows, floating in atop Allen Street's summer breezes and exhaled Marlboro smoke to join the Costa Rican aromas inside. When the noise settled, I looked to Finn again and adjusted myself on the stool. Comfortable, I cradled Deirdre's rosewood neck in my left hand and strummed my first chords of the night with my right. Slowly, delicately and smoothly, I varied from an E to an E/A and E/G on the lead before reverting back to an E for Gray's first verse. I repetitiously fluttered across the strings, singing about wandering hearts and wings of time, about rising from ashes and stepping from shadows. Finn backed my lead with light rhythm as I implored patrons to remember your soul is the one thing you can't compromise. I closed my eyes while singing, squeezing the lids so tightly shut they ached when I opened them. When I did, I could see the crowd interested and attentive. A man in cargo shorts and navy Chuck Taylors tapped his canvas soles through chord shifts; a young woman in a yellow sundress nodded her dark brown locks to the romantic lyrics. With every note of music that eased from my Martin's mahogany, the song was becoming my own, just as hundreds of songs had before.

After I strummed Gray's last chord, applause streamed forth. I let it die down before I motioned thanks and turned to Finn.

"Ready?"

He looked to me, smiling.

"Make it happen, kid."

I smiled, then approached the mic again.

"So I've got some new material for tonight, songs finally ready to make their live debut. You ready to hear them?" I paused for some claps and cheers. "Hopefully you'll like listening to these as much as I liked writing them. If you think they're shit, please don't make a scene. Just try to sneak out of here quietly."

Another round of responsorial laughter ricocheted around the café. I counted off with four Doc Marten boot stomps and started into the cheery G, C and E combination of "Nights of You and Me #44." With my fingers shuffling around Deirdre's frets, I sang my scribbled lyrics about brown eyes and family ties, about a pick-up truck and Buffalo's tough luck. I looked down at the floor while strumming chords; I closed my eyelids when I leaned in to sing. Before the last verse, I unclenched my lids and took a peek at the crowd. To the right, a man stood in a Corona T-shirt, rocking back and forth on the balls and heels of his blue Nikes; to the left, a red-haired college-aged woman sat tapping her tabletop while her friends joined her rhythm with fingers on their thighs.

I looked to the two young boys sitting at the nearby table, the one that flanked our stools. Mickey smiled and waved when I glanced over. Brendan sat expressionless. He didn't connect with my gaze, and he didn't raise a hand or grin. Instead he seemed lost in a hypnotized stare fixated on Deirdre's frets. When I switched chords, his concentration moved to my fingers' new spot on the rosewood, like he was taking mental notes of the transitions. As he watched, he operated his own air guitar, twanging invisible strings and imprinting an imaginary finger-board with his slim fingertips. Finally, as if he could feel my stare scratching his forehead, he glanced up, stopped his motions and smiled.

I picked the song's last note and I kept my head down, staring at my boots' leather toe-tops. Looking past their laces and into the grooves between the café's floor tiles, my head was raised by a wave of claps and stomps and shouts, rolling from back to front and then back again. Scanning the crowd, I found

Butch Strombone, standing on a chair in a weathered leather vest as he repeatedly stomped his seat between blue-collar hoots. I found Pete and Tracy, clapping and whistling at a table. I found Sues in the back corner, crowded with cheering Nighthawk patrons. I peered through the faces to the café counter and found Sam, leaning on the cash register and nodding in my direction. When we connected, she raised her coffee mug in my direction, then set it down so she could cup her mouth and join the vocal barrage, validation that lifted my head, heart and soul.

And this is what it feels like to be alive. This is the love that turns Buffalo's harsh winter mornings into beautiful embraces; that turns Lake Erie's numbing winds into soft, romantic kisses. This is the support that balances exhausted bodies, that props open heavy eyelids. This is the encouragement that inspires, infuses and ignites childhood ambition toward a life of passion and purpose. This is what it feels like to step into the light.

"Thank you, Buffalo," I said into the mic. "Ready for another one?"

24

When the lights go out
You fight through the black
To turn on the lights
And take your life back
-"When the Lights Go Out" by J. Nolan

B rendan and Mickey would typically resist being inside on
the last Saturday of August. They'd prefer to be outdoors
with their St. Stephen's cohorts, crashing around Cazenovia Park
or other neighborhood locales in a street hockey game as their
summer vacation raced to its end. But weeks after my Cigarettes
& Coffee performance, they each decided to spend their last sun-
drenched summer Saturday somewhere else. They came downtown with me to fill seats next to a dozen young, aspiring guitar-
ists inside a small classroom at St. Jude's Community Center.

Sitting atop the teacher's desk at the front of the room,
I could see this semicircle of tweeners and teens, each with an
acoustic guitar resting on a lap or between legs. There were
scuffed Yamahas and Epiphones, beaten up Hohners and Taka-
mines and First Acts. There were guitars fashioning no brand
names at all, anonymous secondhand instruments in the grip of
neophytes raised among family room echoes of old folk heroes. They'd listened to strings picked by artists like Dylan and
Young, Morrison and Mitchell, Waits and Springsteen. And as
one particular song escaped stereo speakers, an emotion was injected into their bodies they couldn't explain or forget. It floated

into ears and shivered the roots of mussed hair, flowed down their necks and tickled their chests. One by one, they were transformed by a few minutes of chord progressions. One by one, these kids found their own guitars, intrigued by the possibility of jangling souls by strumming six strings.

I volunteered my musical services for these community center kids shortly after the café show. With that night's take and independent donations solicited from the show, St. Jude's earned enough cash to keep the center's programs rolling. I also had Sam selling the night's recorded performance at the café's counter, with all funds earned from sales going directly to program funding. Things were still tight, but the monies raised bought me, Finn, Sam and the rest of St. Jude's staff some time to come up with some bigger fundraisers in the future. In the interim, the center was open—and had a new music teacher.

"Okay," I said, hoisting Deirdre up to my waist. "Everybody grab your guitar and set your fingers on the fingerboard for a G chord. That means index finger on the A string, second fret, middle finger on the lower E, third fret, and ring finger on the high E, third fret."

One by one, each kid fumbled with his or her instrument, getting comfortable before aligning their fingers on the copper strings and twanging a cacophony of inharmonious racket through the room and out its windows. I cringed through the noise. I looked to Mickey as he sat watching his brother line up the chord on my old, childhood Yamaha. The guitar was scratched and chipped, but it was still good enough for a kid picking up a new hobby. When I listened to Brendan strum the chord a few times, I was thankful to hear at least one guitar in tune.

"Good, good," I said. "Now, take your fingers from the

G and set them for a C chord. That's your index finger on the B string, first fret, middle finger on the D string, second fret, and ring finger on the A string, third fret."

Relaxed kids in concert tees and cargo shorts balanced their axes, lined up the chord and strummed it repeatedly with teardrop-shaped picks. Some hit it just right to send the appropriate tone floating off mahogany, up to the St. Jude's classroom ceiling and out the windows to Delaware Avenue. Some struggled to strike the strings or plant their fingertips properly, sending a variety of off-kilter twangs and blongs bouncing off tiles. It was a start. It was their attempt at a functional transition between two sounds, between two places.

With time and patience and effort, each one could get there. All of them would be able to pick up their guitars, swing the straps over their necks and let the instrument dangle around their waists before sending out the G to C progression necessary to dance through the first verse of a song by Neko Case, Jeff Tweedy or Justin Townes Earle. With chords come confidence, and with the confidence will come presence. Boys and girls will become men and women, going from G to C and uniting with an A. They'll trade in their First Acts and Hohners for Gibson electrics, for Les Pauls and Fender Stratocasters. They'll down-pick power chords as sweat drops off their hair and soaks their fingerboard, playing with a speed so dizzying that it drives crowds to stomp floorboards, smash shoulders and inhale sixteen-ounce cans of Genny Cream Ale. And every now and then, one may look out through the hot shine of the red, blue and yellow bulbs. They'll gaze out into the multitudes to see the frenzy they've created, a mania generated from their fingers and wrists and, if only for a moment, they'll feel lifted higher than they've ever been hoisted. If only for a moment, they'll feel whole.

I stood watching the students get comfortable with the chords when I heard a knock at the classroom door. I turned to see Sam, Finn and Meg, all standing and smiling in the shadows from sunlight that beamed through the windows behind me. Sam waved me out into the hallway, so I put down my guitar and left the kids to continue their exploration.

"What's up? What's going on?"

"Well," she said. "Actually, Finn you tell him."

"Got a call this morning from the program director at WJCU, the radio station for John Carroll University outside of Cleveland. Apparently, some student from Buffalo brought a copy of the Cigarettes & Coffee show back to school with them, and the station's been playing it on air since classes started up two weeks ago."

"And?"

"And some of the songs have gotten pretty popular," he said. "Guess 'Nights of You and Me #44' and 'First Second Chance' are two of most requested songs at the station."

"That's great, but what does this mean?"

"It means they want you to come to campus and play," he said. "They're having a fall festival show there in October and want you to be a part of it. What do you think?"

"Sounds great, but what about the boys? What about Meg?"

Meg stood next to me, balancing on crutches as her facial bruises and scrapes had faded under an August tan.

"We'll be fine for a weekend," she said. "Besides, Sam has agreed to be on call that weekend for any emergencies."

I eyed Sam, who tilted her head and flashed a sweet grin.

"She has, has she?"

"Of course I did. This is a huge opportunity for you," she

said. "A college festival show with an established out-of-town audience? Some of the best musicians around here have never gotten that far."

"Name one."

"How about Luther White," said Finn. "Guy never broke through in Cleveland."

I looked to my uncle and matched his subtle grin. I turned back to the nascent strums of St. Jude's aspiring six-string saviors. Standing in the glow of Buffalo's August sunlight, I enjoyed the start of something beautiful.

Acknowledgments

Clash co-founder Joe Strummer once famously said, "Without people, you're nothing." The same is true about me. Without the collection of helpful family members, friends, professors, students, co-workers, and musicians who helped and/or influenced me over the last six years, I'd be nothing—and this novel simply wouldn't exist.

First, to my wife, family and friends. Thanks for your kindness and insight throughout this process. Your help was as simple as buying a round and as complicated as critiquing chapters. You listened to the whining and cursing and all the ideas that went with it—yet your support was constant. Please know how much I appreciate it.

Next, to the faculty, staff and students of Pine Manor College's Solstice Program. Whether in workshops, independent study or cafeteria meetings, your instruction and artistic guidance put this story on the path toward its conclusion. Without the aforementioned—or extended time in Pine Manor's library—I wouldn't have a second novel. Your imprint on this story is permanent.

To the ownership, management and staff of both Brighton Music Hall and the legendary Paradise Rock Club in Boston. Aside from the aforementioned literary professionals, no one was more influential in the construction of this story than all of you. We served thousands of drinks and watched hundreds of bands together. Through it all, you helped paint the scenes, sounds and spirit of this novel, and also colored my own life in ways I'll never be able to repay. Thank you. This book is for you.

Finally, line up for the roll call. Thanks to the beautiful cities of Buffalo, New York and Boston, Massachusetts; the lasting influence of St. Bonaventure University; Starbucks, Spot Coffee and the South Boston Public Library; Newbury Comics, Record Theater and the late Home of the Hits; Mohawk Place, Showplace Theater, Nietzsche's, and any other Buffalo joint that's given upstart musicians a chance; Jeff Tweedy, Dan Auerbach, Jim James, Bob Dylan, Neil Young, George Harrison, John Lennon, Levon Helm, Ron Hawkins, Gord Downie, Sam Roberts, A.A. Bondy, Neko Case, Andrew Bird, Ani DiFranco, Tom Waits, Jeff Mangum, Shannon Hoon, Ray LaMontagne, Van Morrison, Howlin' Wolf, Otis Redding, Bruce Springsteen, Willie Nile, Justin Townes Earle, Dave Rawlings, Ryan Adams, David Mallett, Glen Hansard, Sam Beam, Justin Vernon, Elliott Smith, Elvis Perkins, M. Ward, Fiona Apple, David Gray, Susan Tedeschi, and any other musician whose work surrounded me while writing this story.

And to every bedroom or barroom artist who's ever spent even a minute creating a picture, song or sentence—keep on keeping on.

About the Author

Michael Farrell is a graduate of St. Bonaventure University and earned an MFA in Creative Writing from Pine Manor College's Solstice Program. His work has regularly appeared in numerous publications, including *The Buffalo News* and *The Boston Herald*. His debut novel *Running with Buffalo* was originally published in 2007, then re-released in 2013.

He now lives and listens to music in his hometown of Buffalo, New York.

For more writing from Michael Farrell, visit farrellstreet.com.

www.ingramcontent.com/pod-product-compliance
Lightning Source LLC
Chambersburg PA
CBHW021323250626
47155CB00002B/597